KIOWA KILL

Eli Holten jumped up, fully exposed to hostile fire, and furiously cranked round after round through his Winchester as he charged the Kiowa war party. Smoke rolled back from his busy gun muzzle and savage blood soaked the rocky soil.

Grabbing cover behind a granite outcrop to reload, the Scout spied a Kiowa running toward him, his huge gleaming trade knife raised in the noonday sun. Holten dropped his Winchester and pulled the pistol from his holster, quick-aimed, and fired.

The Kiowa brave stopped cold and folded, falling on his own sharp blade to end his scalp-hunting days forever.

#32:

THE SCOUT

STIFF JUSTICE
BUCK GENTRY

ZEBRA BOOKS
KENSINGTON PUBLISHING CORP.

Special acknowledgments to Mark K. Roberts.

This episode in the adventures of Eli Holten, the Scout, is dedicated to *R. C. House* in appreciation and gratitude for his advice and assistance.

—BG

ZEBRA BOOKS

are published by

Kensington Publishing Corp.
475 Park Avenue South
New York, NY 10016

First printing: February, 1991

Printed in the United States of America

1

She had worn a dress that left her shoulders bare, with a plunging neckline that also left no secrets about her upper endowments. The occasion had been the monthly Ladies Night at the officers' mess at Fort Rawlins, Dakota Territory. Against the chilly evening, she had worn a long, white, knit shawl, what the women in Tucson would call a *rebozo*, Eli Holten noted. It draped gracefully around her shoulders and fell in waves to her elbows. A small purse, which looked like a puckered sack, dangled on long strings from her wrist. Holten considered her one of the most beautiful women he had ever known.

Impulsively, Doreen Thorne swung the ends of the shawl and quickly made a loose single knot at the back of Eli's neck, then pulled the ends. It forced his head—and he willingly allowed himself to be pulled—into direct contact with hers. Holten didn't need that kind of persuasion. Their lips crushed together with driving, pent-up passion. Doreen surprised him in that she didn't immediately open her mouth and begin flirting with her tongue.

Second oldest of the Thorne sisters, Doreen usually exhibited the most aggressive attitude toward amorous endeavors. At nineteen, her older sister Malissa had taken on the refinements of a mature woman. That didn't prevent her, or any of the Thorne girls from being wildcats in bed. Wisely, Holten now let Doreen lead.

In a consciousness only slightly dimmed by champagne, he decided to let her drive herself loco before he picked whatever divine delights presented themselves. While the kiss burned on, he reached behind her and opened the door of his cabin on Officers' Row. By leaning forward, he got Doreen off balance and backed her inside. Thank all the good spirits of the Sioux, he'd convinced her to distract her sisters for the evening. Another bizarre night with five naked, wriggling, female bodies in his bed would be too much to endure. Especially with a new assignment pending. Doreen's lips became more demanding and Eli concentrated on their erotic combat.

His hands slid along her back, hugging her close as they fenced with their tongues. He felt the lean flesh of her upper ribs, and the tips of his fingers registered the start of the swell of her breasts under her armpits. Sufferin' Judas, he thought, she's bare, nothing under this dress. His hands, passing over her back, located a row of buttons. Intent on prolonging the buildup, he had stroked right over them. Later he'd have them open in no time.

Although he swam in ecstasy, Holten remained ever-conscious of his technique. Tantalize. Girls with as much experience as the Thornes could easily have become jaded. Holten acknowledged the need for inventiveness. Take time. Do it right and this woman of vast carnal knowledge would treat their night together like it was the last one in this lifetime.

Their bodies clung in full contact in the darkness of the cabin. Through his thin cotton shirt, Eli could feel her breasts heaving against his chest. Below his belt, his ample member quickly grew to twice its flaccid size. Already it rose up to meet Doreen's

6

compelling V of crotch and the gently protruding, welcoming mons veneris. Doreen lightly worked her hips, but not overstating the movement—enough to let Holten know her womanhood was there . . . and willing.

"Would you care to come into my parlor?" he whispered, his lips still brushing hers.

" 'Said the spider to the fly,' " she quoted in soft reply. "I'm not afraid of flies . . . especially if they're open. Nothing wrong with this for now. You don't seem to be in any hurry, Eli, so why should I?"

"The night is young," he said, avoiding mention of his pending departure from Fort Rawlins and Dakota Territory. He'd told the girls already. "And I'm feeling younger by the minute."

"Oh, goodie," Doreen teased. "Keep at it and maybe we'll be of an age."

"Growing tired of older men?" Holten riposted.

"Not . . . this . . . older man." Her hissed words clung warm and moist to his ear. Doreen's skilled fingers worked the muscles of his shoulders, plied down his shoulder blades and gently massaged his lower back muscles. All the time she held him close to her with the shawl and brought him to the peak of his need.

Holten let his hands slide down her tapering, lean, and curved back to savor with a tingle through his body the slight swell of her tight, round rump. His fingertips now sought the beginning of the rear crevice through her dress material. He encountered nothing that announced undergarments. This filly, he thought for perhaps the thousandth time, is about as audacious as they come.

His hands eeled lower until he held both cheeks cupped in their broad, square grip, encouraging them with a gentle hug. He marveled at the firm, flawless globes of flesh. He clasped her to his erectness as it found the cleavage in front despite the

7

thin layer of dress, and his heavy whipcord trousers. He took care not to push too hard—fly buttons rudely shoved could hurt and the passion of the moment could easily cool. Listening to her coos of delight, he gently rocked himself up and down against her mound; Doreen responded with a slow, languid, and rhythmic grind.

Fantastic moments passed. Doreen gasped and ran her hot tongue against his earlobe. Better take it easy, Eli told himself, or she'd be wasted right here. The hell, he thought, let 'er come. He knew from long experience she was a woman who could burst again and again and come crying back for more. Damn, he thought, still marveling at it, nothing but a dress!

He had but to reach up, undo a few buttons, and Doreen would be before him in the altogether, nothing but high heels and that idiotic shawl and her dangling little purse. A whimsy-induced imp compelled him. He had to satisfy its mischievous urge.

He kept one hand encircling her tight butt and slid the other up to the equally plunging back of her dress. He found the row of knobby, cloth-covered buttons as he again forced his lips against hers in a new hunger. Almost as though to fool her that he was not doing it, he slowly and stealthily undid the buttons, though not fooling her in the least. Craftily he followed the curve and contour of the small of her back. The bulky shawl still clung to her shoulders, the tag ends draped over his. Holten inched back to let the dress fall away. It landed gracefully, in a crumpled circle, at Doreen's feet.

Still in his waggish humor, Eli made as if to lean one hand down to the low table beside the door, where the thin edge of lampwick allowed only a fine yellow ribbon of light. His fingers found the small stamped metal wheel on the stem and he rolled the wick upward. A tall spurt of light leaped into the fragile glass chimney.

8

Instantly the area around them became bathed with its light. Yellow brightness revealed Doreen Thorne in total nakedness, the snowy white shawl framing the familiar, and what he considered spectacular, pair of knockers and a totally compelling wedge of chestnut hair. Holten backed away, chuckling.

"Eee—liiii!" Doreen shrieked.

"Couldn't help it," Eli snickered. "I had a sudden urge to see you." His hand went back to turn down the lamp again to its low glow.

Doreen feigned anger, protested in murmurs, then sighed sensually. Still kissing her, Eli slid his right hand and arm under her armpit, the other across her velvet butt, and lifted her bodily in his embrace.

"A man likes to have a good look at the merchandise before he buys it," he explained in a cooing voice in her ear. In his supporting arms, Doreen's lightly tensed body relaxed.

"You've seen it plenty of times before," she whispered in mock anger. "And you've never had to pay for it."

"Granted," Holten breathed back softly. "But with you, lady, it's always as though I've a new, delightful experience at hand. Now hush!"

Holten pivoted and strode with her in his arms the few steps to the bed and tossed her into the air to plunge to the center of it and bounce once. Doreen made a little squeak as the sturdy rope supports made resisting sounds and the frame groaned in protest. It could probably be heard in the next cabin, that of bachelor lieutenants Baylor and Sturgis of the 12th U.S. Cavalry.

Poor boys, Eli thought absently. This'll put lead in their pencils and no one to write to. Doreen lay silently in the soft light and watched as Eli peeled off his shirt and shrugged down his Sunday-go-to-meetin' whipcords to his boot tops. He hopped first on one foot then the other to pull off the tall, black stovepipes and shake his legs out of his britches. She watched the ritual with rapt attention, eyes riveted on the more-than-ample, stud-sized organ between his legs.

She had turned loose of her earlier inhibition about performing without at least one of her sisters, as well as the shawl, purse, and shoes. Her words rustled like leaves in a soft breeze. "What'er you gonna do to me, mister?"

Accustomed to the wide variety of fantasies the Thorne sisters liked to play out, Holten got into this one quickly. He went to his knees at the edge of the bed and shuffled close to her. Slowly he leaned his lips toward the spongy, copper-furred passage between her creamy thighs. "I'm going to . . . eat . . . you . . . up."

Doreen squealed with delight. "Dessert before my vegetables," she cried, clapping her hands.

Eli encountered the heady musk of her moist and ready opening. His senses reeled. Edging closer, he extended his tongue and ran it along the fevered outer lips of her honeycomb. His arms snaked around her firm, young butt and clasped her tightly. With a groan of self-arousal, Holten began to lap at her like a greedy kitten in the milkhouse. Doreen gasped and panted.

Holten developed a rocking motion, working himself deeper and deeper into her plantation of joy. Doreen shivered and laced fingers behind his head, drawing him further into her steamy jungle of delights. Eli could feel his heart pounding. This was only a beginning. He drew back slightly and began to slaver the stiff little rod in the upper arch of her portal. Doreen howled with delight.

"Oh, hurry, Eli. Take me, take me now," she begged in a frenzy of pleasure.

Industriously, Eli worked on until she had peaked

three times. Each glorious surrender increased in its reward. Doreen thrust out her legs, quivering and parallel with the floor. Her toes curled under. When Eli judged her arousal to be at its ultimate, he broke free from his suppliant's position and entered the downy softness of the thick mattress. Rigid to the point of aching, his fabled lance blushed a deep crimson in its readiness.

The words of some old adolescent, early-saloon-days doggerel flipped through his head. As he straddled Doreen with her eyes on the blatant length of him, arched upward and proud, the limerick came out softly, almost whistled.

"There once was a fellow named Morgan; Who said to his girl, 'You're a gorgon; For gorgons are known; To turn things to stone; And look what you've done to my organ'!"

"You're terrible, Eli!" Doreen squealed. *I wish Helen*—no, she wouldn't say that—*Helen's so hungry for you*—she wouldn't say that, either. Tonight was *her* night, like last night had been Malissa's, tomorrow Samantha's, then Susana's, and finally Helen's. Their good-bye to Eli Holten. But they so loved to do it together.

In the dim light and softness of the bed, Holten sprawled on his belly beside Doreen. His full prong reached up in the general area beyond his navel. He angled toward her and leaned over to kiss her. His left hand under her neck, he savored the lush, clean-smelling, long auburn hair. His lips close to her, even in the low light, let him see deeply into her eyes. They stared intently and romantically into his as he began a nibble of her lips.

"You feel good," she whispered huskily. "Even if you ain't where you ought to be."

"You're not ready yet." His words, too, were whispered. His mouth hovered close enough to her ear that merely the soft suggestion of words proved

11

loud enough.

"I was ready the minute we stepped out of the officers' mess."

"Maybe you think you were," Holten taunted. "There's a lot left to be done."

"Let's do it then, for my sake. I'm burning up."

He brought his free hand to Doreen's chin, held it firmly. "Don't get your pretty little butt in a frenzy, madam. I'll let you know when you're ready."

"Y—you've never been so—so masterful before, Eli."

"You're growing up, Doreen. You're a full-fledged woman now."

Doreen responded; beside him she relaxed and quit trying to lead the goddamn cotillion. Eli continued to hold her chin loosely, though firmly in his control, and planted his lips squarely and strongly on hers. Tasting and testing the soft, savory fullness of her lips in his hungry devouring of them, Holten felt her hand, which rested on the bed between them, probe along his side and try to slide under his belly pressed against the mattress. He eased up, allowed her long, skilled fingers to find his maleness and, without gripping, to caress its length.

Her strokes sent shivers of delight and need surging through his body. Doreen had always possessed a knowing, instinctive style. Her lips slid slightly free of his, though still touching.

"I guess *you're* ready," she observed, the movement of her lips and her hot breath tickling him.

Centering his thought totally on her gratification, he had to play out his string. "The point is you're not," he said as he slid his free hand away from her chin and stroked her throat. Women, an old whore had told him in his callow youth, were more properly excited by a man who didn't jump right into the chore the first thing like it was a job of work to be over and done with as soon as possible.

12

Eli brushed his fingertips over her delicate throat and along the cleavage of her breasts, then down the low, sloping curve of her lean, tight belly and into the silken hair of her pubic triangle, lightly, gently, gracefully. Doreen shivered.

It worked as it always had. Doreen gave her consent by pulling up her heels and spreading her knees in mild encouragement. The tips of Holten's fingers slid along the warm, wet opening. The pads of each digit grazed the moist, parted slot. With his middle finger, he gently teased the lump of flesh in the crevice above it. His action sent tremors of sensitivity through the body under him.

"Oh, God," Doreen moaned. "Now, Eli. Now!" Her fingers stroked the hard, fleshy rod between them, kneading it and pumping it with vigor, eager and waiting to guide him to a ready access. He refused to move and she moaned in frustration, powerless to do more.

His lips found her ear, his words so soft he was hardly aware of their utterance. "Will you for godsake, Doreen, slow down?"

Still he responded by sliding one leg out and locking it over her knee. He felt her legs spread wider in invitation. With her hand still gripping him, he slid more of himself over her eager, heaving body. With the hand that had been behind her head, he reached down and took hers by the wrist and away from the hard shaft of flesh. Gently but firmly he pinned her arms against the bed. His own need had come up magnificently now and he didn't want to spoil it. Determined, he moved slowly, deliberately.

Eli supported himself over her on elbows and knees. His position right, he bent to his goal. In one try he found the wet, pouting opening that burned with fervent need. The bulging ruby head found her tight, wet pocket and his entire body reveled in the sensation of a constriction, a drawing-in, an all-powerful sucking-in to get the full length of him within her. The effect on Eli was electric! The depth of the saucy, inviting cavern squeezed and impelled him further . . . ever further.

Here was a woman of acknowledged championship style in matters of mating, brought to a frenzy of ultimate need. Eli knew now she'd perform with all of the skills and nuances she'd learned or invented over her years of being bedded by tyro and expert alike. Eli allowed his engorged member to work deeper, propelled by his own languid, light thrusts and rotation. Doreen still had the tightness of youth, though well oiled—if he could believe it—since her preteen years.

He'd partly seen to that, he acknowledged. Against his ear, the girl's moans, groans, and gasps fell hot and compelling. He backed out partway, bringing another tremor to the quivering, surrendering body beneath him. Doreen always wanted deep thrusts and she sure wanted them now.

Doreen's rhythmic moans in time with his pumping cadence grew louder in his ear, the ecstatic signal of her approaching summit of joy. The nails of her taloned fingers dug into the flesh and muscles of his back. Hot flares erupted along his nerves. In abandon, Holten beat against her, felt his own cargo building in the channel, like a race to the top of some supreme hill on a magnificent stallion. Doreen's screams roared in his head, encouraged him, pleaded with him for full measure. In a cataclysm of completion he blacked out, his consciousness centered on the thrill of the slippery tube that tugged and gripped at him for more, more, more.

With an almost brutal lunge, his first spurt coincided perfectly with a sharp exhalation of extreme ecstasy from Doreen as the dam of her desire burst once more and overflowed. Still hammering into her, Eli felt himself emptying in strong, pulsing

14

cascades and knew that each thrust and each powerful response brought a wail from Doreen.

Then it was over and he shoved his still hot, hard extension into the quivering cavity. He felt the backwash of their mutual completion. Most women he'd known and loved savored the moments of tender contact as they both wound down in the slow ebbing of these glorious aftermoments. Timing by heartbeat, Eli again pulled up his weight to his elbows and knees, still strongly encased, and bent over to kiss Doreen warmly and lovingly.

"Lord, Eli," the lips under his hissed. "When you finally got around to it, it was short, but oh! So fine. Our best ever."

"That comes from having my undivided attention. But I will second the motion."

"I'd rather not just now," Doreen said, teasing over his making light of a pointed remark, and giggling about it. "Give me at least ten minutes to recover."

"Suits," Eli agreed, an amused, gratified tone in his voice as well.

"On second thought," Doreen drawled, "make it five minutes."

2

Since his recovery from the grievous wounds from an assassin's bullets, Gen. Frank Corrington made it a practice to hike two miles around the sprawling military cantonment of Fort Rawlins, Dakota Territory, each morning before going to his doctor-enforced half day of desk duty. He remained a mite feeble, he admitted to himself, for much riding, though he vehemently denied it to the post surgeon. Walking roused the blood—and the spirits—he maintained, and made him ready to face the day.

Unlike most, this day offered something to look forward to. Eli Holten was due to report this morning and Corrington eagerly anticipated their get-together. They had campaigned a fair bit together, and fought Indians shoulder to shoulder when the deck seemed so stacked against them they feared they might walk the same trail as Custer.

And they had caroused, the two of them, before the general took a wife, from gold camps to trail towns, from the northern Dakota extremes to palatial sporting houses in Omaha. Together they'd sampled the tenderloin from the glittering honky-tonk sin capitals of Kansas City and other eastern meccas to the wicked fleshpots of Junction City, outside Fort Riley, Kansas.

16

Not to forget, General Corrington added with gratitude, that Eli had taken leave from his assignment in Arizona Territory to come and avenge the attempted murder ordered by the Pierre Ring. Right then, three-quarters around on his daily constitutional to rebuild his stamina, and nearing the main gate, Frank Corrington caught a glimpse of Eli Holten riding on Sonny to their meeting.

Dear, beautiful, magnificent Sonny, his own gift to a treasured friend and army scout without peer. Holten, the by-God man, the scout, proud as a Sheridan or a Stuart in the saddle, the morning sun shining gold in his abundant blond hair. Muscled shoulders squared above his slim waist, Holten's broad forehead and wide-set, gray eyes confirmed the suggestion of force showing in his blocky jawline. The determination in those smoky orbs was deep seated and of long standing, a trait which set him apart from lesser men. For a fact, and from wide experience, Frank Corrington knew that Eli Holten would only be getting his second wind when field-hardened and battle-seasoned campaigners around him were caving in. Corrington walked slowly out, aware of a slight pained limp, to meet Holten.

Although Eli Holten saw his companion of many a back-trail nearly daily since his recovery from a deep coma, he still gasped. Pain from frostbite, his wounds, and long drift in unconsciousness traced seams in Frank's face, and his dark eyes, that normally flashed with vigor and undaunted courage, were dull, sunken orbs surrounded by dark rings. A man nearing sixty should not have to endure such travails.

Corrington, a brilliant field commander, Holten knew, had only been allowed temporary desk duty while he recuperated and could once again ride at the head of his brigade. It had been done against the best advice of the post surgeon. Holten still found it hard to see his old friend this way. Corrington was still a long way from full recovery. Sighing, Eli rode up to within a few steps of the general and stepped out of the saddle.

"I didn't think I needed a by-your-leave to get down, Frank," Eli said, in acknowledgment of frontier protocol and military custom.

"In my presence you should know you never need to ask, Eli." Corrington's eyes gazed beyond the scout and took on a vague, filmy quality. When he next spoke the words seemed a part of another conversation, another time. "Eli, by God! How are you?"

"Coming from good times. Some old friends have been on post. Remember?"

"Of the female persuasion, am I to assume?"

"General Corrington, you are a master of perception."

Corrington abruptly snapped back to the present. "It seems ages since that's been my good fortune, Eli. This wound and then this eternity of healing have altered my priorities. Simply not up to it, nor in anything like the proper frame of mind."

He knows, Holten thought. *These slippages, these vagaries*. "Patience, Frank. You'll be back among the living before you know it."

"You're reassuring. Seeing you is worth two weeks of recuperation, I'm here to tell you. You look good, man. Let's go into my office. I've some excellent Napoleon and as fine a box of Havanas as you've ever put match to."

"Lead on, General," said Holten, suddenly resigned. Brandy and cigars meant a bad job ahead. And *he* got only the bad ones.

They walked along together to the brigade headquarters office, Holten leading Sonny. The big, black Morgan peeled back lips and whuffled interrogatively at a few comely mares on the parade ground, ears atwitch with interest. The remount sergeant and his two corporals glowered at the stallion; then, recognizing the animal's owner and the general beside him, produced tolerant, patronizing smiles.

"My old Morgan charger there looks good," Corrington said, observing the byplay. "Whatever care you can give him out in that blasted desert certainly must agree with him."

Holten chuckled. "The rules and regulations you laid down when you made me that gift are hard to ignore. Not that I would. Besides, I learned a great deal about keeping a horse hale and hearty from you. As I told you before, I have a contingent of Apache volunteer scouts. They manage to keep Sonny well supplied with oats, one way or another."

"The tools a good cavalryman learns to maintain properly for his survival are his issue arms and his horse. An unhorsed cavalryman with a jammed weapon is, well . . . remember Custer."

They reached the building and Holten looped Sonny's reins over a convenient hitch rail. Brigade Sergeant Major Flannigan bellowed the orderly room to attention when they entered.

In Corrington's office they sipped excellent Remey Martin and enjoyed the pleasurable smoke of the general's stogies. Frank Corrington blew a perfect smoke ring and watched its ascent to the ceiling.

"So, you're headed back to Arizona, Eli?"

"You know that, Frank. Or you wouldn't have asked me here. When Texas, New Mexico, and Arizona are properly tamed, I guess my type will go the way of the dinosaur and the old beaver men."

"That day will be a few years coming."

"Like your full recovery, they'll be here before we know it."

"A paradoxical statement if I ever heard one, Eli."

"One thing I know about you, Frank. When you call a man like me in, uncork a bottle of brandy—which is an excellent treat to this old palate by the way—and set up the see-gars at eight in the morning, trouble's a-brewing, and that's for certain."

Corrington brightened and broke into a low chuckle. "You've seen through me all these years."

"Hell yes," Eli answered, joining the laughter.

The general sobered his countenance. "Could be all smoke and no fire, Eli. The army needs a man of your caliber to guide a detail headed into Arizona to augment and reinforce Crook's presence there."

Corrington regarded Holten with dark and cavernous eyes. Despite his lingering infirmities, a lot of the old spark returned to them, probably because he enjoyed having Holten handy to solve his problem. A recently unused timbre came back into his voice. Gen. Frank Corrington seldom needed to raise his voice to command attention.

Equally laconic in speech and action, Corrington was unaccustomed to having to issue orders more than once. "A full troop is shortly to be on its way from Jefferson Barracks, Arizona bound, via the old Santa Fe Trail."

Holten had as little use for the new designation of "troop" in place of the old, familiar "company" for cavalry as he did for untried soldiers headed for a combat zone. "Cherry troopers for General Crook, learning along the way, eh?"

"I'm afraid so. There's, ah, more. Trouble could be brewing along their route of travel. Crooked Leg and a band of Kiowa misfits is off the reservation. Where exactly we don't rightly know. As you know, wherever Crooked Leg walks, devastation and death are certain to be in his wake."

Corrington strolled to his office window and looked out reflectively at the fort's high stockade and the flat roofs of barracks and support buildings. A tall, yellow bluff rose behind it, the whole place hemmed in by a welter of civilian shanties, road ranches, and raw-board buildings.

"You're sure he's not raiding down in Texas?"

"Who's to say, Eli? For that matter, since the coming of the railway, the Trail's about as useless these days as tits on a boar. We're figuring he'll pop up in New Mexico, anywhere from the Cimarron south. Or maybe in Kansas," the general added reluctantly.

"Which means the Trail, which means the rookies. Where do I fit in?"

Corrington turned back to him and scowled. Chewing his stogie, he shot Holten a quick glance.

"The army wants you to rendezvous with the troop at Bent's Old Fort and guide them south through the Cimarron Cutoff to Santa Fe, and on into Arizona to their frontier post assignment."

"Why backtrack like that? I should meet them at the Little Arkansas crossing and take the Cimarron from there," Holten protested.

"Man proposes but the War Department disposes," Corrington said airily. "Or like that poet wrote of our brothers in the famous Light Brigade: 'Ours not to reason why.' More time on the trail means, to some desk-soldiers, more time to gain experience. You're right about their being green troops. The pundits in the War Department decided that the ride to Arizona would serve as well as a field exercise to toughen and acclimate them. A small cadre of seasoned troopers is going along, a sergeant major, two corporals, and about five experienced troopers."

Holten made a face. "Green troops possibly coming under fire. Dicey business, Frank. If they lock horns with Crooked Leg, that could be a hazardous situation. If they lose their mettle, it'll make Custer look like a Sunday school picnic."

"I understand the risks involved from your

21

viewpoint, Eli. It's those desk-bound fog-heads on the Potomac. That's why the army's authorized me to offer you an extra-risk bonus if you'll take the assignment.'' Corrington named a figure, then rolled his chewed stogie to the other side of his mouth, looking every bit the used wagon salesman. "Interested?"

"It's . . . tempting. I'll not deny that. How many braves bolted the Nations with Crooked Leg, any idea?"

"Thirty at the most."

"Crooked Leg won't chance an attack on a cavalry troop. Better than four to one against him aren't odds he'd savor. He'll ride the other way and find some poor nester heading into town for groceries. That's more his meat."

"Our greatest fear is he'll do just that, only on a grander scale. Somehow the news will get back and fire up other Kiowas at Fort Sill to bolt the reservation. I'm in constant touch with Granville Scott at Jeff Barracks as we monitor the situation."

"How is old Scotty?"

"Due to pick up his first star any day now," Frank said, pleased.

"By God, Frank, when he does, let's go down there and pump him for drinks."

"I'm for that. I'm due for some furlough after this wound. You go get that troop into Arizona safe and sound and attend to whatever else has to be done there and let me know. I'll pull some strings with George Crook to get you off, and we'll go down there and see what we can do about wearing out our welcome with General Scott."

"Who's commanding this troop out of Jeff? You said a sergeant major is with them. He's the key to the whole shebang, forget the officer in charge of the detail."

"An old friend of ours, Harry Adams."

22

"That puts the seal of approval on it. I'm your man, Frank. When do I leave?"

Corrington glanced at his desk, reluctant to bear bad news. "Just as soon as you get fresh socks for your war bag."

"Already have. All that's left is to say good-bye to my visitors."

Corrington raised an eyebrow at the use of the plural. Then his trick memory provided the answer. Oh, yes, the Thorne sisters. Eli had his hands full there. "I can allow you only two days for that duty, Eli."

"Thanks, Frank. Oh, I said to forget the officer as long as Harry Adams is on the scene. For curiosity's sake, though, who's the C.O.?"

Again Corrington hesitated, bit his lip, his eyes reflective for several moments. He shrugged, sighed. "Major Randall Covington."

"Holy Hell!" Eli exploded.

"Ginny, don't take the banty's eggs. You know Momma told us not," eleven-year-old, freckle-faced Cindy Nichol told her younger sister.

Ginny made a face, stuck out her tongue. "I weren't gonna take 'em, bossy. You lemme alone, or I'll tell Momma."

A tomboy, Cindy went barefoot and wore nothing at all under her faded, worn bib overalls. The hot Kansas sun had browned her exposed skin and tough callus protected the soles of her feet. She had spent all of her life she could remember on her father's homestead farm thirty miles south of Dodge City. Winters she made bushels of popcorn, strung some for the Christmas tree, ate her share and then some, and tried to avoid the squabbles of her brothers and three sisters. Being oldest of the girls only saddled her with more responsibilities, Cindy believed.

In the summers she went swimming buck naked with her brothers and two younger sisters in the Little Arkansas River. Not much of a river, she considered, it only came up to her belly button. So far they had been twice this year and Cindy had noticed her older brothers, Lenny, who was fourteen, and Jimmy, twelve, looking at her in a different way than before. Maybe it was those bumps pushing out sort of soft and round on her chest. Or it might be the way her little purse opened up all wet and pink when she looked at Lenny and Jimmy.

If only she had one of those . . . "Cindy, Ginny, hurry up," Momma called. "Breakfast in twenty minutes. I need those eggs."

"Coming Momma," Cindy yelled back. They'd go swimming today. Maybe she'd ask Jimmy what it was like, having a stick instead of a little bald mouse.

Crooked Leg smiled mirthlessly. The white-man farm looked prosperous. Many cows, horses, some of the noisy, dirty animals that tasted so sweet when roasted in a big bed of coals. Those girls looked tender and ripe. Long yellow hair. Not like the woman, all angles, who had come to the opening in the back of the white-man lodge and made cawing noises at them.

White man's talk. Crooked Leg had learned some of it during the five years he had been confined at the fort called Sill. It would serve him and his warriors well on this war trail. That he knew to be a true thing. He had some boys with the war party, adventurous youths with not more than two hands and three, two hands and four summers to their lives. If they did their duties well, if they acted brave and did not turn away from the bloody work at hand, Crooked Leg mused, perhaps he would give the tender little girls to them for their pleasure. Now, he sensed, the time had come.

"The man and boys in the big animal lodge first," he commanded in the gutturals of the Kiowa language.

Seven Kiowa warriors seemed to materialize out of the tall, waving, green grass and glide soundlessly toward the barn. They reached their objective without an alarm being given. One stepped into the opening created by the wide-flung double doors. He drew his bow and it twanged musically.

A muffled scream followed, then the soprano of a boy's voice. "Pa! Oh, Pa. Oh, my God, Injuns!"

Yelping in their bloodlust, three braves leaped into the barn. Lenny Nichol impaled one on three tines of a hay fork. Disciplined to endure great pain stoically, the warrior grunted as steel slid into his guts. Lenny wiggled the deadly tool in an attempt to free it and even the courage of the Sun Dance deserted the Kiowa. He screamed hideously and went to his knees.

At once one of his companions loosed an arrow that struck Lenny in the belly, an inch above his navel. He shrieked and clawed at the buried shaft with his free hand while he continued to torment the mortally wounded brave. Another projectile hummed its eerie tune. Propelled by a seventy-pound war bow it went to the fletching in Lenny's throat. Two feet of the shaft protruded from the back of his neck.

Lenny's eyes crossed and he gargled in a rising pool of blood as his knees sagged and he dropped to a level with the Indian he had wounded. Glazed orbs gazed on a similarly dimming pair as the white boy and his red victim sank forward to fall in an obscene embrace of death.

"Stinkin' Injun, dirty fucker!" Jimmy Nichol shrilled, white gobbets of spittle at the corners of his small mouth. His blond hair swayed about his ears while he sought frantically for a weapon, or a means of escape.

His stubby, nail-bitten fingers closed around the lower handle of a scythe. He yanked it free from the support post peg and sent the keen edge swishing through the air. The tip caught the taut flesh on the outside of a Kiowa's left thigh and sliced through cleanly. It continued, hooked into the loincloth and horribly emasculated the brave before Jimmy over-balanced and sprawled on the ground.

Rendered immobile by the physical and psycho-logical damage done his reproductive system, the warrior could only look on in terror and bitter resignation while the white child crawled to the scythe handle again and forced himself upright. The curved blade swung again, this time at the paralyzed Kiowa's neck.

Shock and pain from the impact ran up Jimmy's arms as the scythe made contact with the thick, muscular neck of the Indian. An old trade rifle banged flatly from the double doors and Jimmy thought an invisible fist had struck him in the stomach. His gut ached with a hot fire, then slowly went numb.

What was he doing on his knees again, he wondered driftingly. Then he saw a warhawk raised before his round, soft, child's face. He lived long enough to hear the crunch when the steel axe bit into his skull. Then blackness descended.

The hurting had stopped. Only the pain remained. Cindy Nichol lay naked on the ground. Silently she prayed that it was over. It had hurt so awful. Though, perhaps not so much that first time.

She had been terrified when she heard the screaming from the barn and realized that real, live Indians were attacking their farm. She didn't see Pa,

26

but she watched in fascinated horror while Lenny plunged the pitchfork into one redskin's belly. She almost threw up when Jimmy cut one of the savages with a scythe, saw the Injun turn and reveal how Jimmy had sliced off his stick and sack. Then Jimmy cut off his head. Sick at heart, she watched the painted warriors murder Jimmy. Cindy tried to hide her smaller sisters, to protect them and preserve some of the family. Too quickly the Indians had swarmed into the house. Momma had fired the old Greener shotgun at them.

A ten gauge, it sprayed a large cloud of prairie chicken shot. Number Six, she recalled her father calling it. One Indian lost most of his face, another, blinded in both eyes, ran from the kitchen. The other two withdrew. It gave Momma time to reload with buckshot. Two barrels, four dead Indians when they charged again. Then the front door slammed in and glass tinkled. Ginny screamed and ran like a frantic bunny for the loft stair. A brave caught her and hauled her, howling, out of the house. Cindy never saw Ginny again. Cindy's turn came next.

Two braves grabbed her arms and dragged her from the kitchen. Behind her she heard her mother scream and cloth tear. Outside the warriors yanked off her bib overalls and idly pawed her body. She didn't understand the words, but she knew they remarked about the difference in how white the covered parts were compared to where the sun had browned her. Momma's screams went on a long time. When the braves came out of the house, one of them adjusting his loincloth, it had gone deathly quiet inside. Cindy began to cry.

Then the one who had been fooling with his breechcloth, the one with a stick like Grover Gaines's big stallion that stood to stud, pointed to them and grunted some of those turkey-gobble words. Some boys, near to Cindy's own age, came over. Laughing, the chief—for that's what he had to be to have these wild savages obey him so promptly—groped the crotch of one redskin lad and said something more, then laughed. The boy turned and looked at Cindy's naked body.

Body taboos had not been a strong issue with the Nichol family. Everyone had seen everyone else naked more times than the eleven-year-old girl could count, if she had cared to. Cindy didn't even blush at the examination. She crossed her arms over her bare chest and folded them. Legs widespread, she faced the grinning boy.

"Don't touch me, you red nigger," she challenged.

"Go on, Little Elk," Crooked Leg urged. "She is yours first."

Little Elk, a Kiowa boy of thirteen, had little idea of the mechanics of what Crooked Leg expected of him. It wasn't polite to watch while one's parents coupled in the lodge at night. He had heard the sounds, though, and caught glimpses. That alone, and the sight of the naked white girl, brought a quick response.

He felt his flesh lance elongate, stiffen, and rise inside the pouch of his loincloth. It tingled with anticipation, like it often did on a hot summer's day when he threw aside his sole garment to hurl himself in the tepid water of Caane Creek, or late at night when he wrapped fingers around it to ease the persistent itch. He stepped forward and pulled off his only clothing.

Two braves grabbed Cindy by the arms and threw her to the ground. She saw the dark bulb peeking from from under the coppery hood of the Indian boy's stick and knew what surely must come next. Cindy wriggled and fought the constrictions of the warriors who pinioned her to the earth.

"No!" she yelled. "Don't you do that!"

28

"It will be fun," Little Elk responded in his own tongue.

Fire erupted in her purse. Cindy screamed and forgot about writhing on the ground. Gravel had already scratched her bottom raw. The Indian boy kept on pushing with his hips, driving his rigid stick deeper inside her. She shrieked again. Grunting, he began to pump. Then, suddenly, it was all over. She felt his hot spurt within her tight, sore passage and he pulled away from her.

It should have taken longer than that, Cindy gauged from memories of muffled sounds that rose from her parents' bedroom to the sleeping loft for the children. Another boy approached, bigger, and exposed himself. Red and ready, his stick swayed before her. Then it disappeared as he dropped to his knees and forced himself between her legs. The pain came again. More this time.

Another boy followed. It went on for the longest time. Then the first boy came back to her.

"Me called Little Elk," he whispered into her ear as he pumped away on her slippery body. "What you name?"

"Cindy," she surprised herself by answering.

Blood and semen had been augmented by her own juices the moment this boy entered her. Although fiery and pain-wracked, her tight passage didn't convulse in an attempt to eject him. With this boy it was different, better. She—she even . . . sort of . . . sort of *liked* it. Then the horror of her family's murder, the long, terrible assault by the other, rougher boys came back and Cindy began to weep uncontrollably.

"Cin-dee. It's pretty name," Little Elk cooed. Then he noted her tears. "Don't cry, Cin-dee. Little Elk like you. Make you his slave. Much pump-pump. You like it with me, yes?"

29

"I—I—I don't knoooow," Cindy wailed in abject misery and utter emotional confusion.

When it ended, the warriors stood around her, looking down. Little Elk came forward, an expression of eager appeal on his young face. "This one, Cin-dee, we keep? She can be mine?" he asked Crooked Leg pleadingly in Kiowa.

"Little girls are of no use to us. Crazy Knife, when everyone has had his fill, kill her."

Mercifully for Cindy, she couldn't understand him.

3

Rain seldom cooled or dampened the incipient, burning impatience within Maj. Randall Covington. The incessant drizzle since he'd left St. Louis for Jefferson Barracks, Missouri, had only peaked the furies that regularly resounded in the darker corners of the major's makeup. The fact that Missouri was always cold and wet at this time of year did nothing to mitigate his rage.

So, his mood darkened as he began the last few miles of his ride and the gray daylight did little to burn away the depressing morning mists and tendrils of ground fog. Crows mocked him from their hickory trees. Small creatures startled him and his mount as they scurried to find escape. His appointment with Col. Granville Scott was set at 7:30 and Scotty, Covington knew, could be a stickler for punctuality, a military tradition to which Randall Covington had never quite adjusted.

It was common knowledge around the officers' lounges, and particularly in Washington, D.C., from whence Covington had come scant days ago, that a War Department promotion review board was about to award his first star to Granville Scott, Covington's old West Point classmate. That, in itself, only served to heighten the bad feelings that bounced around inside Maj. Randall Covington. To make matters worse, half of his luggage had been lost on that infernal stern-wheeler and this, his second-to-best, had become bespeckled with mud and Missouri fungus.

Thinking back, Covington knew that he had dallied too long in St. Louis, necessitating this ungodly discomfiting dark-hours ride the last twelve miles to Jefferson Barracks. He'd stayed the night before at a wayside tavern and hostelry where the roast beef was gristly and tasted tainted. He was sure the biscuits contained weevily flour.

Worse, to his fastidious nature, he awakened abruptly during the night, an hour before his call, aware that his sleeping accommodations were occupied by others. And not two-legged bedfellows either. The creatures that invaded his nightclothes were miniscule and itch producing, and walked on a multitude of appendages.

Livid with rage, Covington rid his naked body of the lice as best he could, dressed in his uniform after checking it for similar habitation, and went down the darkened hall. With a loud bellow he abruptly brought the night manager rudely awake. The startled fellow nearly pitched from an oak captain's-chair he had tipped back against the wall behind the front desk.

Not so much as allowing the mousy little man to rub the sleep from his eyes, Covington launched into a tirade of fury, punctuated with obscenities and profanity that would have blistered the hide of a rhinoceros. He invoked not only the infinite powers and wrath of the secretary of war but the threat of presidential economic sanctions for the indignities he had suffered under this miserable roof.

Covington had stormed from the place to look to the condition of his horse with not only his hotel bill and dinner free and clear, but with a twenty-dollar gold piece for his abandoned nightshirt that had been coming apart at the seams anyway. Shrewdly, he had insisted that the flustered clerk write him a receipt for the lodging and food as well.

Before securing his belongings on his horse, Covington stowed the paper away among his travel receipts and entered the cost in his per-diem compensable expenses journal. He considered it a sound tactical engagement.

He had done the same with the invoices for his out-of-pocket expenses during three days in St. Louis, much of the time in the company of a not-unattractive streetwalker. Covington had spent three monotonous, uninspiring days with the insipid chippie seeing the city's sights, the time only mitigated by four positively phenomenal nightly romps in his quarters at one of St. Louis's better hotels. So responsive, demonstrative, and recurrently vocal in her sexual abandon had been his bedmate that twice the management had been constrained to come to the door to complain.

They had interceded on behalf of the tranquility of neighboring guests. Flattered, Covington considered it more a bonus than a detriment. When the two lovebirds parted on the morning of Covington's embarkation for Jefferson Barracks, the ungrateful hussy had had the temerity to seek compensation for her long days—and nights—of companionship. In response, Covington used his fists to beat the poor woman senseless and made his way, whistling, to the livery stable.

Randall Covington of the Back Bay Boston Covingtons, through the good offices of his politically influential father, had gained an appointment to West Point. Covington had excelled in cavalry tactics, was among the highest in strategy and grand tactics, strong in physics, math, and composition, but low on general merit. He was graduated in 1861, twelfth in a class of thirty-four, ahead of Granville Scott and head and shoulders above a midwestern boor named George Custer, aka "Fanny" and "Curly," who finished thirty-fourth.

Good riddance, Covington thought, for the strutting Ohio-Michigan martinet. Scott was a born leader of men, while Custer gained his laurels becoming a *beau sabreur* in the Army of the Potomac's cavalry contingent through his typical audacious flair and dash.

Covington was only too painfully aware that he shared some of Custer's negative characteristics. Except in Autie Custer's case, they turned him into a hero and "Boy General" in Civil War cavalry skirmishes and major campaigns while Covington's command was plagued by malingering in the ranks and full-scale desertions under fire. A pompous dandy, Custer grew in favor with both McClellan and Sheridan, while Covington only retained his commission and gradual advances in rank by hobnobbing with the politically ambitious in the War Department and by dropping the names of his father's friends in high places.

He yearned to be back there now, in the bosom of its comforts and warmth, mingling in his congruent and congenial circles in Washington, as he slogged through the rain toward Jefferson Barracks. A rain not accompanied by wind, he noted sourly. It simply rattled down, drenching everything in sight, and turned the already rutted road before him into quagmire. His horse's cannons and legs were heavy with mud, which had the facility of being transported upward clear to the knees and hocks.

The rain eased as Covington passed through a dense, dark, and sodden forest of Missouri hardwoods. He reckoned that the web of limbs and leaves over him kept the precipitation at a drizzle. In truth, the rain had wound down to a demoralizing,

34

dripping grayness that promised to give way to stationary moisture that clung to everything. Aside from the suck of his horse's hoofs laboring through the mud, the only sounds came from the drip and patter of water as it beaded up on leaves overhead and plummeted to the dead humus below.

"Halt!" the sentry challenged. "Who's out there? Er—ah—who goes there?"

Jerked back from his sour reverie, Maj. Randall Covington instantly had enough of the foolishness. "I am here to report to Colonel Granville Scott, and you *will* call me sir."

The sentry looked confused. "Identify yourself, *sir*."

"I'll want the name of your troop commander," Covington growled.

"Advance and be recognized." The nervous picket stuck to the comforting routine.

"Of all the incompetent nincompoops! I am Major Randall Covington, with an appointment with Colonel Scott at seven-thirty. It is now seven thirty-four, you idiot, and—"

"Beggin' your pardon, sir, you don't look like no major to me. Corporal of the Guard, Post Number Three!"

"Damn you, look again!" Covington shouted, and then became suddenly aware that his poncho covered all insignia of rank. With a grunt of impatience he pulled the rain gear aside to display the golden stylized oak leaf on his epaulet.

For a moment the kid-soldier gaped. "Yes, sir, Major, sir," he responded as he dropped his carbine to his left hand unmilitarily and threw a hand salute. "There's something I'm s'posed to say to let you pass, but I forget. So you can go ahead . . . sir."

Covington rode up to the sentry and leaned down

to give the man the best scowl he could muster. It had been said in some quarters that Maj. Randall Covington's scowl could scorch the bark off a tree. He made the best of it this time.

"Thank you, my good man," he purred, patronizingly. "And as you walk your post in a military manner, consider this. When I report this unsoldierly conduct on your part to Colonel Scott, he'll have your troop commander in front of his desk in five minutes. Then, the C.O. will have your troop sergeant up to his desk. And your troop sergeant will have your guts for garters." Covington paused to gather his most scathing tone. "And you, my good man, were you under my command, would with the same degree of alacrity be up for company discipline at least, a summary court-martial more appropriate, and the very best of all in the interests of the good of the service, dishonorably discharged."

Gloating inside over his spontaneous eloquence, Covington directed his horse toward the large, red brick building that housed the post commandant's headquarters. Tying his horse in the drizzle, Covington clumped up the steps to the door to the orderly room and fumbled for his watch. Secured to his vest by a nonregulation gold chain and fob, it read 7:40. He squared himself and grabbed a deep breath. Ramrod straight, he opened the door and marched inside to stop in front of the only man in the office. That pigeon-breasted individual wore corporal stripes.

Sensing that he would be in for another demonstration of lower-echelon incompetence, Covington saw that the corporal had a pinched-up, clerical face, into which a snotty look seemed to have been burned at birth. Engrossed with his paperwork, the corporal did not look up through his eyeglasses. He allowed Covington to stand several moments before the desk. Covington's seething continued unabated.

"Corporal, if I may be so rude as to ask for your attention for one moment, I have orders to report to Colonel Granville Scott."

Still the stuffy little clerk did not look up. Instead, one hand reached out. "Let's have a look at those orders, soldier."

Out of his poncho now, Covington again set his bark-scorching scowl and leaned down close to the corporal, hands on the edge of the desk. "Corporal," he barked, "you have those glasses on your face for a purpose. Use them to see if you can remember your insignia of officer rank. And then . . . address me as . . . Major!"

Gulping, the clerk shot out of his chair and came to astonished, rigid attention beside the desk. "My apologies, sir. My mind was occupied."

"Scant space for much by way of occupation, I'll warrant," Covington snorted. "Show me to your commanding officer and be damned quick about it."

"Sir, the sergeant major is out of the office for a moment, sir. I . . ."

Covington moved directly toward the closed office door at the back of the room. The corporal barely beat him to it. Biting a lip in total frustration, the clerk opened the door and Covington stormed past. He strode halfway across the room before he came to a rigid stop in front of Colonel Scott's desk. He drew himself up to full attention, lightly clicked his heels, and locked a perfect West Point salute against his hat brim. Staring straight ahead, he waited recognition.

"Major Randall Covington, reporting as ordered, sir," he belted out crisply.

Scott looked up from his papers. "At ease, Major."

Covington smartly brought back both hands to clasp them at his back, turned his right foot at a slightly oblique angle, and bent his right knee, so that his fury-rigid body appeared to relax. Colonel Scott glanced beyond him and gave a casual nod.

"That will be all, Gibson," Scott called to the corporal who had stopped just inside the open door.

"Yes, sir, thank you, sir," Gibson blurted and slunk out of the room, still cowed by Covington's outburst.

Shedding his military formality, Colonel Scott got up from his chair and came around the desk smiling, shoved out a hand. "Good to see you, Randall. As you were, Major." Even then, Covington never fully relaxed.

It's only protocol, he thought in envy. Scotty lied in his teeth. He'd never had much use for Randall Covington since they left the Point. Too dratted ambitious, the bitter major's thoughts ran.

"Your servant, Colonel," he said as he forced a smile and shook Scott's hand.

"I'll send for coffee. For now, let's get right down to business," Scott began, some of the old fierce glitter in his eyes.

When he got right down to it, Covington knew he respected Granville Scott more than he had the late, lamented Curly Custer. Scott went back to his chair.

"Have a seat if you wish."

"I'd prefer to stand for the time being, Scotty. I've been long in the saddle."

Scott produced an understanding smile. "You look cold and drenched. Eight in the morning is hardly time for cordials, but I've some fine brandy that ought to take the edge off the chill. What say?"

"I'd be obliged."

"Brandy without a cheroot is like fornication without a kiss," Scott quoted from some obscure wit.

Faithful to his *bon mot*, as he hauled out the brandy bottle and two glistening cut-glass tumblers, Scott broke out a cedar box of stogies and offered them to Covington. In moments they had lit up and sipped the first of the rich throat- and digit-warming

Napoleon. It swept away the dismal damp of the day like a new broom, rousing ragged spirits.

Scott appeared more relaxed with his drink and smoke, inclining him to small talk. "Hours in the saddle. I know what you mean, Randy. I don't know that General McClellan's creation has been all that much of a boon to the cavalry. The McClellan, you know, was inspired by the design of a saddle tree used by horse combatants he saw when he was with a team of our observers during the Crimean War."

Covington hated to be called "Randy." Scott's familiarity prompted a stiff-lipped response. "I've always found the McClellan saddle to be a right proper outfit for officers and men alike, Scotty."

Covington had also grown up knowing "Little Mac" as a frequent house guest and close political friend of his father. During the war, Covington had despised Lincoln for his publicly voiced displeasure with General McClellan's style of command. The gaunt Illinois president's remark about headquarters and hindquarters had galled young Randall Covington.

"I've no data to support it," Scott went on, "but I feel the high incidence of inguinal hernia among cavalrymen, particularly in the West, spending long and hard hours as they do in the saddle, may be traceable to the design of General McClellan's inspiration."

"Interesting speculation, Scotty," Covington said, tactfully allowing both of them their opinions.

"And speaking of long hours in the saddle, I hope you'll soon be up to it again, Randy."

"Sir?"

"Major Covington, I think we both know that the reason for your transfer back to Washington since Crook's summer campaign of two years ago may be directly attributed to your rather outspoken disapproval of General George Crook's methods."

"I did not intend it to be a personal attack, Scotty. That's not my place as a junior officer. Yet, Crook *did* listen too much to his civilian scouts, two in particular, Jeffords and Holten. Instead of seeking an overwhelming military defeat of Geronimo and his heathen baggage, he dwelt too much on a peaceful solution. Unfortunately, some of my suggestions, which reached the press and were distorted and twisted by them in the name of scandal and selling papers, were intended to be for the good of the service."

"Don't alibi, Randy," Scott chided gently. "It ill becomes you, or any officer of the United States Army." He paused. "So, now you are transferred back to the field and to the West, aspects which I know must be somewhat repulsive to you."

"I have always felt my greatest potential lay in some capacity with the War Department in Washington, Colonel. I have difficulties with the general level of incompetence and indifference I see all about me in the West among noncommissioned ranks. Including two glaring incidents here on your post this very morning."

Scott dismissed with a fierce glance the latter accusations, which he knew to be Randy Covington again making mountains out of dung heaps. "Then, Major, may I suggest that you will simply have to order your mind to alter your style, your thinking, your prejudices, and your approach." Fire had returned to Granville Scott's voice. "If such is the case with your sentiments, your upcoming assignment has every element you normally find repugnant."

"I am a soldier, sir, and duty is duty," Covington answered stiffly.

Scott studied him, pulled thoughtfully at his chin, let his hard-glittering stare lance into Covington's eyes.

"For Lord's sake, come off the posturing, Randy. Be real for a change. This is the West, and whatever we accomplish is due to our key proposition, our, ah, first general order if you will. We *make do*. With the caliber of soldier we have joining up, with whatever scant equipment the War Department and a penurious Congress sees fit to send us, with Mr. Lo and his wily ways, with the harshest climate anywhere in the United States, through all of it, we make do.

"I'm under orders, too, and frankly, if I had my way, I'd leave you back there with the Washington nabobs." Scott paused, gulped down the last of his brandy. "You'll be taking a troop of recently trained enlistees out to the Arizona Territory."

"Sir?" Covington simpered. "Green recruits?"

"Randall, I didn't ask for this assignment any more than you did." Scott's eyes lost some of their glitter.

"From here," he continued, "you leave as soon as your troop is checked over and properly outfitted to your satisfaction, quartermaster stores drawn and such. You will pick up the old Santa Fe Trail west of Independence, which is still a reasonably clear-cut thoroughfare all the way to Santa Fe. You are to proceed along the trail to Bent's Old Fort out near the Purgatory River." He gave it the French pronunciation, "Purgatoire."

For the first time, Covington came up with a sincere grin. "I've heard the enlisted horse-soldiers refer to the river as the 'Picket Wire.'"

"Yes," Scott acknowledged with a similar smile. "The old place has been long abandoned, but the enormous walls still stand. Quite an affair in its time, all manner of recreation, billiard parlor, grand dances, and excellent victuals, wines, and brandies. But the company of Bent and St. Vrain—Ceran St. Vrain, ah! I went down the Santa Fe Trail under him when I was just a sprout, long before I went off to the

41

Point. Marvelous man, Randy, marvelous. We all could learn about leadership from him. A fine business sense, but a supreme backwoods scout as well, a man without peer.

"The Bent–St. Vrain venture fell apart. George, William Bent's brother, was American governor in Santa Fe, massacred along with his family in a Mexican uprising. That took some of the starch out of William. And William's son, Robert, a half-breed, united with his mother's people and rode the war trails, I'm told. That, in itself, must have caused old William Bent untold discouragement."

"Ha-ummm," Scott arrested his chatty flow. "Here now, back to business. Your troop will rendezvous at Bent's Old Fort with your assigned scout, who will conduct and help safeguard your command through the Cimarron Cutoff, and down the trail to Santa Fe and to your new post in the Arizona Territory."

"Scout?" Covington blurted angrily. "I hold a low opinion of civilian scouts. In particular one who implicated me in my differences with General Crook and was, I'm sure, responsible for some of the defamation I suffered at the hands of those conspiratorial scamps and scribes of the fourth estate."

"At ease, Major," Scott barked. His voice moderated then down to a flat tone, hardly more than a murmur. "I have no more use for spies and misfits than you have, Major Covington. I am persuaded that the man who will be assigned to guide you from Bent's is in no way guilty of such divisiveness."

Scott leaned forward on his desk, brushed aside reminiscences and service small talk, aware again of the glaring chinks in Randy Covington's armor. "Your troop is under the ex-officio command at the moment of Sergeant Major Harry Adams, as fine and as seasoned a campaigner as you'll find in the West. The men worship him—when they are not grumbling over his stern command and strictness to discipline. You'll find Harry Adams indispensable in every conceivable way in the field."

"I'm glad to hear that, Scotty. In the field, I brook no swerving from adherence to military discipline as well."

"I've heard," Scott said knowingly, almost sadly.

Enlisted men openly called Randall Covington a prick. Even in the field, where most officers least insisted upon it, Covington was known as a strutting advocate of unrelieved spit and polish. No buckskin jackets like Autie Custer, nor evening campfire sing-alongs for Maj. Randall Covington.

"May I ask, sir why we are marching the extra hundred or so miles to Bent's Old Fort and then backtracking to the Cimarron Cutoff? It seems such a waste of time," Covington queried.

"Don't ask me," Scott snapped. "Ask your friends in the War Department." Instantly he regretted his petty outburst. Scott sighed and framed his conclusion.

"Treat your men fairly, but with sound principle, Major Covington, and you'll find they will follow you through hell." Scott knew he might as well have been baying at the moon for all the effect his advice would have on implacable Covington. "And speaking of which, on the final legs of the journey, keep your outriders and patrols alert and don't for a moment drop your guard."

"Is there something about which you haven't apprised me, Colonel?"

"The Kiowa tribe has never had much of a reputation for meekness. Yet, they are out on their reservation at Fort Sill in the Indian Nations and across the board appear to be acclimating to the path of peace right properly."

"Uh-huh. Do I sense the emergence of an im-ponderable?"

"Yes. The fiercest of all their old living war chiefs, Crooked Leg, bolted the agency some weeks back, taking with him an estimated twenty-five or thirty of the most willing and savage hotheads. Evilest of the evil if you want to think of it that way. They in no way represent the consensus of the present Kiowa tribal council."

"I remember him."

"I'm sure you do, Randy. As for those with him, they kill for the sheer sport of it, better when they can pillage and rape the weak and vulnerable. The problem is—and I'm sure Crooked Leg is viciously scheming at this very moment—that one good raid with fascinating spoils for the boys back at the agency to hear about, and Crooked Leg's hostile band could be reinforced on the order of fifty to seventy-five percent. Pray for good weather and that Crooked Leg sees the error of his ways and goes back home to the Nations. Godspeed, Major Covington."

Without another word, Covington saluted, about-faced, and strode out, his boots drumming a hollow tattoo on the colonel's office floor.

4

Filled with anticipation, the tall, rawboned man left his horse on the downslope of the scrub-choked ridge while he had a look-see into the commotion rising up from the valley floor. Ben Gross shoved back his hat to dry his gritty forehead sweat, exposing a shock of prematurely silver-white hair, long though reasonably tended. His equally lengthy, stringy beard revealed the same exposure- and dissipation-bleached color. Benjamin Gross edged like a slinking snake to the lip of the rimrock, crouched to keep low against the gnarled, thick, shoulder-high brush. The Mexican wagon trail, the one he'd been hunting, lay down there a mile, maybe two, yet in full sight.

Over it, Mexican *carretas* toiled along, each drawn by a span of oxen in crude wooden yokes. The four nearly equal-sized sides of the rough carts flared slightly outward for greater load capacity. Turning on a single axle formed of a ponderous timber beam, great lopsided wooden disk wheels about four feet in diameter and eight to ten inches thick squealed in protest. Each had been fixed to the axle's outside protrusion with a tapered, roughly square peg which served as a cotter key.

On the heavy log perches at the front of each

carreta box stood dusky, coarse- and black-haired teamsters in grimy, off-white outfits of equally coarse material, crude sandal-like *azóteas* on their feet and great voluminous *sombreros* shading their heads from the unrelenting sun. They cracked whips and shouted Mexican obscenities at their plodding ox-teams.

Typical Mex inefficiency, Ben Gross mused, observing the heavily laden *carretas* lumbering noisily along below him. More weight in the gawdamn carts than the loads they should carry, and probably killing an ox every three months if they even got that much good out of them. A former teamster, Gross knew the trade well. Cussed *carretas* were about as worthless as a whorehouse in a leper colony, he thought, chuckling to himself.

Gross had tracked the small caravan to this valley to see what he could make off with by stealth, or by gaining the Mexican teamsters' confidence, or perhaps by bushwhacking the whole lot of chili-eaters. Clearly, Ben Gross lived by his wits, which because of his extreme limitations in that department, caused some to wonder how he had survived this long.

And there, thought Gross, come those gawdamn woolies, trailing behind the ox-carts, bleating and generally raising one hell of a ruckus. It all brought an annoying ache to Gross's ears, even at the distance. The column of stinking sheep, hundreds of them, formed a seething, ever-changing circle that sometimes went round, sometimes oblong, other times strung out in a long file. The hated sheep were tended by little boys, scaled-down versions of the adults of the train, and herded by scattered, busy dogs, which barked and nipped, everywhere at once, to keep the bunch-quitters in line.

Shouts of the teamsters, the agonized creak of the great lopsided wheels, the shrill yells of the boy shepherds, and the hateful bah-baahs of their wards,

continued to assault Gross's ears as he pondered his
moves to exploit what he could of the situation. At
least the oxen would be worth something somewhere
even if the carts didn't contain anything convertible
into coin of the realm.

Over the clatter and the bleating, muted by
distance, Gross's ears shot him an abrupt spear of
warning with the crisp, three-staged click of a six-
gun hammer being cycled to the business notch close
to his head. He froze, his hand poised to skin his own
worn Colt, slung low against his right thigh and tied
down.

"Go for it," a gravelly voice behind him snarled,
"and you're dead meat."

Gross stared straight ahead, unmoving, eyes
walling at the heavens in anger at his own stupidity,
dumber than one of those greasers down yonder.
Intent on discovering the nature of the noise in the
valley, he'd allowed himself to be stalked from
behind, violating the first law of the wilderness:
Watch your back trail.

"Jist leave it be," the voice commanded. Discon-
certingly it held a note of familiarity. "Ease up and
let's have a look at you."

Gross complied, turned to face his challenger.
Recognition flooded him, yet didn't make these tense
moments any easier. It had been a long time, yet bad
blood was bad blood.

"Ames?" he gusted. "Norville Ames?"

Ames's face had cured the color and texture of old
saddle leathers from exposure and rough doin's since
Gross had last seen him in Westport, Kansas. Ames
was also bearded now.

"Ben Gross! I'm a son of a bitch." The seamed,
weathered face twisted in open contempt. "This *is* a
hot one. Six months is a long time for the worm to
turn."

In a flash, Gross remembered his last glimpse of

47

Norville Ames, humiliated in the garish moonlight of Westport, naked save for a thick dressing of tar and fluffy goose down from a convenient pillow. A hooting mob of vigilantes, laced with a goodly crowd of angry townsmen and an equal portion of carousing drunks, were escorting Ames to Westport's outskirts on a handy fence rail.

At least Ames was a known quantity and once a friend and a partner, and probably wouldn't shoot him down like a dog for his Colt and his horse and the small change in his poke as he might with a perfect stranger.

"I'm sorry for what happened, Norv," Gross whined.

"Like hell you are!"

For Gross, memory burned bright. The two born opportunists had been business partners briefly in Westport. Gross ran a mercantile, selling staples and necessities for the trail at three times the back-East value to westering immigrants. Ames, meanwhile, operated a consulting service on trail routes and conditions, about which he knew absolutely nothing. He also asked exorbitant prices for his handsomely printed and authentic-looking maps of areas and trails he'd made up out of his head with only sketchy information from a few years of scavenging and trying to convert meager opportunity into almighty dollars in the sprawling expanse that was the Great American West.

"And you stood by and let 'em ride me out of town on a rail, Gross. I'd oughtta put one th'ough your head right here and now, but I got my eye on that train down yonder, same as you. There's no point in sendin' 'em skallyhootin', which the sound of Judge Colt's gavel'd do right enough."

Gross remained caught up in the unpleasant memory. "I had no choice, Norv. It was you they were after. Somebody should've scouted those sand bogs the McAllister party got snarled in and so many got sucked under and lost. Not to mention all their other problems in being totally confused in the desert and folks dyin' by the day. When that word got back, there was hell to pay in Westport. What'd you want me to do? Ask them to tar and feather me, too?"

"You were too busy savin' your own miserable hide," Ames growled. "As for the McAllisters, I didn't invent heat. Or thirst. Or quicksand. People die out here all the . . ."

Gross heard a thud and a choked, garbled gasp out of Norville Ames. Ames dropped the Colt and his jaw went slack, his eyes popped big, and were unblinking in abject astonishment. A small, glistening crimson pyramid at the end of a blood-red shaft jutted out of his belly, just below the rib cage. Ames's hands groped for the arrowhead that had impaled him as though clutching it would ease the pain and justify the surprise. His knees buckled and Ames fell forward with his hands still gripping the shaft.

Facing the direction from which the Kiowa arrow had come, Gross still could not see the assassin. With no decent cover in any direction, he stood his ground, prepared to fight it out with whoever had struck down Norville Ames.

He had barely started for his Colt when a violent impact socked into his throat with the force of a blue norther. His wildly staring eyes looked down at a feathered shaft along which rivulets of blood leaked. Most of the arrow's length protruded out the back of his neck.

Lucid, though with a throat that had become a trunk of immobilizing pain, Gross dropped to his knees, unable now to resist their attacker. He continued to grope at his neck behind tight-clenched eyes, futilely trying to rid himself of the intense, unbearable pain. Red flashes streaked through the dark behind his clamped eyelids. A dusky Indian figure in buckskins, crude osage-orange bow in one hand and a long-bladed Bowie knife in the other, materialized out of the land below the two dying white scavengers.

Quickly and silently he covered the few steps to Gross, who remained much alive, yet unable to resist. Crazy Knife, himself scouting the Mexican *carreta* train for his Kiowa chief, Crooked Leg, sent Gross's Stetson sailing with a cuff of his hand. For a moment he stood marveling at the long, glistening silver-white hair. Such a prize and conversation piece he would have to show in the camp of the Kiowas. He grasped a long hank of the silver stuff at the back of Gross's head and virtually lifted him bodily off his knees.

Deftly, Crazy Knife drew the razor-sharp Bowie blade to describe a circle the circumference of an over-large coin at the back and top of the head. He yanked and the disk of bloody scalp and long white hair came away in his hand with an audible popping report.

Gross's hands came up to deal with this new source of incredible pain. His throat injury prevented him from sounding an involuntary shriek against the agonies in his neck and head. Huge tears formed in his eyes.

Crazy Knife waved the bloody trophy before his victim's horrified eyes, his own obsidian orbs glittering in triumph. As Gross knelt in agony, holding his throbbing head, Crazy Knife drove the long Bowie edge into Gross's abdomen and sawed the blade upward through the viscera as he retrieved it.

Face ashen and aghast, Gross knelt there a long moment while he died by slow degrees. Blood pumped out of him in dark vermilion gouts, intestinal gasses belching through them. Staring at Crazy Knife with wide eyes, he pitched forward into the gravel to complete his death contortions.

Norville Ames's hair, dark and greasy with filth and accumulated oils, smelled rankly. Crazy Knife stepped to the task all the same. As he pulled up Ames's head, the dead face and eyes and gaping mouth formed a mask that stared as though fascinated at the horizon. Ames's eyeballs, open in death when he fell, were dotted with small, terra-cotta–colored pebbles of decomposed granite. His scalp came off with the same degree of ease as that of Benjamin Gross.

Crazy Knife had been stalking Norville Ames as he neared the vicinity of the moving Mexican wagon train since the previous afternoon. Legendary as the best scout and tracker of Crooked Leg's renegade band of Kiowa braves, Crazy Knife loved being off the reservation and out for blood. The way he had of sticking to a man's trail proved he took his work seriously. Even as Norville Ames slept the night before, Crazy Knife maintained his watchful, sleepless vigil. It had paid off.

Known as the fiercest of Crooked Leg's band and a favorite of the old hellion, Crazy Knife felt good only when raiding. Because, as escapees from the reservation life they were marked as hostiles with instant death their penalty if caught, the agency jumpers reacted with as much venom and hostility as they could muster. Crooked Leg would give no quarter to the teamsters and peons, nor the little shepherd boys. Crazy Knife looked down at the tableau in the valley again. Perhaps there would be great treasures in the crude and careering big-wheeled carts. He must get back to Crooked Leg with his report and to proudly display the two white scalps.

To Crazy Knife's amazement and dismay, down below, shattering the quiet morning, a sudden flurry of gunfire crashed out. Whooping screams and howls of attacking Kiowas pierced the ragged vollies. Crooked Leg's command had found the train before

Crazy Knife had been able to ride in and report its whereabouts. Anxious to join the attack, Crazy Knife still took time to briefly go through the pockets of the dead men.

He found only coins and the white man's precious green papers, and pocketknives. Proudly he strapped on their holstered Colts and cartridge belts, one to a side, the left one jutting butt-first. He abruptly raced back to take their horses and ride his own mount down to be in on the battle. Hardly a battle, he thought. The poor Mexicans, never great gun handlers, would be largely defenseless. Still, Crazy Knife yearned to be there to count coup and take fresh scalps.

He knew the horse of the man with the dirty hair. He quickly found the other one. The rich wood sheen of the butt of a fine rifle projected from the saddle boot under the stirrup belonging to the white-haired one. Crazy Knife saw a long, narrow tube of dull brass sticking out over the breech. When he withdrew the weapon, he saw it ran nearly the barrel's length. A sees-far sight. Truly this had to be the finest rifle he had ever seen and he vowed to become good with it, better even than the white buffalo hunters whose guns, like this one, could kill at great distances.

Now he had more immediate game to attend to. Crazy Knife, from horseback, led his two prize animals up and over the ridge, then down the steep slope. They slid and scrambled and raised great dust clouds, hoofs digging, and rolling to the bottom in a smother of sand and gravel.

Crazy Knife and his three horses hit the flat at a high gallop and raced across the desert floor to his part in the attack. Already the great sheep herd had been scattered and the butchery of the shepherd boys was nearly complete. Frantically bleating, wild-eyed woolies bounded and leaped in panic around him, causing Crazy Knife great difficulty as he raced to join the massacre.

To Crazy Knife's ears, as he charged in, came the shouts and yells of beleaguered Mexicans added to the confusion as they tried to outdistance their mounted attackers in the clumsy, lumbering carts with jaded oxen. Another element to astound Crazy Knife involved the method of defense.

One or two men in each of the carts, armed with some manner of long gun, fired at the fierce Kiowa attackers on two sides and at their rear. From the looks of their method of loading and firing, the train's meager defenders fought with ancient muzzle-loading fusils. The outmoded weapons gave them little, if any, advantage over the arrows of the Kiowa.

When the Kiowa horsemen gained the final advantage and the two forward elements merged ahead of the train, the Mexicans had little choice but to try to circle the clumsy carts and make a stand of it behind such breastworks as the carts provided. As they did, the Kiowa horsemen dismounted.

Quickly they took stations behind rocks and wash banks. In seconds they began to pour lead and flint arrows into the besieged Mexican party. The defenders lacked accuracy and proved quite slow in firing at muzzle flashes from the rocky terrain around them. They grimly tried to hold out. Still, one by one, the Mexican teamsters dropped. Before Crooked Leg's braves could finally rush the ox-carts, two Kiowas had been wounded, another three lay dead.

By the time Crazy Knife secured his trophy horses and made his way into the final battle zone, all coup had been counted, and all scalps taken. Crazy Knife remained consoled. Not only did he have two white-man scalps—not worthless ones like those of the timid Mexicans—and two fine horses and their trappings, but a wonderful rifle he would become proficient with to make him the stoutest, fiercest Kiowa warrior of them all.

Quiet settled on the bloody grounds. Crazy Knife saw that the sheep had been scattered to the four winds, the little shepherd boys all butchered; their six dead dogs promised a bounteous feast in the Kiowa camp that night. The Kiowas felt only mild distress in that, aside from the emaciated, worn-out ox teams, the miserable *carretas* contained nothing of value. Nothing whatsoever.

Crazy Knife knew all this before he rode up to the hoof-scarred ground around the carts and their cargoes of dead Mexican riflemen. The place reeked of death. Crooked Leg dismounted, his disappointment over the spoils of battle keen in his set features and his flashing black eyes. His great barrel chest heaved outward, then sagged in dismay. His thick lips folded back from his teeth to make a savage mask of his face. Yet he did not speak the anger he had in his mind.

Crazy Knife chose that moment to walk to his great chief and mentor. His heart sang, full of the knowledge he could bring good news to ease Crooked Leg's discouragement. He brought the two horses and saddles as a gift to Crooked Leg to assuage the chief's bad feelings.

"You are true Kiowa," Crooked Leg praised with the highest compliment a man could pay, his spirits lifting.

Crazy Knife reserved the great rifle and its stock of ammunition for himself in return for even greater heartening information. "Four, at the most five, sleeps to the west lay a large sheep rancho high in the hills. It is filled with Mexicans and is where this sheep flock would go. There are more, many more men's scalps to be taken there. Little boys to be used and then killed. More of the smelly beasts to be scattered and a great feast of many fine dogs."

Wise in the ways of his protégé, Crooked Leg produced a slow smile and put a hand on the younger

54

savage's shoulder. "There is more?"

Crazy Knife had wisely saved the best until last. He knew Crooked Leg had not been much excited by tidings of just another sheep rancho to attack and despoil. Now Crazy Knife went off a ways to crouch apart from two of the dead Mexicans, a jerk of his chin signaling Crooked Leg to join him. The old chief bent down; his rheumy eyes sought those of Crazy Knife for his good news and found it there. The other braves clustered around to listen.

"Near the rancho," Crazy Knife explained, "is a small village with a white man's prayer place and a cantina. The chapel will have treasures of gold and silver and the cantina will have much mescal and pulque for our celebrations."

Crooked Leg's eyes glistened in reverie, seeing the place and the easy fight in his mind's eye.

"Small children play all round the village," Crazy Knife went on.

"What use have I for Mexican nits, but to bash out their brains to halt their infernal howling?" Crooked Leg spoke with an impatient grunt.

"Don't you see, oh great chief?" Crazy Knife queried. Crooked Leg studied him expectantly. "Where there are young children are also"—Crazy Knife paused for effect—"women!"

5

Eli Holten hired a buckboard to take the cargo of valises and barrels of supplies the ten miles to the railroad's spur-line depot to catch the train to the station nearest their wilderness home. Doreen rode to the station beside Holten in the rig while Malissa, the twins, Samantha and Susana, and their kid sister, Helen, flounced happily with twirling parasols on the tailgate, chattering like young squirrels at hickory-nut time.

"When will we see you again, Eli?" Doreen asked, invitation loading her husky voice.

"They're sending me back to Arizona," Eli exaggerated slightly. The destination had definitely been of his choosing. "That's pretty much where the frontier line is these days and where my work is. It could be a while. And after the past months, I need a while."

"Why, Mr. Elias Holten, whatever do you mean?" Doreen's offense was not feigned.

"It ought to be as evident as the rings under my eyes. Three nights anywhere in the vicinity of the Thorne sisters inclines a man toward three more days and nights of solid sleep, followed by two weeks of total recuperation."

Flattered now, Doreen abandoned pique to share

56

the banter. "The effect was that devastating, umm? Your impact on us is no less intense. You bid farewell to five women you've again shown the summit of delights, who are all a-quiver about the whole thing. Each of us in her own way loves you . . . well, I of all people, shouldn't have to draw you pictures.

"Among and between the Thorne girls there is only love and no jealousy where Eli Holten is concerned. We all want to see you again. And soon. We older girls are all agreed that this time you definitely slighted poor little Helen."

"But, she's . . . only fifteen," Eli protested.

"And you've known her—in the biblical sense— for two years," Doreen snapped.

"That's only because the rest of you tricked me," Eli defended his self-image.

"Fair's fair, Eli, and we all want you so."

"Surely you must not really need me all that much, Doreen. There's certainly other eager, excited young men moved into your neck of the woods by now."

"Hardly!" Doreen denied. "At least, those who have brought wives with them and stick to that old-fashioned idea of monogamy. Granted, we Thornes have entertained a variety of manly lovers in our chambers. Some are amply endowed, others make up for what they lack in performance. Yet, as far as we Thornes are concerned, Eli Holten excels, nay, is the world's champion, on both counts."

"Much obliged for the kind words, dear madam," Eli responded drolly.

"Then just you remember that obligation, Eli. Get your responsibilities dealt with in Arizona and catch the first train for Dakota Territory just as soon as humanly possible. There will always be a place for you in our hearts and in our . . . well, you know."

At that moment, it would not have taken much more urging for Eli Holten to have packed up, gone

AWOL from his obligations, and set off with the Thorne sisters. It was a compelling thought. Albeit his leave-taking had not been dull.

His grand evening of drinks and dinner and rousing conversation with Doreen, followed by her absolutely magnificent performance as his bedmate, had been only a preamble to the next night. It had been what his French friends in St. Louis and New Orleans extolled with superlatives and plenty of "ooo-la-lahs" as a *ménage à trois*.

Well after the entire post had settled in sound asleep, a slumbering Holten responded to a light rapping on his door to find the Thorne twins, Samantha and Susana, in their nightcaps and sleeping gowns, waiting all nubile and expectant. They eagerly pushed in and quickly hoisted his coarse cotton nightshirt off over his head. Twittering, they shrugged out of their own nightclothes and ushered him to his already warm bed, accepting no protests.

It had been a heavenly encounter with the two teenage redheads. While Samantha kissed him ardently and saucily, Susana began making a path with her slow-coursing lips and warm, moist tongue over his chest, moving in the direction of his navel and points south. At that moment, both sisters had a fist around Holten's endowment, stroking in concert. Still there was shank to spare. Blissfully, Holten could anticipate the target of Susana's warm, tender lips.

They closed like moist velvet over the hot, ruby tip of his rigid member and engulfed a generous portion. Eli shivered at the contact and pumped his hips slightly. Susana cooed and ingested more of his silken shaft. Samantha began to nibble on his nipples and flash her tongue against his bare skin. While her twin worked away on his organ she slithered atop him and the juicy petals of her puffy cleft spread on his belly.

She bent forward and Eli took one globular breast into his mouth. The other he kneaded with willing fingers. Susana changed her position and began to slide her own fevered purse up and down the protuberance of his shinbone. In a flash he knew exactly why little girls liked to ride horses bareback. Susana's lips and tongue brought him near to a frenzy.

Eli was wild-eyed and goggly when Susana playfully shoved Samantha away and bent forward to kiss Holten long and hungrily. She swung herself over and with a cry of delight impaled herself on his enormous prong. A few moments of churning action brought Susana to a foaming, moaning explosion. Then she took in a bit more of the sword of Eros and rode it to another cataclysmic climax.

"Greedy, it's my turn," Samantha demanded.

For the next two hours each girl took turns riding him from the top, each registering her gratification time and again and graciously allowing her sister a turn on the great peg while herself recovered enough to have Holten's great weapon again plumb her depths. Well past the stroke of three, Holten went to sleep with a warm, tender cherub under each arm.

Next day, Holten had taken the five sisters on a prairie ride of several hours in a rented, six-passenger shay, drawn by a team of gleaming bays. They picnicked in a grove of lodge pole pines and found a delightful pool formed by an abundant spring. Before Holten could yea or nay, he had five buck-naked, shapely, and desirable girls cavorting in the water. It took little encouragement after the first five minutes for Eli to join them. On the way back, Doreen and the twins, in unspoken agreement, allowed Malissa the privilege of riding up front with Eli and pursuing a seduction.

That night Holten entertained Malissa, savoring her warmth and her charms and her willing, soft, and demanding body. He knew the encounter to be his last with the desirous Thorne sisters for perhaps ever. Often the last, he considered, under such circumstances, could be the best.

Malissa had not disappointed him, attaining her climax volubly and voluminously again and again in true Thorne tradition; and when Eli approached his own thrilling apex, she more closely attuned her rhythms to coax the greatest ecstasy for her lover as she could possibly deliver. Sated after three monumental contests, Holten dropped off to sleep with Malissa's gentle head on his shoulder, trying to rate the Thorne sisters, realizing there was no scale of good, bad, or indifferent. Each had her special style and each, in her own way, viewed Eli Holten as the supreme lover. Staunch friend first, protector if need be, lover always.

He awakened to the indominable capacity of the eldest Thorne. At least he thought so until he opened his eyes. In his deep sleep he had not heard Malissa open the door and admit the youngest of the Thornes. Helen rode his upthrust pole now, not Malissa.

She clung to him like a bronc rider, head thrown back as she keened her terrific enjoyment of his magnificent member, fully encased in her tight, slippery tube, which contracted and expanded in perfect tempo to draw deeply of his reserve of lust. Grunting, groaning, grinding her hips with the superb talent that only vast experience could bring, Helen guided him up the steep slopes of Olympus to the ultimate blending of their souls.

Little yelps of joy came from the slim girl's throat as she impaled herself over and over. Her utter involvement soon banished Holten's reticence and he surrendered himself to her charms. Every bit as good as any other Thorne sister, Helen gave him waves of euphoria until they crashed together into

60

oblivion. With happy resignation, Holten spent the rest of the night savoring and being savored by the oldest and youngest of the Thornes.

These pleasant memories still tingled when they reached the depot.

To the full astonishment of onlookers at the station platform, big, handsome, bronzed Eli Holten delivered a passionate kiss and body-hugging to each of the Thorne sisters in turn as the train's engine whuffed and chuffed in impatience to be off again. He started with Malissa, the eldest, then on to Doreen, Samantha and Susana—Lord, he thought, what those twins have known for so long about delighting a man!—and finally a warm kiss and hug for luck for Helen. He still tingled from the tightness of her passage.

"Two years, li'l darlin'. Two years and then we'll have some times."

"Not until then?" she blurted. Then she whispered, "You'd better make it before then, Eli Holten, or I'll come looking for you."

With a flurry of skirts, the Thorne girls clambered aboard the chair car teary-eyed, then waved at him from windows as dust closed around the platform and the train clacked and wheezed away into the gathering night. Eli had never felt so alone in all his life.

He also felt draggy as he strolled back to his quarters at Fort Rawlins with twinges of loneliness still nagging, an emotion uncommon for a loner. They had been there, giving themselves to him so many times in so many ways, and now, suddenly they were gone. A void remained. Something tangible he could experience in its barren hollowness. A precious commodity had left his life and he missed it. Missed it to beat hell.

Yet, tomorrow, as the Mexican residents of Arizona were wont to say, was another day, and Gen. Frank

Corrington had an assignment for him as he made his way back to Arizona Territory. The small cabin on Officers' Row Holten entered seemed gloomy in the gray of a nearly departed day. That desolation got down inside him as well.

Concepcion Madrid had heard it from Lupe Ramirez, who had heard it from Maria Ortega, whose husband, Armando, was the *alcalde*—mayor—in the little village of twenty-five God-fearing, devout Catholic souls, men, women, and children. *Los indios* were raiding, would probably come to their small village. Concepcion shivered at thought of it.

A sheep-herding rancho, a rude collection of hasty shelters high in the hills, had been attacked by marauding Indians. Jose Valdez was dead and Lupe's husband, Juan Ramirez, was wounded but escaped to bring the bad tidings to Alcalde Ortega. Juan was badly injured and would die before nightfall. Worse news was to come from Lupe Ramirez.

The men of the village, at word from the alcalde, gathered in the cantina where they had taken the hemorrhaging Juan Ramirez. Lupe had been allowed to be there to look after Juan's wounds while the men deliberated in a council of war, a situation foreign to all of them. Lupe wept in frustration, powerless to help her husband.

Repeated applications of clean cloth pads failed to staunch the flow of blood from two grievous belly wounds. Juan had become irrational and thrashed against his pain as she tried to calm him with cool, moist cloths on his forehead, which flowed with sweat. The cantina was a large and empty place that showed signs of going downhill. To Lupe's usual way of thinking, it had sunken to the depths the day it opened. Darkness pooled in the corner where the

62

townsmen sat, gravely digesting news they didn't want to hear.

"Kiowa Indians," Armando Ortega reported to the men after his hasty talk with the dying Juan Ramirez. "The Kiowa have not come here in a generation. Yet, now they come. They will follow Juan here. We must prepare for an attack."

With his ominous words, eight sombreros around him came off, eight gnarled and brown right hands traced crosses on chests and foreheads. Quickly murmured supplications for divine intercession momentarily took precedence.

"We must get busy and be ready for them," Armando warned as Father Dominguez, summoned from his meditations at the tiny whitewashed adobe chapel down the street, rushed in to hear Juan's confession and to administer the last rites.

For a moment Armando's eyes and those of the good padre locked. The town's legislative and religious leaders, they had often spoken of just such an eventuality. Those times the menace had always been the dread Comanches. Who knew anything about the Kiowas? their glance seemed to say. Then, as quickly, the padre turned away to attend to the departing soul of Juan Ramirez.

Their little town represented not much more than a cluster of crude, widely spaced *jacals*, squatty, cramped little cubicles, dominated by the whitewashed chapel, a two-story *mercado*, and the good-sized but poorly kept cantina. How could such a place withstand an Indian attack?

"Our rifles are poor, alcalde," whined Estevan Valdez, brother of the slain shepherd. "We are simple people who do not believe that God's way is the way of the rifle and the killing of other men."

"I am told the Kiowa believe exactly the reverse, friend Estevan," Armando counseled. "We must do the best we can to protect our homes, our wives, and our little ones. Go quickly and clean what guns you have and ready your supplies of powder and shot. Gustavo, do you still store the sticks of blasting powder in the stone cave behind your mercado?"

"*Sí, alcalde.* Only it is old now and . . ." Gustavo Obregon shrugged expressively. "Who knows if it will go off?"

Momentarily, Armando's mind conjured the grim company coming up the valley from the south. Vicious they would be, and would give no quarter. They might outnumber the villagers two to one. Hope just now, for Armando Ortega, seemed an elusive commodity. Armando Ortega had lived too long not to be realistic about the impending attack. And particularly the legendary viciousness of the marauding Kiowas.

They could shoot like it was solemn business and never seemed to know when they should call it a day's work and time for a refreshing, relaxing drink of pulque. They would kill without mercy, through the night if necessary, until all vestiges of resistance had vanished. And, for the women, the dying would come too late.

The village men they would ride over and slaughter swiftly, like so many sheep. Screaming terrorized children would be shot or their heads dashed against trees or buildings, if only to shut them up. The larger ones, Armando had heard, would be sodomized. Then the savages would turn their attentions to the real prize of the impending attack: the town's four women, five if he counted old Señora Franco, the aging, wizened-up blind woman in the falling-down *jacal* on the outskirts. She was well over eighty and would hardly be appealing to ravaging Kiowa braves but . . . *madre de dios,* he thought, one could never anticipate what a blood-maddened Indian would do.

Armando shuddered over his thoughts. His men

would be outnumbered. Yet with preparation, they might stand a chance. What they needed was a reliable defensive position. Best, he considered, to confine his efforts to their defense and for the moment try not to speculate on the consequences.

Through the afternoon the men labored under Armando's direction to fortify several stout, adobe-walled buildings. The sun had only begun to set and grow large and orange in the west when thunderous hoofbeats south of town proved all of Armando's fears to be correct. Within moments of the stilling of the invaders' hoofbeats, rifles began to crack out of the shallow arroyos that surrounded the village.

Armando knew who commanded them, at least had heard of him. Crooked Leg, the most vicious and heartless of all Kiowas. He had been taken to the gringo Fort Sill in chains. A renegade, he had left the reservation to the east to seek the old Kiowa ways of war and pillage.

Now Crooked Leg sent his braves on two attacking salients which would swiftly thin the opposing force of Mexican villagers. They would be wiped out as quickly as prudent with concern for Kiowa life and limb—a condition not strongly considered by vain warriors who believed they went to glory if they died in battle. Then the Kiowas would get to the real work of the day, the village's supposed riches in its chapel, in the much-desired mescal and pulque in the cantina . . . and its women.

This was a new, young village. Crooked Leg would be well aware of that from its appearance. That meant the women, too, would be young, plump but not fat, with smooth and dusky skins and tender with juices and warm sauces in the right places when a man unlimbered his pole to try to find its depth between compelling Mexican legs. Armando suppressed a shudder.

He had arranged that the women and children be

secured in a place of refuge, safe from bullets in the chapel. Perhaps, he thought without real hope, the Kiowas would respect the house of God and allow the women and children to live. Perhaps, too, he considered bitterly, he had only made the Kiowas' task easier by gathering the innocents in one place. The roar and concussion of battle dinned all around Armando, shattering his reverie.

He tried to focus his attention on leading the men in defense, yet sadly he had simply too many weak points to try to fill. He would no sooner direct men to a vulnerable point, than firing would intensify from another quarter and he would try to rally his puny resistance in that direction. He fought against panic while his fear and inadequacy poured sweat all over his body and his mouth grew dry as a desert pebble and sour tasting. Sadly he kept a count of the toll.

In the opening volleys, Armando's nephew fell immediately with a shot through the throat. Armando's brother, Rudólfo, dropped with a wound in the chest. Armando remained too busy organizing and rallying his defenders to know their condition. Through it, he fought savagely with the only weapon he owned, a great and ponderous Dragoon revolver brought home by his father before Armando was born, after the great war with the gringos that secured the entire Southwest for the despised Anglos. The firing of his untrained defenders proved ineffectual against a superior force of skilled, seasoned, and rapidly advancing Kiowa killers. Leaping from place to place, Armando encouraged his men and rallied them. He rose from the protection of a hasty breastwork to try for a shot at an exposed Kiowa he could see far out from the village's limits on the gradual hillside. Fire from that man's rifle had been extremely effective and Armando had never known of a rifle so dangerous at such a great distance.

He sped two shots into the spot from which gray

puffs had risen, if only hoping to keep the man from being so brazen with his shooting. The Indian marksman on the hill answered and Armando Ortega slumped, still clutching his smoking Dragoon. His mouth sagged open and his eyes stared skyward in death. A huge bullet hole, like a third eye socket, showed itself grotesquely in the center of his forehead.

Their alcalde down, the remaining handful of Mexican peons burst now in panic for the sanctuary of the chapel. One man tried to use a terrorized burro as a shield to escape from the village and the firefight. The big-bore rifle that had struck down Armando Ortega belched like a sick buffalo from the slope.

The same bullet gut-shot both burro and man. In falling, the small donkey pinned the unfortunate campesino beneath it. Three remaining defenders sprinted for the chapel to be quickly picked off. Not a one of them gained the steps to the thick oaken door that hung on great, black-iron hinges.

6

Hurry or no, Eli Holten decided to spend a while alone, away from the routine of army garrison life, free of the sweet, delicate, yet demanding company of lovely ladies, apart even from the companionship of friends. He needed time to think about Maj. Randall Covington. He chose, then, to ride Sonny to Pierre to take the Union Pacific spur south to Omaha, and the MKT line on from there to Kansas City and the AT&SF.

How fast civilization moved, he pondered as the miles slid slowly past at Sonny's best walking gait. Early that spring he had taken the steam packet north from Independence, Missouri to Pierre. Now the mail boats had become a thing of the past as the final rails had been laid for the new spur. Before long the entire frontier would be partitioned off into neat parcels by the twin steel ribbons and neither man nor animal could roam free.

Like the damned farmers in Kansas and their barbed wire. They claimed the vicious strands only served to mark their holdings. Any cowman could tell you they existed solely to keep Texas cattle out and secure the market for locally raised beef. The Jayhawkers and Red Legs had outlawed liquor, now they seemed determined to outlaw Texicans as well.

Holten wished them the joy of it. For himself, he welcomed the return to the rough and untamed reaches of Arizona.

"Only I got a feeling we'll be goin' through hell to get there," he advised his horse.

Considering the person of Maj. Randall Covington, well that might be, Eli mused. He had first met Covington upon arrival in Arizona Territory. He had reported in to then Fort McDowell. Crook was in the field, served by Tom Jeffords as chief scout, to powwow with Geronimo. Geronimo wasn't another Cochise and held Jeffords in low esteem. He felt the scout, despite his Apache wife, had betrayed the people by leading them onto reservations unsuited for human habitation.

In fact, Jeffords had nothing to do with the placement of the Chiricawa, Mescalero, White Mountain, Jicarilla, and other Apache bands. He had stood by helplessly, cursing, while the bewildered people got herded onto malaria-infested swamps and river bottoms that flooded yearly during the brief rainy season. When conditions grew totally intolerable, Geronimo, Naiche, and old Nana rebelled. They led the young men off the reservation. Nelson Miles, for all his skill in dealing with the Nez Perce and Sioux, failed utterly to understand the Apache mentality.

When Crook returned, many of the agency jumpers gave up. He had even been able to recruit a company of Apache scouts. It was to these volunteers that Eli Holten had been assigned. The officer in charge had been a staffer, the training officer, Maj. Randall Covington.

Jealous of his position so close to the famed general, Covington took an immediate dislike to Eli Holten, whose reputation as a crackerjack scout had preceded him to the Southwest. Newspaper men and dime novelists had extolled the courage, skill, and amorous adventures of the 12th U.S. Cavalry's civilian chief of scouts for several years. Most disconcerting to Covington's way of thinking, the real thing outstripped the fabled product of sensationalist journalism.

Holten fit right in, got along. He even began to learn the Apache language. Fluent in Sioux, passable in Cheyenne and Arapaho, with a smattering of French, Eli Holten fit the requirement of linguist far better than did the protégé of the ambitious, albeit unremarkable, Randall Covington. In Crook's absence, Covington contrived to make life miserable for Eli Holten and his assignments impossible.

Assisted by the willing cooperation of Ski-Be-Nan-Ted—the Apache Kid—and seven hard-core Apache volunteers, the scout company shaped up into the best trackers and most able fighting men in any army department. Covington raged in private and plotted other means for Holten's downfall.

At each turning, Holten came out of it with laurels, Covington with another black mark on his efficiency report. Gen. George Crook began to court the scout. Covington became critical of his superior. Injudicious words, dropped among fellow officers, and eventually to the press, brought for a time the possibility of censure for General Crook.

Then, in typical manner, Eli Holten pulled the general's rump roast out of the coals. In reprisal, Covington conceived a suicide mission for Holten and his Apache scouts. Holten and all but five of the company of volunteer scouts came out of it alive, with a dozen of the most wanted renegade Apaches as prisoners. The notorious Bacoon they brought in dead. In the end, it had been Randall Covington who had been relieved.

Everyone fully expected the disgrace to end his career. Holten actually did all he could to see the board of inquiry got the correct impression. When

70

Frank Corrington informed him that Major Covington would be traveling with the company—damn, troop now—of recruits, Eli had been genuinely surprised.

Now his ruminations brought him to the conclusion that Randall Covington, scion of one of those "proper" New England families, had used family influence to not only keep his commission, but to prosper with a posting to the War Department. Now someone, thinking they did Covington a favor, had given in to the old adage that a field command looked good on an upwardly ambitious officer's record. The army, Holten reflected, was about to find out the extent of their error when they failed to dismiss Randall Covington from the service. Somehow, Eli contemplated, he would have to find a way to make a temporary truce with the malignant martinet for the good of the service and the safety of the cherry-troops.

Before that, he would have to make it safely into Pierre and on to Bent's Old Fort. Something, he chided himself, he wouldn't do if he continued to daydream.

Almost as suddenly as it started, the firing ceased. A deafening silence crept in to fill the void left by the violence. Minutes passed as the waning sun cast shadows over the clumps of valiant but inexperienced defenders, randomly scattered in death. Like wraiths rising from ancient graves, figures emerged from behind hummocks of gravel and clumps of sage and chaparral.

They moved with slow, measured strides from two sides of the village. The Kiowas had outnumbered Armando Ortega's defenders by more than five to one. Crooked Leg's force now numbered over forty braves. Padre Dominguez, the village's only surviving male adult, grabbed a large, gleaming crucifix from

71

the altar screen and raced out to meet the oncoming, merging Kiowa force.

He sought to appeal, to plead, in his innocent belief in mercy, for the lives and safety of the women and children. As he swung open the great chapel door and stepped out into the dying sunlight, the Kiowas stopped and stared blank-faced at the black-robed priest.

"*Pax vobiscum*," the padre intoned.

One Kiowa snickered. Another hefted his Winchester repeater.

"I come to prevail upon you to spare the women and children," the cleric declared in a broken voice.

None of the Kiowas spoke Spanish. Growing impatient, Crooked Leg shook the feathered lance he carried.

"Go forth now, leave this place in peace and none will pursue you. I must tend the dead and dying. Go now. I command this in the name of Christ. *In nomini patris, et filis—*"

A volley cut him down. The good padre's body slumped on the chapel steps. Blood began to pool on the stone risers.

At once, the invading force, turned loose now to their own devices by Crooked Leg, began to ravage the town. Some entered the humble, abandoned *jacals*, searching for riches or spoils, or women who might not have been herded into the chapel. As they looted and despoiled each *jacal*, the braves set it afire. The crackling of flames and dense gray-black smoke oozed up to fill the sky with an inky blackness which hastened the dark of night.

Others charged to the cantina to begin a night-long savage revelry in mescal and pulque. Crooked Leg sent men to the chapel to butcher the children and to make certain none of the women escaped.

*   *   *

Concepcion Madrid, huddled beside the altar, saw them enter. Terror rendered her heart numb. The faces she found on the savages moving through the place of worship seemed wooden, impassive masks. Yet their fierce, black eyes went over the women like exploring fingers. Concepcion shivered at the touch of their gaze. They appeared evil, ugly, dirty, and altogether repulsive and terrorizing. All around her, children cowered and shrieked before being dragged away out of the chapel. Concepcion never learned their fate.

Lupe Ramirez leaped up with a scream and rushed for the door. Three Kiowas caught her and Concepcion saw Lupe go down with a shriek under the trio. As four other men advanced toward Concepcion, she shoved herself back as far as she could against Padre Dominguez's lectern. Concepcion saw great flashes of colorful cloth fly in the air where Lupe lay in a swirl and tangle of arms and legs as her clothing was ripped from her struggling body.

Elsewhere in the chapel, similar fates were shared by the others of her woman friends in the village. A few terrified howls came from the women. Only high-pitched whoops of delight and anticipation came from the Indians thronging through the door. Concepcion, thoroughly frightened, tried to make herself smaller against the lectern. The three crouched over her. One pulled her away from her refuge, his companions stretched her prone on the altar.

Rude hands easily ripped away her white, low-necked bodice. Coarse hands groped up her dusky thighs, raised next the colorful skirt she had been so proud of. It shredded away in tatters and her chemise got pulled from her bare skin. A burly arm swept the candelabra and Bible stand from the altar. Exposed to them, plump and coppery, Concepcion knew they had revealed the wedge of soft, black fur at her crotch.

A man knelt beside her and while one moved to

thrust himself between her legs, the one at her side angrily jerked her head toward him at a painful, awkward angle. Her eyes widened in abject terror as he drew aside his loincloth to expose a massive, engorged, copper rod of flesh. It was tipped by a giant, ruby head, with a pouting little mouth set vertically; sight of it made her stomach churn.

Concepcion's head was pulled toward the repulsive thing that loomed larger and thicker than any snake she had ever seen. The evil cap was rammed against her lips and when her mouth resisted, a filthy, callused hand yanked her lower jaw down and the loathsome object forced its entry. She gagged and coughed as her assailant rammed its length in her throat. The suffocating monster began vicious lunges over her lips and down her gullet. Concepcion grew certain it would kill her.

She remained only vaguely conscious of another massive shaft's cruel penetration between her legs and the same brutal thrusts pounding against her tender groin. For a long time, an eternity it seemed, the vicious thudding beasts pounded into her bruised lips and fevered loins. Suddenly these monstrous *diablillos* spurted their obnoxious venom and withdrew. Nausea gripped her, yet nothing came up.

Others of the war-painted Kiowas took the places of the first pair. For countless hours, Concepcion's only release from these moments of terror, agony, and degradation came in an occasional glimpse of the great colored crucifix high above at the rear of the chancel. Clinging like a drowning victim to the sight, she shared in her Blessed Savior's ordeal on His cross. She tried, when her anguished mind allowed it, to pray for understanding that she was in no way party to the depraved indignities being forced upon her or to the desecration of the church. She begged, pleaded for His forgiveness.

Again and again they mounted her. Concepcion

74

became aware only of the shuddering lust of whatever man pressed his suffocating bulk on top of her at any given moment. Hard hands yanked her from the altar at some time in the night. She recoiled in horror as yet another of the bronze-skinned savages approached and knelt between her legs.

She wanted, as she had time and time before, to shout out for mercy, yet somehow held herself above it as futile and dangerous. Roaring in her ears came the lecherous cackles and grunts of approval from eager spectators, as the man spent himself and rolled up to stagger drunkenly away through the nave. His ugly mouth made meaningless words and giggles of delight, shaming her to her core. Why didn't she die? Why didn't God let her die?

Then another approached and flung aside his breechclout. Concepcion saw another gnarled instrument of torture and knew she must endure yet a further agonizing round of torment. As the swollen organ came closer her awareness became mercifully numbed by the onslaught of unconsciousness.

At dawn, Concepcion got only a brief moment of relief. Through the broad open doors to the chapel her heavy-lidded eyes could see a gray morning breaking. For but a second she could ponder the fate of her children, certain her husband lay dead. Some Kiowas around her whooped in mirth and chattered drunkenly among themselves.

At once they thronged toward the chapel's nave where Concepcion had seen Lupe go down under a trio of bellering Indians. They bent low and grabbed flaccid arms. Lupe, naked as Concepcion, blood streaming down her legs, was pulled up and dragged along the aisle to the chancel, barely conscious. Two brutes flung down Lupe's battered body beside Concepcion and slapped her to awareness.

While she responded groggily, the demons draped Lupe over Concepcion, her legs straddled Concepcion's head, her face pushed down into the sparse triangle of sodden black fur at Concepcion's crotch. Fully conscious now, Lupe scrambled off her friend's inert form in rebellion against this final, unconscionable indignity. A Kiowa appeared with some sort of great gun with two barrels and fired at Lupe. A bright, concussive explosion rattled the chancel.

Lupe's head vanished in a red mist of brains, hair, skin, and bone that spattered all over the floor and walls. Lupe's naked, blood-soaked remains contorted and writhed beside the hysterical Concepcion.

Her body numbed beyond pain, brain drugged with horrors and shame, Concepcion struggled to take her gaze off Lupe's twitching corpse. Willing herself with prayer and untapped fortitude, she riveted her eyes upon the thorn-crowned image of her Blessed Savior on the wall above her.

"Oh, my God, I am heartily sorry . . . ," she began to pray. Then her heart, gentle, innocent, and trusting as that of a little fawn, burst and Concepcion Madrid expired close to the throne of her Lord.

7

Holten had "ridden the cars" throughout the West to scouting assignments for Gen. Frank Corrington and others. He traveled from badlands to mighty pine-furred mountain ranges and from blistering sun to raging blizzards. He had been hauled to destinations by old "diamond stack" Baldwin No. 4s, American Locomotive Works 4-4-0s, and modern, streamlined 4-6-2 and 4-6-4 locomotives capable of breathtaking speeds up to sixty miles an hour.

Of all the railway lines that now spiderwebbed the West, Eli found he most greatly admired the Atchison, Topeka and Santa Fe, which was a mouthful despite its lyrical lilt. AT&SF proved almost as hard to say casually, so travelers simply settled on "the Santa Fe." These days if someone said he rode the Santa Fe, he meant the railway and not the tradition- and legend-soaked overland trade route from western Missouri to Santa Fe in the newly admitted state of New Mexico.

In almost constant use after 1825, long before Holten was born, and nearly obsoleted by the westering railroads, the Santa Fe Trail remained a memorable stretch of nostalgia for mule skinner and mountain man alike. Many an immigrant family had passed through the Great American Desert along its rutted path. Now it was either essentially grown over or plowed under as far west as the Lower Spring on the Cimarron Cutoff. The mighty route of commerce had given way to the corduroy of ties and the dual thin stripes of gleaming rails.

Two Bulls, Eli Holten's Oglala Sioux foster father, described the immense sweep of the Santa Fe Trail as "many sleeps." Except for some idiot in the War Department, it slept now in memory. Holten favored the new Santa Fe for its clean, well-lighted coaches, the unflagging but unfawning courtesy of conductors and porters, and the facility of a smoking car on each run for the convenience of its adult male passengers, where a man could also buy a drink. With his thoughts turned to travel, instead of the sinister Major Covington, Holten's mood improved.

Heading back for Arizona this time, he planned as he strolled through Pierre, he first would be exposed to the lesser amenities of a Union Pacific spur line, taking him out of Dakota Territory via Omaha, Nebraska, and on into Kansas City. There he would pick up the Santa Fe for the run to his jumping-off place for points farther west, Dodge City, Kansas.

With Sonny and his bedroll in a stock car toward the head end of the train, Holten found a spot on one of the thinly upholstered plank seats covered by an abrasive, but long-wearing, diamond-shaped, embossed fabric. He adjusted his brain to two days of dull, monotonous travel. The spur line afforded no sleeping coach, so Holten was obliged to stay in his seat dozing now and again, both day and night, and awake for similar pitch-dark or daylight stretches.

Like a whore taking on whatever foul assignment she might get, so long as the money was good, Holten shut off his mind to the hardships of a seat that would make a saddle feel like a sultan's cushion. Hat tipped down over his eyes, he leaned back and spent the endless hours reliving the past and anticipating the future.

Images of the spiteful, pouting face of Randall Covington danced in and out of his reflections. After their first unpleasant encounter, Holten had considered the peevish major to be a small, thoroughly spoiled boy, grown to adult size without the accompanying advantage of profiting from the lessons of maturity. Hell, Eli chided himself, that sounded every bit as pompous and pretentious as Randall Covington in person. He at last came to the conclusion that whatever the immediate future might hold, with or without Randall Covington, he was fortunate that the key to it would be Harry Adams.

Laying over a half day in Kansas City, Holten found a bathhouse and soaked his weary bones, then shaved in the steaming establishment run by a plump, bowing-and-scraping, tight-eyed Chinaman known only as One Hung Lo, a handle hung on him by one of the local wags, a certain Frank Pendergast.

Eli had a washerwoman in the Chinaman's emporium scrub and dry his trail clothes and press the wrinkles from his Sunday duds, which he would save for the K.C. to Dodge run on the Santa Fe. The relaxation of the Santa Fe's ample amenities would compensate for the dubious ride down from Dakota.

"You makee velly clean, Mis-tah Hol-ten," One Hung Lo pronounced the finished product, long fingers of his soft hands polishing each other. "You makee quickee look-see Tenderloin, go rumpty-dumpty with nice white gel?"

"Nope, One," Eli responded. "I got my ashes hauled right proper before I left Dakota Territory."

One Hung Lo produced a lascivious grin. "You go two way, three way, maybe, one girl?"

"Nooo," Holten drawled. He knew from his days watching the railroad creep across the nation that the Chinese held great score with prodigious sexual

79

performance. "I go four way, maybe more with five girl. One time all together."

Lo's almond eyes went round with appreciative wonder. "Aie! *Dzwày cháhng chyáng!*"

"What?" Eli asked, unable to understand Chinese.

"I make talkee, say, the longest rifle. Ho-ho, you makee big mans allasame."

"Hummm," Holten responded noncommittally. *Well, he had made time with all five Thorne sisters once long ago.*

His afternoon in Kansas City proved every bit as uninspiring as the ride down from Pierre. Perhaps, Holten reflected, he shouldn't have avoided the Tenderloin District.

Lurching through the coach as the Santa Fe clanked, wheezed, and chuffed out of Kansas City, Eli Holten tossed his war bag in the iron-rod rack overhead and settled his now-happier bones, sighed, and sat back. Unless they took on more passengers down the line, he'd have the double seat all to himself clear into Dodge. A nearly empty Pullman car also offered promise. His spirits ran high. He'd gotten clean and well fed in K.C., and as far as Eli Holten could be concerned, all was right with the world.

He had bought a newspaper during his layover and now leaned his long legs across the ample space afforded him. Leisurely he began to read up on the day's events, a luxury his life-style seldom allowed.

Over the top of the tabloid, Holten eyed one of his traveling companions, alone like himself, in the double seat across the aisle. She had blond hair, the rich gold of dried straw, and unlike most blondes, had a complexion that would only deepen in the sun. Perky in a starched white percale frock, she wore a modified sunbonnet-style hat. White lace gloves clothed her delicate hands and supple fingers.

Holten considered her features to be pert, petite,

80

and piquant. Probably belying her true age, he considered cynically. Her face said she could scarcely be out of her teens. But the body that went with it revealed mature lines, well filled in all the proper places. It prompted animal instincts in Eli Holten as he studied her over the dark columns of newsprint and the off-white top margin.

Apparently sensing Holten's gaze on her, the girl lightly shifted her head and her eyes, blue and deep as as a mountain pool, found his. She smiled sweetly, unabashed by his bold stare. Eli felt a familiar stirring in his loins.

He reddened at being caught ogling so openly and reached up to tip his hat. Belatedly remembering only when his fingers brushed his forehead that his Stetson rested above him in the rack with his war bag. He turned the gesture into a courteous salute.

"Ma'am," he said politely.

Her voice came soft as a dove's breast, unheard over the rumble of the railway coach, yet he could read her lips saying, "Good morning, sir."

Holten acknowledged with a thin smile. Embarrassed, he went back to the columns of his paper. His attention again shifted from his reading to movement at the front of the car. A man had gotten up and, grabbing the seat backs to maintain his balance against the carriage's roll and pitch, made his awkward, staggering way to where Holten and the young woman sat midway in the coach.

He was a tall, big-boned man of dominant presence, with glacial black eyes set in a dark face. On first impression, Holten surmised that the man would be no stranger to a life of wading through crime and sudden violence.

Though ample in proportion, he had been hawkishly leaned by short rations and little sleep, emphasized by a long and austere, black, broadcloth

81

coat. He doffed his short-crowned hat of the same color and held it in one hand.

His hungry eyes feasted on the blond morsel across the aisle from Holten. His close-set, black eyes said he'd take any desperate chance that came along, whether for women or gold. His teeth were yellowed, from inattention or liberal use of chewing tobacco, and he showed them abundantly when he tried to fix a friendly smile on his face.

He ignored Holten to move to the empty seat beside the young woman. "This taken?" Holten heard him ask in a deep bass, with a note of foregone conclusion.

The girl's eyes fixed with the lingering fear of a trapped rabbit, much too polite to refuse. She nodded shyly, and the intruder swung himself heavily into the seat beside her.

"Th' name's Flint. Leander Flint," the rawboned man introduced himself.

"How do you do?" the blonde responded coolly, without giving her name.

Holten had not heard him give his name and went back to his paper, assuming it to be none of his affair. Nonetheless he felt a burn of resentment rise in him. Over the clack and rattle of the train as it made its way over the rolling hills of eastern Kansas, Holten grew aware of the deep drone of the man's voice, the words indistinguishable.

That the man made small talk as precursor to a hard sell was evident. Holten figured it wasn't up to him to legislate the cute blonde's preference. Unless the boorish bastard became ungentlemanly, Holten figured to let nature take its course.

His eyes caught an item about famine among the Indians and he read to acquaint himself with the particulars until he reached the word Calcutta. He realized it involved another kind of Indians halfway around the world. The big man now appeared to be making his pitch in shrewd but unrelenting terms, Holten observed.

The young girl politely though firmly declined. Eli now took it all in. The two seemed deeply engrossed in the rowdy's game of cat-and-mouse, paying scant attention to the man across the aisle. The ardent suitor dug into his clothing to come up with a thin silver flask, offering a dram to his unwilling seat companion.

Demurely, she again declined. It was obvious she did her best as the well-bred young lady she was to rid herself of this leech while retaining her dignity and composure. When her erstwhile admirer swept back his coattails in the grope for his hip-pocket flask, Holten caught a glimpse of a mahogany-leather tie-down holster and the rich, well-rubbed, smooth grips of a gleaming blue-steel Colt, conspicuously much used.

The incessant drumming of his bass droned on as he finished his own slug of whiskey from the metal container and returned it to his rear pocket. His words became more demanding and the girl's rejections of his advances grew louder, more strident, and less polite. Any minute, Holten prepared to launch out of his seat to put man-to-man teeth into the young woman's refusals of the man's advances.

Before that became necessary, the boor said something rude and cutting and lurched up to make his way down the aisle toward the doors that led to the smoking car. As he left his seat beside her, Flint gazed with freezing eyes at Holten, who had obviously witnessed his failure at seduction.

Recognition of Holten, if only fleeting, also flamed in the man's gaze as he turned to storm away. Reaching the car's vestibule ahead, he turned once to stare, not at the girl, but at Eli Holten. Close-set eyes narrowed in some kind of conclusion, signaling some link with the past. For all his remarkable memory, Holten could not recall seeing that vile face before. Still it left something there to be reckoned with.

Herself embarrassed by the display of raw emotions that had been thrust upon her, the girl glanced apologetically at Holten. Other occupants of the coach had been oblivious of the scene. That fact seemed to heighten her discomfort. It moved Holten to lean across the aisle and speak to her.

"Beggin' your pardon, young miss," he drawled. "I hasten to reassure you there are one or two gentlemen left in this world. That gent wouldn't have gone much farther without my steppin' in and takin' a hand."

Her eyes fluttered. "You're very kind, Mr.—?"

"Holten, ma'am. Eli Holten. Where I come from, they send out a committee to negotiate with hombres who are forward with our women. Some of those improper jaspers have been known to wind up in trees, if you know what I mean."

The girl blanched, but only momentarily. "I appreciate your concern, Mr. Holten. My name's Redmond. Rose Redmond." She courteously offered her lace-gloved hand. Holten gripped it as daintily as his pawlike hands would permit and quickly released it. "And I love the scent of white camellias."

Her remark seemed a non sequitur to Holten, who gave her a warm smile. "He'll not bother you again, Miss Redmond. And to make sure, I believe I'll go forward to the smoking car and take a cigar, and . . . if need be, have a little chat with our gentleman friend."

"That shouldn't be necessary, Mr. Holten, much as I appreciate your chivalry." Her eyes gleamed at him and in them, Holten felt he caught some sort of message. "And please do call me Rose."

Patting himself to be sure he had at least two of Frank Corrington's fine Havanas, Holten rose.

"Your servant, Miss Rose."

"Thank you, Mr. Holten . . . ah, Eli." She made his given name sound like the music of angels.

Holten made his way out of the car, opened the door to the vestibule on the deafening clack-and-grind of the tracks and roar of wind of the moving train. Conscious of the ill-matched tread plates that slid across each other with every rocking motion, he crossed the short walkway over the couplers and swung open the door to the smoker. Slamming the door behind him instantly shut out the blast of sound as tons of steel and wood plummeted across Kansas. The car, he saw, was nearly deserted.

Toward the front of the coach, a great distance from Holten, two men at a bolted-down table bent toward each other, deeply engrossed in conversation. Close to his position, a prissily dressed, slender man with the face of martyrdom tried to restrain the activities of a rambunctious six-year-old while puffing furiously on a pipe and trying to read a newspaper. Behind a short, curved bar, a Negro in a white linen jacket and a black, woven rattan cap with gleaming visor and brass nameplate reading Porter, stood ready to serve drinks or otherwise accommodate the Santa Fe's passengers.

Midway in the car of tables, chairs, and smoking stands, Leander Flint stood at a window, braced at a waist-high rail below the sill, looking out. He had a thin cigar in one hand and his silver flask in the other. He still had, to Holten, the looks of a hard hombre with his holster tied down for business concealed under the knee-length, black broadcloth coat.

Holten took a seat near the rear of the car and rolled his green wrapper Havana between wide, thick fingertips. Blue-tipped lucifer matches were available in crystal cylinders secured in a hole in the tabletop. Holten bit off the end of his cigar and fired it with one of these while he regarded the big, mean-faced man.

Lee Flint had been aware of Holten's entrance, yet so far had ignored him. Now, almost as if on impulse, he left his place by the window and strode back to where Holten sat calmly smoking as he watched the unending prairie roll past the window. Holten's peripheral vision fixed on the tall man approaching him.

"Mind?" Flint asked as he stopped by Holten's table and made as if to pull out a chair.

"Help yourself."

"Purely hate to smoke alone," Flint allowed, sitting down. He propped his elbows on the glossy veneered surface and dragged on his Marsh Wheeling.

"Were I inclined that way, I wouldn't smoke as much," Holten told him.

"Take a jolt?" Flint asked, offering the silver flask.

If there existed one paragraph in Holten's code in boldface print it was that he only drank alone or with friends. At the moment he would have preferred the former, and was well persuaded this bastard would never be counted among the latter. He knew it to also be time to move on this rough-cut specimen.

"No thanks. I make it a practice never to drink on a full stomach."

For a moment, Flint ignored him. "The name's Flint. Leander Jacob Flint." Holten put teeth in his contempt by not taking the proferred hand. Flint drew his back insulted. "I don't understand you, sir. You mean you don't drink on an empty stomach?"

Holten flared. "I meant exactly what I said. I never drink on a full stomach, and just now I've had a belly full of you."

"Wait a minute, wait a minute, friend," Flint gobbled, hands raised slightly as though fending off a physical assault. "If you're referring to the young lady in the Pullman back there, I was merely passing

86

the amenities of the day with a fellow traveler."

"In a pig's ass you were. I know a mangy coyote scenting fresh meat when I see one." Holten's voice grated like old iron.

Flint was easily angered. "Why you're not even decent. I know you, Holten. They say you steal like an Injun, fight like a wildcat, and ain't got no respect for nothin', as you have just amply demonstrated. They tell me they found your last victim dead next morning near the river with his pockets turned out."

Leander Flint proved not too good at fighting talk. Still, under other circumstances, Holten might have accommodated him just the same with fists or side-arms. His thoughts went to the girl in the next car, on his enjoyment of Santa Fe, and the gentle Negro porter watching with large, luminous eyes a few steps away. He considered this neither the proper time nor place for a fight. Yet Eli Holten would never be a man to be pushed past his limit.

"I'll not respond to that, Mr. Flint. I only ask that you go and leave me in peace."

"You're backing off? I'm a son of a bitch. I'm backing down the great Eli Holten."

"Don't push your luck, Flint."

"Ha! The great scout. You rode with General Miles. I'm truly surprised at his poor taste in civilian personnel. I was there, too. Only I called him Colonel Miles then."

Wait a minute, Holten thought. Leander Jacob Flint. Recollection fled back like a shred of nightmare remembered.

Jake Flint. Yeah. Sutler at Fort Robinson. Holten squinted his gray eyes at Flint reflectively. A man who moved wherever the tide of easy profit took him. Fired by Congress as an Indian agent for, among other things, deducting horrendous sums from the Indians' annuities for snake-head whiskey, weevily flour, and decaying pork. When food poisoning from

87

ancient meat and spoiling staples killed fifteen Sioux men, women, and children drawing rations at his agency, the subsequent investigation by the Bureau of Indian Affairs deposed Jake Weller as an Indian agent.

He received a reprimand, was chided really, for mismanagement, though more likely for having been caught out. Then, because of the threat of his knowledge of shady deals in high places, Flint gratuitously received the sutler's post at Fort Robinson. There, argued the powers-that-be, his scheming wouldn't likely kill his customers—the post's cavalry troopers—but rather only skin them of their meager wages through grossly inflated prices.

Since then, Flint had shown up in, and been run out of, Arizona Territory. Jake Flint and Maj. Randall Covington were as if cut from the same leather. Shrewd, vicious, and scheming, they each sought to rise through the misery of others. Little wonder, Holten thought, that they had been bedfellows and confidants in frontier treachery and chicanery.

Jake Flint—no way to know what he was up to these days—wasn't about to walk away from a man whose reputation he despised and whom he now perceived as a rival for the favors of the tenderloin in percale perched in the first coach back.

"You forget, Holten," Flint sneered, "that I was there when your precious Chief Crazy Horse hatched his dastardly plot to assassinate Colonel Miles, one of the greatest cavalry officers America has ever produced, Sheridan, Stuart, and Custer be damned."

Holten looked at Flint again. Now standing, big fists clinched, big mouth to go with them, Flint towered over him. Holten had been loyal to Miles, and still respected him. Still he also had strong allegiance to the Sioux. Also a keen—nay, acute—understanding of the betrayal of all tribes and the duplicity of the many beyond numbers of scheming representatives of the White Father in Washington.

"I have already suggested, Mr. Flint, and yes, I know of you and your nefarious history only too well and too painfully. I have recommended that you not push your luck. I will so state again. Crazy Horse, under whom my foster father, Two Bulls, was a head man, was himself viciously murdered at Fort Robinson, not for plotting against General Miles, nor for his role in devastating the Seventh Cavalry, but more because he was a persuasive spokesman for the Sioux in their times of trouble."

"Pisswilly," Flint interjected.

Holten ignored him. "Crazy Horse sought to maintain some kind of equilibrium and forthright negotiations with the White Father at a time when the War Department and the Indian Bureau preferred annihilation to coexistence."

"Folderol. Crazy Horse—as his name suggests—was a savage, ruthless killer lashing out with no more thought for his people than raising hell and white men's hair," Flint snarled.

Holten eased up from his chair. His glance caught the eye of the black porter. Holten spoke through anger-thinned lips. "I apologize in advance to you, sir. I will be responsible for any damages."

Lee Flint regarded Holten with astonishment. By now the prissy gentleman with the pipe hugged his little boy to his chest and the two gentlemen at the front of the smoking car had broken off their conversation. They watched slack-jawed at the two in confrontation some distance from them.

"And gentlemen," Eli called, "my respects. Stay where you are and you shan't be hurt. The drinks are on me after this gentleman and I have settled our differences."

Saying it, Holten had a fist built and for an instant stood bleak-eyed and somber as he scanned the black, glistening eyes of the hawkish face of Lee Flint and slowly edged toward him. Flint had made no moves toward his gun, and Holten responded in kind, though his gunfighter instincts leaped alive, urging and insistent.

"Crazy Horse wore handcuffs and leg irons when he was stabbed in the back with a bayonet wielded by a young, white soldier under orders from your croney, Captain Harvey," he recited in icy calm. "And you, sir, are a lying son of a bitch."

Instantly Eli's fist came up and Flint caught a hard one on the tip of his chin. He reeled back, not losing his footing, despite the careering of the Santa Fe smoker. Licking reptilian lips, he waded back in toward Holten, eyes flashing.

Unwilling to keep it a fair fight, Flint swept back the skirt of his broadcloth coat and a heavy, long-barreled Colt leaped into his hand, flickering with wicked, blue-steel sheen.

8

With the same speed, Holten's hand darted out, caught the gun hand by the thick, steel-corded wrist, and wrenched it back to ineffectual range. Stepping in, Holten glared at the gun and into the iced eyes of Leander Flint, almost nose to nose with him.

"Damn you for the back-shooting coward you are, Flint," he growled. "Drop that thing or I'll break your goddamn arm."

Slowly, Flint loosed his hold on the six-gun. Holten gave a twist to Flint's wrist and the weapon skittered back along the carpeted floor in the direction of the terrorized, white-jacketed porter. Holten pushed Flint away from him without landing a blow. The scout purposely held his fists at waist level, which gave Flint the opening and the advantage. Lean as he was, Flint bested Holten in both height and weight, and sheer muscle.

Furious, Flint charged in, aiming a haymaker at Holten's head. The scout ducked and felt the arcing fist whistle over him. He landed a solid one in Flint's hard armor of belly muscle. Holten sensed that Flint endured no pain while his hand and wrist speared fire from the blow to his elbow. Flint's lips curled back from his yellowed teeth in a gloating grin as he pressed in again.

This time he landed a one-two on Holten's cheek and his midriff. Eli felt the man's formidable strength in the blows and knew his hope of victory lay in avoiding a straight give-and-take. He had to win, and fast, or his opponent would trample him to a pulp. He couldn't expect victory by matching his strength against Flint's power blows.

The big man lunged and Holten sidestepped. Instantly he set himself to try one cut to finish the fight. Feet set, Eli brought it up from his swiveling hips. It was an inspiring blow that flooded Holten with euphoria. Cracking Flint on the chin and jaw, it tipped him backward. As though to defy Holten's delight, Flint caught himself and waded back.

Holten went for the head. Flint's torso simply absorbed too much punishment without effect. This time Eli nimbly ducked blows from both Flint's fists, which came at him from either direction. Holten danced back a couple steps and grinned evilly at Flint, further infuriating the giant.

His arms flailing, Flint again offered his head as a vulnerable, ready target. Holten's rock-hard left caught Flint on the cheekbone and eye, splitting the right eyebrow, which instantly splattered blood. For all the battering Holten had given him, Flint still had the solid strength of a buffalo bull.

Toe-to-toe now, no quarter given, they flailed and slugged at gut and face. Holten landed a solid one that crunched Flint's nose like an eggshell. Driven blood fanned over his cheeks and gave Flint a comical look. Flint stared a moment, astonished at the incredible pain in the center of his face, then slumped to the floor.

"You're whipped, Flint," Eli panted as he stood over the man, fisted arms still drawn up. Flint pulled himself to his knees and then to his feet, weaving in again as the strength of rage flowed back into him.

Holten's expression set grimly as he sidestepped

the charge. He sent every pound in his lean frame zooming along his muscles as he again smashed out a prodigious blow, which took Flint with a solid slam in the jaw.

Flint recoiled, sagged, reeled back, and in falling, tipped over a smoking car chair. For a long moment, Flint lay still. He tried to rise, slumped back again to the floor, his breathing deep and noisy.

Holten rubbed his sweaty face. His hand came away free of any trace of blood, for which he was thankful. He stepped over the inert form of Lee Flint and tossed a silver dollar to the porter.

"This will buy a drink for the gents at the back with my apologies for the disturbance, and with the balance to you my good man."

The black man's eyes registered his appreciation. Without further acknowledgment of the other witnesses in the car, Holten spun on his heel and strode back to the Pullman coach.

Holten returned to his seat across the aisle from Rose Redmond. Her eyes anxiously searched his face that, despite being unbloodied, certainly told the story of the battering he had taken from Lee Flint. She forced an uncertain smile.

"Eli," she began, gasping as he made his rocking way along the aisle, "you've been hurt."

"A mere difference of opinion, my dear. Only a difference of opinion."

"You fought over me!" Rose Redmond squeaked, her hands clasped melodramatically at her breasts as she looked at Holten with calf eyes.

If she hadn't been prime target for his suave advances later and the woman he had just fought over like a rutting bull at mating time, he might have been tempted to let go of it then and there. He disliked affectations in men and women as well.

"Not entirely," Eli offered glibly. "It turned out that Mr. Lee Flint and I had conflicting viewpoints dating back several years. Your presence, young miss, was probably only a catalyst to bring on a confrontation brewing for a long time."

"But you fought for me," Rose wailed in full histrionics.

"Again, actually, no," Holten stated mattter-of-factly. "It was more for the good name of Chief Crazy Horse."

Rose Redmond looked at him quizzically. Deprived of her gusty motivation she tried twice to form words, her mouth working silently.

"To you," Holten continued, "it's a very small matter. May I?" He indicated the seat beside her. When Flint came back into the coach after his recovery from Holten's drubbing, Holten wanted Flint to know the spoils had been claimed.

Rose reached over with a petite gloved hand to pat the seat beside her, indicating her assent and invitation. Her deep blue eyes bored into his with some kind of undying admiration or fascination. Holten couldn't tell which as he took the seat beside her. Maybe, he thought, she was not as worldly as he had originally imagined.

"*Pop*-corn! Sarsaparilla! Sand-weeches!"

With a bellow the train's candy butcher burst into the coach from the head end, having passed through the smoker where Lee Flint probably sat licking his wounds. The train's car-by-car refreshment vendor had the dark, slick look of an itinerant snake-oil salesman and the nasal-voiced projection of a sideshow barker. Despite the Santa Fe's rumble, he could be heard the length of the car.

"Now, folks, it's a long ride to Topeka. We got hot coffee! If you want it hot, we got it hot, just like you like it! I will pass among you with sandwiches, cheese and ham, no substitutes, please, pie for those

94

who are so inclined, and choice candy confections for the little ones with the sweet tooth, too!''

Well wound up in his spiel, he carried a sturdy flat-bottomed wicker hamper over his arm, a steaming enameled coffee pot prominent as it projected from the basket. Waxed-paper–wrapped sandwiches and pie wedges, and small foil-covered squares of fudge or taffy formed ranks, and a clutch of rosy apples were piled in the center of the hamper.

Rattling off his wares Gatling-gun fast, he made his way through the car, a past master at maintaining his equilibrium while the Santa Fe rocketed and swayed as it made its way across Kansas. He dispensed his products with the same hand that expertly retained a sheaf of bills folded lengthwise between his fingers. He dipped out chicken-feed change from a narrow apron around his slim waist.

Behind the candy butcher, as he made his way through the coach, Lee Flint slunk in from the smoker. He had attracted Holten's attention when the roar through the vestibule door clashed with the relative quiet of the coach. When the portal slammed to, it closed out the cacophony behind Flint. The whipped man planned to get into a seat at the front without being seen by Holten.

He didn't make it. From somewhere, probably the porter's emergency supplies, some court plaster had been found. Flint wore a patch of the white adhesive, bulging with a pad of gauze bandage, over his split eyebrow. Another was prominent in a long strip across the bridge of his broken nose to keep it in place like a splint.

The glaring white of the adhesive tape stood in marked contrast to Flint's exposure-burned complexion. The area of right eye not covered by the white blaze of court plaster was going purple-black. In short, Lee Flint looked a sight. Holten tried to ignore Flint and not embarrass the man any more.

He had kicked Flint's ass and figured that was enough humiliation for one day.

Eli turned his attention to Rose Redmond, who set up a chatter that Holten found enchanting for a while, though after a time it got boring despite his fascination and yearnings for the attractive young blonde. She prattled on about her life, and going to Kansas Normal School for two years. Now she was heading for a schoolmarm assignment in a little town some distance east of Dodge City. When she paused to look over at Eli Holten, his head was back, his eyes closed in sleep.

Taking no offense, she reached over and patted his hands, crossed over his thighs, and thought: poor, dear man, he's exhausted himself protecting her honor from that depraved Mr. Flint. Rose felt strong emotions rise in her breast, and a compelling lubricity anointing her loins.

In his sleep, Eli Holten's hands unclasped and one groped blindly. Rose allowed one of hers to be taken and their fingers entwined, hands resting between their thighs, almost close enough to touch. Rose Redmond leaned her head back, too.

Maybe, she thought, the ride to Dodge City, where she would be met by representatives of the school board from Spearville, might produce a proposition from this blond, handsome giant beside her. Even if it took a little encouraging on her part.

Rose Redmond learned young. She had often parlayed her virginal, innocent looks and refined charms into a fair number of male bedchambers in her time. Since that day, a dozen years in the past, when she had eagerly and giddily surrendered her maidenhead, she had accumulated a vast store of erotic memoirs which would surely shock and scandalize the proprietary ladies of Boston. The strong-jawed, tanned outdoorsman next to her, she mused, would be a pushover. She closed her eyes, contemplating the strong thrust of his hard member, and allowed memory to waft her away to a gently rhythmic sleep provided by the train's incessant movement.

It felt uncommonly like the beat of a strong male thrust, warm and deep inside her. In all her twenty-four years, Rose Redmond had never felt so completely erotic. Behind closed lids, she giggled silently over a small orgasm and went to sleep.

Eli and Rose were jarred awake, still holding hands, by the conductor's entrance with a roar of wind and clickity-clack from the vestibule. He opened his mouth and bellowed with a stentorian voice over the rumble of the trucks and conversation.

"Next stop, Topeka! Topeka, Kansas. We will lay over in Topeka for an hour for the convenience of those Santa Fe Railway passengers wishing to dine at the Fred Harvey House at the terminal, on the second floor mezza-neen! The Harvey House offers full seven-course meals, complete with appetizers, cooked vegetables, elegant entrees and dee-zert! Main dishes include whitefish, capon, beef sirloin, lobster salad, ham, and duck for seventy-five cents. Next stop, Topeka. Topeka, Kansas is our next scheduled stop, la-deez and gen-tlemen."

Blinking, Holten glanced over at Rose, a fleur-de-lis from the seat's upholstery embossed in the red sweatiness of her cheek. "Mornin'," he mumbled drowsily.

She grinned back. "Sorry to tell you, Eli," she said, herself coming awake, "but if you check, that 'dawn' out there is coming from the west."

"That being the case, Miss Redmond," Holten proposed, now fully awake, with the conductor's pronouncement ringing in his ears, "would you take supper with me?"

"Only," she made condition, fixing her gaze on his slate-gray eyes coquettishly, "if we reserve the dessert until much later in the evening."

She pulled his hand, still clasped with hers, over her thigh and released it to fall to the junction of her legs. It allowed Holten's fingers to be titillated by their close proximity to heaven.

He leaned his head to the side, against the seat back, and looked at her intently. "I like my dessert with a lot of sweet sauce," he offered, almost whispering in her ear.

"I believe my dessert maker can accommodate you with just the right recipe to tempt your, ah, tastes, Mr. Holten," Rose barbed back.

A short while later, the train wheezed, slowing in its approach to the Topeka station. With the other passengers, Eli and Rose got up and made their way to the open door at the front of the car. Outside the window Holten could see the lights of Topeka, a view quickly blocked by the large, three-story Santa Fe terminal with its fabled Harvey House on the second floor. Eli glanced back once at Lee Flint, who apparently would stay in his seat and pout.

After an appropriate time to allow the other occupants of the Pullman sleeper car to settle in for the night, Holten heard a whispered call at the curtains shielding his bunk. He parted them and Rose Redmond quickly jumped in beside him. Their bodies touched full length in the narrow bed. Most of the sleeping cubicles around him were unoccupied, Holten considered. Over the constant rumble and creak of the train, whispered conversations and even the sounds of love, discreetly stifled, would not intrude on the sleep of other passengers.

Light from one of two dim brass lamps hanging from the ceiling in the narrow aisleway filtered into the tubular bunk so they could see each other in the ambient dimness. Holten lay nude under a single sheet.

"May I suggest something for dessert, kind sir?" Rose whispered.

"I like your style, Rosie."

"You ain't seen nothing yet."

"Neither have you . . . and it's under the sheet."

Eagerly she reached for his manhood, primed and ready, and he slid closer to let her take him. Rose gasped appreciatively over his size. Her fondling was expert with hands that had superbly soft skin. His silken sheath tingled to her touch. In spite of himself, Eli moved his hips in short ecstatic bumps as she showed her delight with a skillful handjob that encouraged, nothing more.

"Get out of that nightdress," Eli whispered. "This is the moment I've ridden all the way from Kansas City for and beat up a man to get to." He meant it lightly; nevertheless it was the truth.

"And I've waited a lifetime for. You're . . . ," she gulped, "magnificent, Eli."

"I don't like to brag, so let's see if we can do the best we can under the circumstances."

Beside him, Rose Redmond slid off the nightdress. The classic, mildly exposure-mellowed skin he saw in the dim light glowed with perfection. Mature in every respect and every inch of it now shouted supreme sexual savvy. Under his careful manipulation, this would be the piece of least resistance.

Her body proved better than he imagined. Rose, no shrinking violet, worked hard at keeping her form entrancing for a man. The breasts he now saw in full peaked youthfully high with a rib cage surmounting a flat belly she didn't have to worry about sucking in for effect. Her buttocks and hips were tight, thighs and lower legs fascinatingly proportioned. He ached to get closer to it all.

She brought that fabulous form closer to him and they embraced. Mouths fused in their first kiss, her crotch quickly sandwiched his turgid organ between their bellies. His game old campaigner responded with an additional swelling of pride and anticipation.

"Feels like foreplay just got to be five," he said close to her ear.

"Fore-alarm play, you mean," she hissed back, lips close to his cheek. "Get me there, Eli. Lord, I'm hot! Send for the goddamn fire brigade and the pumper."

"I brought my hose, if that's any consolation," he offered. "And I'm the pumper. You do something to me, too, Rosie."

Holten would have liked to contemplate the delightful little form of hers a bit more before taking it. It sufficed in the dimness to have his hands and arms around her, exploring the many sensory delights, feeling the supreme thrills of a supple body he found firm but hardly muscled. Eli slid to his side, back against the window-wall, to make more room for her beside him, and kissed her amorously.

He was ready, more than ready because of the days that had passed since his last bout with the Thorne sisters. Still he stayed in control. Rose surprised him by responding in the same way. He loved a controlled woman. Clingingly he broke from their kiss.

"I don't know about you," he said softly. "Once this starts, it's going to be wild. Time for ground rules. You have any preferences, or things you don't like to have happen, or that dampen your feelings?"

Her quick intake of breath revealed her surprise. "No man has ever-ever-ever asked me that," Rose whispered, delighted. "And I love you for it, Eli Holten. I'm for the old traditional ways, with a little individual variations on that theme. That's about all."

"What sort of variations?" Eli mouthed close to her ear.

"I—ah—well, this is sort of embarrassing. When I was younger, and had a much older lover, one better endowed than the boys in my life, I used to straddle him on top and control the amount and speed with which he entered me. That's about it."

"All the way that way?"

"As far as I'm concerned, unless you prefer something else."

"I'm traditional as hell, too." It was only a little lie, Eli acknowledged, but for a good cause.

He delighted her in their intimate pillow talk. It seemed part of the excitement they both generated. To anyone listening, he thought, it might have sounded like a mere casual conversation. In its openness and frankness, Holten took great pleasure.

"Maybe there is one quirk I have," Rose continued, her cheek against his. "And you're probably going to find it hard to understand."

"It's hard enough to stand by itself and I can hardly stand it," he said, making a feeble joke. "No, Rosie, understanding is my middle name."

"Why else do you think I'm here?" she riposted.

"What about your quirk?"

"When I ask you to raise on your hands and knees just do it. Don't take the bloom off the rose with questions," said she, making a pun.

"Never, Rosie. Your needs are my needs."

"Then let me feel him again."

Holten arched away from her enough for Rosie's silken palm and fingers to again grace his rigid shaft in a velvet grip. He had seldom felt such a loving, caring touch.

"God, he's fine, Eli," she whispered. Holten felt a swelling of pride in his chest with her appraisal.

"He's got nothing against you, either. That's why

101

I'm holding it against you."

Rose giggled. "Not just fine. Magnificent. And your *double entendres* are terrible."

Rosie's knees spread and the one closest nudged under his belly and he raised himself lightly to allow it room. She pulled him to her and, still clutching his maleness in a gentle but firm lock-grip, she introduced the knob-tip to an eager nest. Holten swept an arm and a leg across her and hung on hands and knees while she guided his contact.

First against the upper slot with its supersensitive center-ridge. Then to the warm, slippery entrance, encouraging only a part of the swollen head to bang at the gate before sliding it back for a light exciting of their respective sensitive areas. Eli murmured his appreciation.

Holten let her lead. He didn't rush, only cooperated with her need to feel him this way. Again she flexed the head into her moist cleft, engaging more this time so that her flexing walls pulled ever so lightly. Rose slid her hand back down the long, rigid shank and encouraged deeper entrance with little twitches of her hips.

Eli's tip had hardly slid past her moist lips, yet already had begun a bolder penetration, with her guiding, leading. Holten waited for the sign of Rosie's need, his senses centering on their contact. Belly muscles rigid, he held himself ready to let go by whatever degrees she seemed to want.

Her hands dropped away, his lance well encased and the trail amply marked. Her silken fingers slipped to his buttocks to give a tantalizing hint of encouragement, revealing her deeper cravings. It would be slow, methodical, and best of all, aimed at mutual pleasure . . . and that's the way Eli liked it.

"Now," she cooed. "Slow and easy. Plenty of time for . . . everything."

Eli was filled with wonder. He thought only the Thorne girls were this expert. "We must have gone to the same school," he whispered. He eased in a tad and wiggled and stroked, holding bountiful length waiting in reserve. "How's that?"

"God, what a man!" Rose squeaked hoarsely. "Y-you're on your own from here, until I tell you."

"I think I've got the trail well scouted," Eli said, deftly grinding another fraction of her slippery passage. "Oh, hell, Rosie, this is heaven."

"Heaven? You've got a whole lot outside there yet."

"Have it your way. I'm still on the golden stairway. How 'bout I can see heaven?"

"Then take a few more steps."

Eli delighted in the little talk and it spurred him to control his actions so as to give this fantastic woman the best loving of her life. And in return, he fully expected to get the same for himself.

"Take it from here. Oh! Eli! *Now!*"

Holten ignored her passion, feeling a slow sink best under the circumstances, and he calibrated his push to probe every bit of the warm, totally snug tunnel with one slow, yet not urgent thrust. The fit was as near perfect as he'd ever found. With a surge of new thrill, he bottomed out, his frontal bone resting against hers, their short hairs entwined. Grunting, he eased back and in again.

With each stroke he pulled out farther, sensing the demand rise in him to have more, to give her more. Only to create new demand when each goal had been achieved. He worked harder now, long, full strokes. Rose's hips responded with a gentle, languid grind that sent thrills charging like a sunburst throughout his system.

Minutes passed which brought Rose ever closer to a peak as he sustained the climb as long as he could.

Each silken slide he designed to give Rosie the opportunity to feel his presence in every fraction of an inch along her well-lubricated passage.

At intervals her body convulsed and trembled. Her arms slid under his armpits, hugged him like a bear. Her legs arched gradually up his calves and thighs in total surrender. At last she locked the backs of her knees over his buttocks, loosening and then tightening with his well-timed surges and withdrawals.

"Now," she hissed in unbounded rapture. "Pull up on your hands and knees."

Eli locked his elbows and planted his knees, virtually lifting her off the thin mattress. Hugging him with her arms, her knees locked over his back, supreme euphoria reached into Holten as she raised herself to him, the strength of her legs pulling her quivering pouch tightly against him. Beside his head, hers wobbled with abandon and exertion. Eli had never experienced such a sensation. The hunger of her passionate technique telegraphed to him, fought for dominance, and filled him with new giddiness.

For long, powerful minutes they surged on. Eli did his best to cooperate and give her the substance and treatment she battled to possess and experience. Deep inside some remote, unfathomable area of his pubic arch a delightful pressure began to build. Wildly, Rosie responded in kind.

He commanded his tumult-driven body to prepare for greater demands, sensing the imminence of a monstrous release. Rosie's new rapture sent her into another paroxysm of climaxes, one merging over the other. Then the world lurched more violently than the swaying train and, oh! Oh—oh—oh how sweet the blaze into oblivion.

At length he returned to their tiny cubicle. He held himself over Rosie Redmond, while still nearly fully captured inside. After yet a longer pause, with slow, teasing pumping motions from them both, Eli rolled over, away from her.

"I wonder . . . ?" he murmured softly.

"What?" she panted into his ear.

"Uh—I was wondering what it would be like to die in this precious afterglow from one of the greatest of all my lifetime bouts with love?"

"Don't you die on me, mister," Rose protested. "It's a long, long way to Dodge City."

"And we haven't anything better to do," Eli completed the thought with a lustful chuckle.

9

For Sgt. Maj. Harry Adams, the sprawling, vacant expanse of the Santa Fe Trail presented a quiet, peaceful face this afternoon. Beyond the more settled area of central Kansas, nature still held sway. Around him, butterflies sported and birds winged in the warm sunlight over grass dried the color of refined gold.

Adams rode alone, apart from the moving troop. Regardless of the three troopers far ahead on point, he scouted, eyes alert to signs that could mean danger. In spite of the delights of the open, sunlit country, where farmsteads no longer abounded, Adams knew his normal responsibilities on the march were nearly quadrupled. Maj. Randall Covington was arbitrary, cold, and demanding of men, even the raw little fellers Adams had done his best to nursemaid, as well as to whip, into field condition and fighting trim at Jefferson Barracks.

Adams's aide, Cpl. Joe Locke, was a tough, wiry little scrapper whose pluck could inspire the rank and file private soldiers. Unfortunately, so far most of Joe's combat experience had been in off-hours saloon scraps. Locke had yet to earn his spurs in actual field engagements. Despite the five long-term troopers assigned to help Adams, Locke, and Major

Covington guide the rookie troop across a wild and generally untamed land, Adams knew that the bulk of the responsibility rested directly upon his shoulders.

His opinions and his decisions had to be discreetly conveyed in a suitably subordinate fashion to Major Covington in such a way as to allow the major to construe them as his own. Such techniques would, in great measure, mean success or failure of the mission. Who cared who came up with the ideas so long as they made it through?

Adams's gaze roved the rolling, sprawling country before him. He kept his horse on the move and maintained a sixth sense on his whereabouts in relation to the moving column. Balmy was the only word to describe the day. A warm, moist breeze toyed with the grass he rode through and combed lightly through the mane and tail of his cavalry mount. There'd be a thunderstorm by nightfall.

Harry didn't need a map to visualize the great Santa Fe Trail spearing like a broad lance through the land ahead. It pulled them inexorably in a southwesterly direction. They would reach the crossing of the Rattlesnake Creek in another day. In Adams's strategy-sharpened brain was the memory of every trail over which he had campaigned throughout the West, merely reconnoitering or actually pursuing hostiles. And of the engagements with Indians, where the guns flamed over red-earth plains or where great rocky prominences were thrust against a hot, azure sky.

He could picture those campaign fields of old, the trails of soldiers long past, of years long gone. His memory clearly saw the sandy flats, the red mud of the wet seasons, the choking dust on hot, dry prairies, and the cold along the northern borders where the wind shrieked down out of Canada with nothing to block it but a man and his horse. At moments like

107

these, Harry Adams allowed himself to savor the richness of the years that had brought him his sergeant major stripes.

That's about all he had to show for thirty years in this man's army, he thought. Nothing much more to represent three decades of dedication to the uniform but chevrons and rockers and a yellow diamond on his sleeves and a thankless job of keeping recruits in line. Of course there were the medals he kept hidden and refused to discuss—even the one on the powder blue silk ribbon with the tiny white stars.

Little more than that to illustrate his life and travails, except possibly bullet and knife scars and old fractures that sometimes came back to haunt him with deep aches on days when it was fixing up to be cold and drizzly.

Medals, he spat, physically projecting a gob of tobacco juice into the dust. He refrained from chewing around the troops, feeling it didn't become the image of a proper sergeant major to be seen with a puffed-out cheek and littering the parade ground or the trail with brown splatters. He reserved the luxury of chewing for solitary scouts such as this one or for the privacy of his solitary quarters. His mind remained on medals, and his opinion that anyone who bragged on them didn't deserve them in the first place.

They were only tokens, symbols of memories of times and campaigns and skirmishes past. Of fights and faces under hard-billed kepis, remembered from barracks camaraderie. Yeah, comrade-faces that sometimes had been shot away or gaped frozenly in horror or surprise at the fatal bullet, saber thrust, or war-hawk blow.

The dead, the valorous dead, they deserved the medals; the living needed only the consolation that they had survived. Such speculation on long-forgotten deeds and men brought another memory rushing back to him in fragments, in swift, flashing scenes of tragic losses, the euphoria of winning, the pain of wounds and the wonder of surviving. *"The Congress of the United States . . . for conspicuous valor . . . Corporal Harrison Adams . . ."*

Hell, ol' Abe himself hung that one around his neck. Memories . . . and medals . . . bedamned! Yet, it was somewhere, he mused, in the making of glory that had been the goal in taking the oath and putting on the uniform in the first place.

That had been before John Brown went to Harper's Ferry. Somehow that glory had gotten misplaced or mixed up. He'd lost it in the shuffle of troops and field assignments. It left only sorrow for comrades buried in rude, hasty battlefield graves, and sadness for years eaten by a force Harry Adams failed to comprehend. Adams's reverie rudely came to an abrupt end at sight of a head and shoulders emerging over a low, rolling, grassy ridge to his left. Adams tensed, prepared to gain as much intelligence as he could from the situation. When no longer safe nor prudent to stand his ground, he'd swing right and hit the gallop back to the troop and Major Covington.

Slowly the walking man grew in stature as he crested the grassy knoll and waded through the waist-high grass down toward Adams. It became plain that the fellow wore a cavalry trooper's kepi, and the blue blouse and yellow-striped breeches of a member of Covington's command. One of the rookies of C Troop.

Where in the everlasting hell, Adams thought, all manner of wild notions flooding his head, is the man's horse?

From the distance, about a hundred yards, Adams surmised, the trooper recognized him as he sat his horse stoically in the expanse of rolling, golden-hued grassy swale.

"Sergeant Adams!" the man called in recognition

and quickened his pace toward where Adams held his mount in check, waiting.

Adams shielded his eyes, hooded the bill of his kepi with his hand to aid him in an attempt to identify the trooper. He knew all of them, though under the glaring sun it was hard to tell.

"Who are you?" he called across the narrowing space between them.

"Cate. Private Alfred Cate. C Troop."

"I know your unit, man," Adams growled. "Why in heaven's name are you unhorsed?"

Cate walked toward him, striding briskly in apparent relief at having at least found someone. Anyone, his relief-filled expression said, even if it was the troop's sometimes stern sergeant major. Cate's face was beet-red and agleam with sweat from the exertion of being lost and walking for some time in the blazing sun. He wiped his brow when he reached the sergeant major and looked up with an eager expression.

"I stopped to rest, got down to take a . . . you know. My horse bolted and I couldn't catch him."

Cursing silently, Adams dismounted, making certain his own horse was secure, to interrogate the trooper. Now he recognized young Cate, a fair-enough trooper as a recruit, though one who would spend eternities advancing in grade—if he ever did. They had a good name for Cate's type in the service: professional privates. Or more accurately, cannon fodder. Still, all-around, Adams remembered Cate as a decent sort who showed a reasonable level of honesty and reliability.

"What the fuck do you think you were issued a picket pin for?" Harry Adams roared. Good, he'd gotten that out of his system. Now he could conduct this in a reasonable manner. "And what, may I ask, were you doing out here alone? Did anyone authorize your leaving the column?"

Cate shook his head sheepishly. "I'm sorry, Sergeant Major. Figured I wouldn't be missed. Felt I needed some time alone. I didn't plan on being gone more than a few minutes."

"You've been in service long enough to know that rests for men and animals are routinely called during the line of march. There is no authority for you going absent without official leave, Cate."

Cate looked wretched. "I know, Sergeant Major."

"Where did you lose your mount, soldier?"

"I'm . . . not sure." Cate waved vaguely. "Back there somewhere. I tried the longest time to chase him and then I was afraid I'd never find my way back to the column. So I started walking back."

"Cate, I assume you know this is a serious breach of military conduct. Departing the column without official leave and then losing a valuable government-issue mount. You're in deep trouble, young sir. We could send out a party to hunt your horse. But that would be a waste of time and there's a few stray Cheyenne roaming these parts taking white scalps. They'd be double-delighted if the victim was in army blues. If we lost a small patrol horse-hunting because of one man's negligence, that man stands liable to be shot himself for dereliction of duty in the face of the enemy."

Private Cate's exposure-reddened face blanched. "I'll do anything to make it right, Sergeant Major. I'll shovel manure for six months in my off-time. Anything."

"I'm afraid it won't be as easy as that, Private Cate."

"I know, Sergeant Major." Cate's downcast gaze made him look like a ten-year-old.

"You've been through an ordeal, son. I can recognize what prompted you to do this thing, even though it's totally against regulations. I'm in your corner on that. That still does not relieve the

111

seriousness of your actions, Cate."

"Is it possible you could speak to Major Covington, Sergeant Major? Please. I'll do anything I can, anything you say, to get myself back in your good graces. Quite honestly, Sergeant Major, I'm afraid of Major Covington."

"Since I found you, Cate, I'll have to make a report to the major. I'll not be your ally in this. I must report what I know of this incident, but also not to overlook your good record to date. You've not, to my knowledge, been guilty of such a breach before. Would that there were more like you. I'll speak to the major when we get back to the column. I'll ask that your punishment be left in my hands. And I may deal harshly with you, soldier."

"But fairly. That's all I ask."

"Thank you, Private Cate."

"I'll be forever grateful, Sergeant Major."

"Don't thank me," Adams said crisply. "The major will expect me to make an example of you. And believe me, young man, I would anyway. All this will not go easy on you."

Cate squared his shoulders. "I'm willing to take my medicine. As long as you dish it out."

Adams looked at the haggard Cate. He was a boy, scarcely out of short pants and not yet out of his teens. His infraction of military code was serious, yet the circumstances understandable. Sometimes a man needed to be by himself; Adams reflected on his own solitary ride. Still, it excused nothing.

"I've a canteen here, Cate." Adams unbuckled it from his ring on the saddle. "Have a swig, and splash some on your face. Then mount up behind me and we'll get back to the troop."

Riding to the column a half hour later, Adams had not altogether persuaded himself that Major Covington would be as charitable as he had been toward Private Cate. He passed a critical eye over the troop, strung out in a militarily proper column of two, the colorful red-and-white guidon at the front, snapping merrily in the ever-present prairie breeze.

One thing was certain. There'd be no shirking his responsibility in reporting the incident to the major. Do so and his role as disciplinarian for the troop would be destroyed. They might like his going easy on Cate, but they'd have no respect for his authority thereafter. Tough as it would be to do, feeling deep in his gut that the major would not take it lightly, it was the thing that Adams had to do.

With Cate behind him on the horse, Adams rode to Covington's position midway in the column. Corporal Locke and three of the Jefferson Barracks cadremen rode at point, within sight beyond the guidon bearer. Seeing Adams approach, Covington swung out of the column and halted. As the sergeant major drew near, he pulled off to the side, puzzled by the sergeant's unusual companion. He returned Adams's crisp salute with a touch of his quirt to his hat brim.

"Returned from patrol, eh, Sergeant Major? Ree-port."

Adams dropped his saluting hand back to his thigh, still holding the reins, cavalry-fashion, in his left hand. "All quiet, sir. Scouting mission disclosed no evidence of hostiles in our immediate area."

"Then may I inquire, Sergeant Major, the reason for the presence of one of the troop's privates mounted with you?" Covington barked his question.

For a moment, Adams pondered a little white lie to make it easier for Cate. There was none. Give it then, he thought, by degrees and it might soften the circumstances in the major's eyes.

"Private Alfred Cate, Major. Unfortunately un-horsed on the prairie."

Hostility edged Covington's tone. "Was Private Cate assigned with you on your scouting mission, Sergeant Major? And may I inquire as to the whereabouts of the horse from which Private Cate was discharged?"

"Stampeded on the plain, sir."

"'Stampeded on the plain'?" Covington repeated, savoring each word. "An entire cavalry troop available to lend aid, and a horse is lost?"

Covington was overreacting, Adams thought. The troop, riding by, witnessed with staring eyes the confrontation in midcolumn where Covington had been riding. Adams drew a deep breath, face crimsoning.

"Sir, that is correct, sir."

"I'll ask again, Sergeant Major Adams. Was Private Cate assigned with you on your scouting mission? I remember giving no such orders. Are you now taking command authority on your own, Sergeant Major Adams?"

Adams could see himself being trapped by Covington. "The senior noncommissioned officer always selects personnel for routine duties, sir."

"*Not* in my command," Covington snapped.

Much as it irked him, Harry Adams had to throw Cate into harm's way. Covington seemed determined to make an issue of it, and his dislike of the major was growing quickly into hatred. He cleared his throat and looked straight ahead.

"I found Private Cate unhorsed on the prairie, sir, and returned him to the column."

"And his mount is lost out there somewhere?"

"That is my understanding, yes, sir." Adams felt like he faced a hostile court-martial board. He saw rage darken Covington's face. Adams braced himself for an explosion.

"Unless you have evidence to the contrary, Sergeant Major Adams, Private Cate is guilty of desertion. . . ."

114

"Sir," Adams interjected. "Private Cate left the column intending to be gone only for a few moments. He—uh—had urgent need to relieve himself. As a recently enlisted man, his record shows no prior evidence of malingering."

Covington ignored him. ". . . and criminal negligence in connection with the loss of a government-issued cavalry mount."

Beside Adams, Cate's face became a mask of humiliation and great fear. His shoulders slumped with the emotional weight he now carried.

"Major Covington, if I may be permitted," Adams offered. "By your leave, sir, I will secure another horse for Private Cate and we'll see if we can return his mount to the column."

"Request denied." Covington said it calmly, and calm for Maj. Randall Covington was an uncommon thing. Covington so far had shown Adams only the fierceness of disposition of a cornered badger. Nothing frayed Covington's temper so much as what he construed as malingering in the ranks.

"Your presence with the column is essential. I can't afford to have you skylarking all over the prairie."

"Then, by your leave, sir, permit Corporal Locke and one or two of the cadre to return for the horse with Private Cate."

"Sergeant Major Adams! *I* will decide whether or not to send a party after the horse. Which is without doubt hopelessly lost or already in the hands of hostile Indians."

Adams realized that Covington had chosen to treat him like a common enlisted man, with no respect for his opinion or his authority. Only a brigade sergeant major or the sergeant major of the army outranked Harry Adams in enlisted ranks. Assured by that fact, he sought to exert that weight.

"A final request then, Major Covington. May

Private Cate be remanded to me for punishment? I can assure you, sir, I shan't treat lightly his transgressions against his military responsibility."

Covington frowned, his frosty eyes ferocious. He cleared his throat, rattling out his words.

"Request also denied. Private Cate will be lashed to a wheel of the commissary wagon and flogged as an example to the troop of the consequences of dereliction of duty, malingering, and incompetence."

Beside Adams, Cate slumped but caught himself before he fell. Adams shot him a quick glance.

"Sir," he said loudly enough for all those passing to hear. "I go on record as opposing the severity of the punishment. It is in direct violation of military regulations. Flogging of American soldiers has been against the rules for decades. Private Cate's actions are clearly a serious infraction, but meaningful penalty can be used as a constructive example to the men. What you propose, Major Covington, will have the most dire consequences in the destruction of morale and esprit de corps among C Troop, if not totally destroying loyalty to command."

"Are you quite finished, Sergeant Major Adams?"

Adams reddened. His suggestions would not be heeded. "Not entirely, Major Covington. Whipping is illegal, as I said. Similar corporal punishment in the field is contrary to regulations. A court-martial, duly convened, must decide on such penalties."

"Then, Sergeant Major Adams, I herewith am holding a summary court-martial at this very moment and, as ranking officer and trial judge advocate, I sentence the defendant to be lashed to a wagon wheel and flogged!"

Adams stood rigidly before the major, livid in his own fury. Not only did Cate not deserve the severity of the punishment, but Covington's actions before the troop could only serve to erode Adams's influence on them.

"Once more, Major Covington, I protest. Only a general court can dispense such punishments as entail physical harm to the convicted soldier. You don't have the rank to convene or conduct such a court. Further, I wish to state that I intend to make formal that protest at our next official post of assignment."

"And you, Sergeant Major Harry Adams, are on report yourself for dereliction of duty and gross insubordination."

Adams stepped forward and spoke his words hotly, close to Covington's face. "You need me too much to tie me to a wheel and rip my back open, don't you?" Adams lost his military bearing and forgot protocol in his anger and saw not a major of the United States Army but a hateful bastard standing before him. "I've seen your type. When I have saved your ass, Covington, and you are safe in a fort in Arizona, then you'll throw the book at me, right?"

Covington bordered on apoplexy. He knew the sergeant major was right. Covington needed Adams, seasoned campaigner that he was, and his sway over the green recruits. Covington realized he had stepped in too boldly, yet to pull back now would destroy him as an authority figure over Adams and the troop. He might as well hand over his gold oak leaves to Adams. Cunning and guile were his favorite weapons. He figured he'd fix Adams at the proper time and place.

"Punishment is set for four this afternoon at a troop formation," the major said coldly. "Sergeant Major Adams, you are dismissed to return to your post."

Adams stared a long moment in Covington's cold, unrelenting eyes. "Sir, yes, sir!" he barked, then tossed a crisp salute and did an about-face.

10

Holten's inner man had been worn to a nub by cities and the stuffy people he found in them. The train rides, the ugly encounter with Leander Flint—even the exceptional delights of Rose Redmond—had glutted him with civilization.

On the eve of his departure for Bent's Old Fort, fed up with Dodge City's annoying sprawl of glitter and noise, Holten made a camp on the prairie to get back in touch with himself and to order his mind for the days and events ahead. Always spectacular, the Kansas sunset soothed his acerbic soul with long bars of purple, magenta, and rose. A fat orange ball slowly slid behind a low sand hill. Eli leaned back against his saddle to enjoy an after-supper smoke and stared up eastward at the star-struck sky that would be his blanket in the days ahead almost without number.

Holten took delight from such solitary moments. His mother's God dwelled up there someplace, as did the Great Spirit—*Wakan Tanka*—of his Sioux foster father, Two Bulls. Despite the Bible-thumping religious missionaries' blind zeal to prove otherwise, Eli Holten was confident that the two spiritual entities were not separate and alien—one good, the other evil—but essentially one and the same.

Some *great spirit* was up there, of that he was

convinced. Who else could have created such beauty for man's eyes to drink in and contemplate? The Cherokees called Him *Yoah,* the Chippewas *Gitche Manitu,* and the Muslims *Allah.* Yet His wondrous works, like the dying afterglow, remained unchanged no matter what name one used. In the sky, from rim to rim now, the stars made their cloudy glitter, confirming Holten's deepest thoughts. In the morning, he would ride on again, solitary and steady, toward Bent's.

His mind's eye could picture that beauty, also born of solitude and a man's time to think and contemplate. Across the broad plains and valleys he'd make his way, the days hot and the nights lonely. Through bouldered mazes of twisted, ugly malpais— badlands—flanked by chaparral-dotted deserts, past lakes dry or laced with alkali, and brushy flats, unlike the lush, grassy expanses he knew in the country to the north. Further south, harsh high-altitude desert would replace even that.

Blue days of quiet and awesome distances would fade into nights of dark so dense a man could scarcely see his hand in front of his face. Yet the stars, ever-present, would be sharp as sparks struck by flint and steel. Even here, in the open, desolate land west of Dodge, even his tiny night fire would be visible at a great distance.

Holten felt no surprise, although alerted and a little angry, when the sound of an approaching horse-drawn wagon, or perhaps a surrey, shattered his reverie. He slid back out of the firelight as a precaution despite a sixth-sense voice assuring him that the approaching vehicle did not present a threat.

The rider led his team quietly through the dense, moonless night, guided only by the light of Holten's fire. The rattling of the conveyance in no way suggested stealth. The team drew up. Outlined by his firelight, they shivered nervously, disliking night

119

work almost as much as did a man. Eli could see a figure on the spring-seat outlined against the star-dusted sky. A woman's voice called out of the darkness.

"Mister Holten . . . ?" Her words were edged with an odd inflection.

Eli couldn't peg it as an eastern or southern accent. He stepped back into the firelight, right arm tensed to go for his six-gun. She could be a shill for a holdup man lurking out in the darkness.

"Who asks?" he called.

"May I get down? It was difficult finding you. I wish to speak with you."

"Come to the fire. Slowly."

He heard the creak of the spring-seat as she stepped down and moved forward. As the soft glow of the firelight outlined her figure, Holten's heart skipped. She was elegantly dressed, wholly out of place on the primitive prairie, in a low-cut red gown that marked the beginning of her cleavage. It tapered to a waist so narrow he might have encircled it with his two big hands. The crimson skirt cloaked the rest of her in folds to near the ankles.

Her skin shone white, with a hint of darkness beneath. Her hair had been elegantly coiffed. Bright, intelligent, dark eyes flicked over him, restless and expectant, sizing up the man across the fire from her.

"Forgive me, Mr. Holten. I am Giselle Robi-deaux."

Her English was impeccable. Now the hint of accent Holten had caught in her voice translated into French.

"My pleasure, Miss is it?, Robideaux."

"You are right. Miss Robideaux. Mam'selle, we say. But you may call me Miss."

Holten nodded in acknowledgment.

"Forgive my intrusion. The man at the livery stable where your horse was cared for in Dodge City

120

told me I might find you camped along the road west of town. I also learned from him that you will leave for the West and Arizona shortly."

Holten's gray eyes narrowed as he looked at her across the low bed of small flames. That's the trouble with civilization, he thought. Mention your plans casually, off-hand, and you might as leave buy space in the newspaper to announce them.

"Forgive me if I sound abrupt, Miss Robideaux. But how can my affairs possibly be of sufficient concern for you to drive out in the middle of the night, across a trackless waste, to find me?"

"You will understand, Mr. Holten. I, too, am going to Arizona. I wish to see that magnificent part of the great American West before proceeding on to San Francisco."

Holten saw it coming. "And so," he anticipated her, "I suppose you're looking for a strong, silent type to get you through the wilderness and shield you from all harm." He didn't mean to sound gruff, or flip, yet in his own ears it appeared that way.

Mlle. Robideaux produced a fleeting frown and tiny pout. "I had hoped so, yes, Mr. Holten. I also heard in Dodge City of your great reputation as a frontier scout."

There it was again, he thought with heat. He reminded himself to be extremely careful of ever again telling any casual stranger anything about his affairs. Or even his name. Among the soldiers and frontiersmen who passed through Dodge, he expected his name might be familiar. His scouting prowess and brushes with the hostiles had frequently been blown all out of proportion in tales around the campfires of others. It might also be possible, he thought, that some of the resentment he felt toward the beautiful French woman across the flames from him grew out of bitter feelings that his privacy had been invaded.

"Your plan to see Arizona," he drawled. "I strongly advise against it."

"And why is that?"

"There's nothing to see except cactus and sand. It's not just wild country, it's wild Indians, too. And snakes, scorpions, Gila monsters, and death by thirst."

"But, what of the mighty Grand Canyon? The Painted Desert? I'll not be put off, Mr. Holten," Giselle stated resolutely. "I'm well aware of the risks. This is the opportunity of my lifetime and I've already weighed the threat against the adventure."

So that was it, a *great adventure,* Holten thought glumly. Lord protect us from adventurers. "Beyond here, the Kiowa Indians are off the reservation and committing depredations in the very territory you propose to ride through to get to Arizona. In Arizona Territory, the Apaches are being chased by General Crook."

Undaunted, Giselle faced Eli, fists on hips. "Will you guide my wagons, Mr. Holten?"

Under normal circumstances Eli Holten would be trying his best to tumble such a lovely young woman into his sugans. This time her bull-head stubbornness scrambled his regular responses.

"It's a dusty, hot country. No decent place for a cultured woman. Travel on the Santa Fe Trail is dull and monotonous. Sometimes it's several days' journey between rivers and even springs where often the water may be questionable."

"If you don't guide me, I will have to find someone else. There are others in Dodge City who will conduct me west. But . . . their reputations, unlike yours, are a bit . . ." She searched for the word. "Unsavory."

"Game is scarce. To stay alive, you may have to eat parts of an animal that ordinarily would make you sick to your stomach."

122

"The French eat sweetbreads and tripe. We also eat snails." She had an amused smile.

"Such a trip would be terribly expensive in terms of lives and equipment."

"I am prepared to pay well."

"Money is not the object."

"Certainly not mine either, Mr. Holten. I can make it well worth your while."

"I guess you're going whether I guide you or not."

"At last you are coming around to my way of thinking."

"Not at all," Eli told her. "The route from Dodge City to Bent's Fort should be relatively safe. I suppose I could guide you that far, but no farther. I have an army assignment. Perhaps there, in the vicinity of Bent's Old Fort, you can hire another guide for the rest of your journey."

"I knew you'd listen to reason, Mr. Holten."

Holten blinked, wondering if he'd allowed a pretty face to sway his better judgment. It had happened before, though not to this degree. He had plenty of time to travel with the woman before meeting Covington and his cavalry troop at the fort. Only minutes before, he had his plans all made.

He'd looked forward to the trip alone with Sonny. It all ran through his head in a matter of seconds as he studied the magnificent, almost classic French features that had an animal slink about it. He could use the extra money. He still contemplated the Thorne sisters' invitation for a lengthy visit with them. And Rose Redmond had promised to keep something warm on her hearth for him as well. Some financial latitude would make it all memorable. He sighed. Oh, what the hell.

"You said wagons, Miss Robideaux?"

"Three fine Conestogas I purchased and outfitted in Pennsylvania. High-wheeled, high-sided, cover bows of prime eastern hickory, oaken wheels by a master wheelwright. They'll never require soaking to keep their tires on."

Don't take a bet on that, missy, Holten thought. "Why so many, Miss Robideaux?"

"Please call me Giselle, Mr. Holten, now that we will be traveling together. I am accustomed to journeying in style and I can afford it."

"You have drivers, I take it? Perhaps they are fighting men?"

Giselle chuckled a sardonic and nasal French-style chuckle. "Ah-ha-ha, M'sieur Holten," she purred, forgetting herself for a moment. *"Mais non.* I drive one. The second is driven by Colette, my lady-in-waiting, as you call maid, and the third by her *inamorato*, Hugh D'Arcy."

Holten gulped. "I'd better reconsider. Three people to be responsible for and not just one."

"Mr. Holten—Eli—the odds against an accident or an attack are essentially the same with three as with one."

"Sounds good standing here outside Dodge City. Two weeks on the trail to Bent's Fort a hundred miles from water but only six inches from hell and it's going to be another story."

"You'll go?" she asked, ignoring his argument.

"This . . . what's his name?"

"D'Arcy. Hugh D'Arcy."

"Hugh D'Arcy. Is he tough? Can he fight?"

"D'Arcy? The *boulevardier* from Montmartre? The man of absinthe and truffles and the lover extraordinaire of my Colette a fighter? *Non*, Eli. A survivor, yes. A small man, a delicate man, but as you say in American, don't judge a book by its cover. For Colette he would walk through walls."

"I still think I'm risking too many lives to satisfy a whim."

That brought a scowl. "Eli, we French are lovers first. If we did not invent *l'amour*, we refined it, and added innovations. We do not seek the fight, but when challenged, we will fight to the death. We are all three—myself, Colette, and Hugh—thoroughly schooled in the Colt Peacemaker and the Winchester lever-action and each has good examples of both, chambered for the same-sized cartridge. We took the time to become proficient and accurate under skilled instructors at Colonel Colt's and Mr. Winchester's establishments in the East."

She certainly did her homework properly, Holten mused. "All right," he said curtly. "I'll do it. It's time to escort you back to town."

"I can drive myself, Eli, thank you. After all, I got myself here. There is only one minor detail."

Here it comes, Holten thought. What else has this French tart got up her sleeve? "Yes?"

"The money."

"It is not important," Holten lied.

"Ah, but we must have a basis. Whatever the government is paying you to guide the army unit from the old fort to Arizona, I will triple to get my party safely there. Fair enough?"

Holten hoped his eyes weren't bugging out. He swallowed, envisioning a long, exciting furlough with Rose Redmond and then on to see the Thorne girls after his work was completed in Arizona. What he proposed to take on would be dicey from start to finish. Awh, hell, he thought, his life had never been without its hazards. "Fair enough," he said.

"And remember, Eli. I'm Giselle. To assure that we cut through the formalities, please come to Dodge City tomorrow, meet Colette and Hugh. Check the condition of my wagons and supplies for the trail, and the health and readiness of the mule teams. You and I can have aperitifs in my apartments at the Dodge House and conclude other, ah, arrangements." Holten read suggestion into her words. Things started to look up. "We can have a late supper,

125

possibly even sent in, and start out early the next day. Until then, Eli."

Holten stood nearly speechless. He watched her lift that magnificent form into the surrey and slap the team into motion across the dark, dense prairie back toward Dodge City.

Next evening in her apartments in the Dodge House, probably the Presidential Suite, two rooms elaborately decorated and furnished, Holten began to wonder just who in the hell this Giselle Robideaux really was. The room had several low-lit lamps with cranberry-colored globes, and the wallpaper, carpeting, and plush-covered upholstery in wing chairs and chaise lounges, carried out the sensual theme in complementary maroons and reds. They were not the lodgings of a poor person.

Eli remembered he wasn't up there to appreciate the hotel's amenities when, with a whiff of the next assignment this close, his mighty organ began to throb a war beat under the tight crotch of his buckskins. Giselle's *robe de chambre*, her dressing gown, also closely matched the room decor as she patted the chaise cushion beside her, inviting him to sit close.

During the evening, over drinks and dinner sent in, they had chatted randomly, informally in a friendly manner about the days ahead on the trail. Now it was time to get down to business. Holten willingly got up out of his chair to go over and park beside the woman, aware of a compelling, beckoning, pleasant woman-animal scent radiating around her. His raging beast barked to get out of the confining pants-crotch. Giselle's smile was come-hither.

"You know, Eli," she spoke softly and sensually, "every time I've seen you, last night on the prairie

126

and here, this evening, I've gotten slimy, you know . . . down here."

He spoke as softly, joining in the game for which both of them knew the rules only too well. "Nothing like my reactions in the same way, a man's way."

She leaned toward him, inviting the kiss, and Holten drew himself closer to deliver. Their lips met and hers pressed close for but a brief moment before her mouth sprang open. Her soft, wet, and hot tongue worked its way through his lips. Holten allowed his jaw to go slack and took her tongue into his mouth to curl his own around and over it.

Their fencing match progressed and he slid into her mouth. Her breath escaped this vacuum like a hiss. Holten grew unaware of any other sensations in his body except this warm and wonderful point of ecstatic contact. And of a still fast-growing bulge centered in his buckskin crotch.

In the quick, tight clinch that went with their embrace, Holten could feel the rapid rise-and-fall of her firm bosom against his chest, as they came into view over his night fire outside of Dodge.

He broke from her hold long enough to whisper, working on her earlobe with sucking lips, "May I tell you, mam'selle, that you have a body men would kill for?"

"I would rather they would stay alive to make *amour.* Wouldn't we be more comfortable, ah, in the next room?"

"Said the spider to the fly."

"I . . . don't understand."

"You will when I open it."

"What?"

"The fly."

"I still don't understand."

"You will. Yes, let's."

The light shone even dimmer in Giselle's bed-chamber, although at the right level to see tauntingly enough to add to the thrills of the moment. She climbed up into the center of the bed to sit cross-legged and left off the dressing gown. As she leaned back to shrug the garment off her shoulders, Holten caught a glimpse of a rosy exclamation point topped by a luxuriant puff of black. The skin around it appeared soft and beckoning, an almost iridescent white that glowed starkly beside the gleaming, jet-black wedge.

Standing over her, Holten peeled off his shirt and worked his way out of his boots. "Leave the pants on," she whispered huskily.

"What the hell?" he blurted, bemused.

"I want to unwrap the Christmas present myself."

"Christmas in September," he quipped.

After he tossed his shirt haphazardly over his boots, Eli crawled to her. He caught Giselle to pull her gently down and lie over her, savoring the warmth and softness of her against his exposed skin. He'd been with many women, yet the experience seemed new each time. Giselle got an arm around his muscled shoulders and drew him off beside her. With the other hand, she slid across his belly. Expertly she worked the top stag-horn button of his buckskins loose and then the second. His bold lance bulked as big as it would ever be. Hot and ready, it strained at the sealed animal hide like a flat, tensed spring waiting to burst out.

With his free hand, Eli gently stroked up a bare thigh that, though firm, had a velvety smoothness. The opening he found already wet, willing, and ready. Still he worked it tenderly with thumb and fingers and marveled at the slipperiness a minimum of attention had produced. Giselle responded to his coaxing with slow yet eager rotations of her lower body.

Feeling light-headed and with a featherweight body, Holten drifted over for full contact with

Giselle's warm satin skin. Her legs went wide and inviting and without any guiding, he slid in easily and delightfully, slipping to a point of honeyed stricture, descending to a full depth by easy degrees. Every silly friction of it brought new, sloppy delights.

Eli felt he hadn't probed and backed out and hunched again more than ten easy strokes before her mouth enveloped his ear and her squealings and sharp sighing intakes of breath signaled the ecstasy of first climax. Her joyful sounds roared down the dark tunnel of his hearing into his brain.

It spurred him to ram deeply and intensely if only to have her breathless cooing again blowing hot in his ear. He began to plow hard and forcefully, deliver the surges as deeply as his almost brutal thrust would push it. Small, sucking sounds accompanied his fast, hard strokes. He slid his hands down, to bury his fingertips into the soft flesh of her butt for leverage. His full cycles thudded into her with the depth and precision of piston-drivers on a steamboat.

Over the sheer thrill of it, he lost track of the times he brought her to full cry in supreme pleasure. Then, quickly drowning in the blindness and deafness of his own rapture, he felt his sphincter muscle pucker tight in readiness and his pendulous sack leap as the crescendo of his own fulfillment surged upon him.

He grunted and groaned in primal delight as the roar and concussion resounded sublimely in his head. Eli's body shook with great recoil as the monster weapon fired its full-charged salute to the most beautiful woman and most exhilarating experience he had ever had. And there had been more than a few.

The battle over, drained of all energy, force, and juices, Holten tensely held himself over Giselle on elbows and knees. Still with his great member confined, his body trembled with convulsive aftershocks. His heart and lungs struggled for equilibrium. The saucy sleeve enclosing him relaxed and constricted again, adding greater ecstasies to his afterglow.

Giselle, too, had been drained. He could feel mutual perspiration sliding where their bodies touched. She, too, had held back none of her abundant charms.

"How long will we be on the trail to M'sieu Bent's fort?" she asked in a tiny voice.

Hell, he thought, after a glorious encounter like that now we get back to business. If that doesn't take the bloom off the rose.

"A week. Maybe less. I don't know. Depends on the condition of the trail and how fast we travel. Why?"

"Let's go slow," Giselle pleaded. "I want to make such *grand amour* with you every night."

Relief, mingled with anticipation, flooded Eli. "And maybe sometimes during the day."

"*Oui.*"

Already the prospects had improved.

11

Grim faces formed a semicircle three ranks deep around a low fire that flickered off the walls of the arroyo. Between the pulsing blaze and the Kiowa warriors, Stone Hand paced to and fro while he harangued his brothers. His squat, blanket-wrapped figure and wolf skull headdress cast a long shadow. The words he spoke were not welcome to his listeners.

"Those with the white man's guns are low on ammunition. Many of us have few arrows. We have done well. All people now know that the Kiowas are still men. We have done all that our leader wanted. It is time to go back to our women and children."

Dark mutters of disapproval rose among the braves. Several shook tortoiseshell rattles as though to banish an unpleasantness. Stone Hand stomped the ground in agitation.

"Hear me. We have done enough running and raiding and running again. The easy pickings are over. Where can we find whites that they will fall into our hands like overripe sand hill plums?"

Crazy Knife rose from his place and stalked into the open space. He raised the long gun with the bright brass tube. Stone Hand yielded to the young warrior's desire to speak.

"More of our brothers join us at each long camp," Crazy Knife reminded his audience. "We are strong. The ways of our fathers are good enough to let us triumph. The bow, the lance, the stone war club, and the tomahawk will lead us to victory. Even my shoots-far rifle is not important. We must drive the white-eyes from the land. That is the destiny of the Kiowa."

Stone Hand adopted a patronizing tone. "And where will we find these whites to drive them off? We are not strong enough to attack the big villages, and killing a family here, another there makes no difference to the whites."

Crazy Knife produced a winning smile. "I know of a place. It is the great white-man trail that leads to the sunset."

"The Santa Fe Trail?" Stone Hand gulped, his tongue tripping over the white-man words.

"Yes."

Now Stone Hand became condescending. "You are young, Crazy Knife, and your blood runs hot to avenge our people against the whites. In our fathers' day, I would say you are right. Now there are too few people who use the trail. Again, we would be killing strays, taking little of consequence."

"I say the trail will provide for us as it has for the whites. Food, ammunition, weapons, and many bright things to take to our women. The trail is long, much of it in empty land. I say we can make the name of the Kiowa feared by all whites by raiding along the trail."

Murmurs of approval and interest sprang up in the crescent of warriors. Enough so that Crooked Leg rose and tightened the reservation trade blanket around his shoulders. He strode to Crazy Knife and put a paternal arm around the young man's shoulders.

"You are our best eyes and ears, my son. You are a

fierce fighter. Your words have weight. We will listen and consider. Tomorrow we will decide.''

Rugged, sparsely vegetated, the rocky terrain rolled on and on, sometimes below them when they rode the long finger of a ridge, and sometimes obscured behind a slope of rock and sand. But always there ahead, beckoning to them. It dipped away and rose again to merge with the sky at the edge of sight, a vista made clearer by the air that sharpened all a person's senses with its clarity.

At Holten's approach to the three toiling wagons, Giselle pulled her sweat-wet, blown team to a much-needed halt. She waited patiently until the guide rode up to her. She had packed away her sexy red dress in favor of a colorful calico blouse of cotton, a leather divided pants-like skirt, and glossy boots. Her heavy black hair was tucked up under the high crown of her hat. Colette—cute, demure Colette—drove the second wagon.

Coquettish toward Holten since the trip began, she remained careful about overt displays in deference to her mistress, who seemed to have staked out Eli Holten as her private preserve. Then there was Hugh to consider. Hugh, her diminutive lover who, as a man, rated much lower than the magnificent specimen that was Eli Holten. Yet who, as a lover, and a cook, was *magnifique* in his own right.

Holten waved at D'Arcy in the far wagon as he rode up from a morning scout of their perimeter. The women's little companion wore tight black riding britches, his English boots impeccably polished despite the harshness of the Santa Fe Trail country. He wore a shirt bleached to snow whiteness and starched board stiff, sporting a voluminous tie Holten learned was an ascot.

Only midmorning and the day had grown hot.

133

D'Arcy went coatless. He reminded Holten of paintings he had seen of European duelists, a pint-sized fighter with rapier or saber. Holten had learned that the European dueling saber bore faint resemblance to the long, curved, thick, metal-sheathed issue sabers of American fighting men in cavalry and artillery units. Holten hadn't sized up D'Arcy as much of a fighter, though he'd learned that the little Parisian gigolo had sand.

D'Arcy worked like a crazy man at his responsibilities, and—impervious as a wad of jerky—could handle the reins of his wagon from morning star to moonrise without a whimper. Then the little dandy would be ready to quench his insatiable thirst for absinthe and to stroll away into the night with a blanket over one arm and Colette's arm over the other. Or he would climb into one of the wagons with her and set the cover bows to jiggling and the axles squawling in unison with Colette's ecstatic screams, while Holten and Giselle grinned knowingly at each other over the fire.

"Everything going all right?" he asked Giselle as he brought Sonny to a halt beside her wagon.

Giselle winked and smiled provocatively. "I would rather ride with you into the prairies and make *le grand amour* like Colette and Hugh. Aside from that, *M'sieur* Eli, everything's proceeding properly."

"Nothing could suit me more, mam'selle," he allowed. "Let us put that down on the agenda as one of the recurring necessities of the trail. Meanwhile, we've been a while without fresh meat. There's some game hereabouts and I believe a-hunting I will go."

In fine, high spirits this morning, Giselle comically mimicked an English hunting horn. The effort broke down into a flurry of titters.

On his dawn scout, Holten had seen a small herd of buffalo grazing in ragged formation against the fading green of summer's end. Beyond them, a band of antelope streamed light as if not fastened to earth, moving soft as leaves driven before a mild breeze. He decided to report first before shooting, or being gone for a long time if a chase for meat became necessary.

"Go forth, mighty huntsman," Giselle commanded.

"And bring home the bacon," Holten added.

"Bacon?" she asked quizzically. "There are wild pigs here in this wasteland?"

"No," Holten stated. "Not that I've ever seen. On mountain slopes, maybe. Bringing home the bacon is only another American way of speaking. Sort of means acquiring the necessities." He glanced at the sun, which still climbed its way to the zenith. "I'll be back in maybe two or three hours. Long enough to track and kill some meat, skin and butcher it."

"Then tonight we have *le grand* feast, *non?*"

"I've been a while without fresh meat," Holten allowed.

Giselle feigned a pouting lower lip. "Do you forget Giselle?"

He couldn't miss the inference in her words. "I mean the other kind of fresh meat. How could I forget the juicy morsels of my Giselle?" By the Great Spirit, Holten thought, now he was beginning to talk like a Frenchman.

Giselle smiled sweetly, pleased that her hint had reached him. "Bring us back some choice roasts and racks of ribs, Eli. We will be fine until then. The day is magnificent, and the road is clear. We'll stop at noon to refresh and let the teams rest. Maybe you'll be back by then."

"We'll see." Eli refrained from adding, *"Adieu."* He reined Sonny around and back up the slope into the ocher, rocky plain in the direction he had seen the game. At the top he looked back at the three

135

diminished wagons. Giselle dropped the hand with which she shaded her eyes while watching him, and waved.

Out of sight of them, Sonny moved up the next ridge. His hooves slid on the loose shale footing. In the distance, some taller hills rose, clothed thickly with sage, mesquite, and the deep green of wizened, parched cactus. A roadrunner emerged some distance ahead of Sonny and invited the rider to a race.

Holten slid out his Winchester from the projecting under-stirrup boot and levered it partway to slip down the bolt mechanism. A gleaming stub of .45-70 brass cartridge, with its silent, gray Galena messenger of mortality, waited faithfully. He closed the breech and rode with the rifle over the pommel, ready for anything.

Even though he had taken on unexpected responsibilities on the trail to Bent's, he mused, he still had time and opportunity for hours of solitude such as these. He savored the moments, thinking also of the opportunities for bedtime frolics with Giselle which he hadn't counted on otherwise. His reflections came full circle when he contemplated the sky above.

Blue and big, and dotted with tiny puffs of white, the vast dome answered him with silence, as did the somber land, stretching off to infinity under the hooves of his horse. Holten now rode between sky and land, feeling free with no one about with any kind of request or challenge. The azure sky formed his ceiling, and the land his floor, with no walls in this place he called home.

Sonny took an easy lope while Holten stayed alert and let one corner of his mind daydream as the distance widened between the scout and his wards back along the Santa Fe Trail.

*　　　*　　　*

In a thicket of tall sage with the advantage of a slope dropping sharply behind him, the Kiowa, Crazy Knife, hid from all eyes. By parting the mingled branches of savory sage, he had an unobstructed view of a mile of wide coulee through which ran the vacant, abandoned Santa Fe Trail. Abandoned, he thought smugly as he remembered Stone Hand's word, aside from the three parked, giant white, canvas-topped wagons. Crazy Knife struggled to keep this vindication from making him foolish.

He had dropped his horse's reins back downslope to reconnoiter the big trail ahead. Around his waist he still wore the holstered six-guns of Benjamin Gross and Norville Ames. He had not expected to so quickly discover a profitable-looking target.

Watching the wagons from concealment, Crazy Knife's eyes narrowed, as much to extend his vision against the blinding sun as from sinister lust. Three people could be seen, a little man and two women. As he watched, the man and one woman walked away into the gorse, the man carrying a blanket.

For a long time, Crazy Knife watched the pair disappear, sometimes down into a slow fold in the land, and then reappear smaller on the next slope. At last they vanished into the sunlit chaparral altogether. Crazy Knife felt confident they would not even hear the screams of the other woman, if he even allowed her to scream, which he intended not to do.

Left beside the wagons, the woman had the lithe form of youth and Crazy Knife became conscious of a persistent itching under his breechcloth. It had been three weeks since the attack on the Mexican village. Crooked Leg's braves had taken down four young women in the white adobe place where they had killed the man with the black robe.

Crazy Knife had amazed himself by rising to the occasion, drunk and staggering on the Mexican mescal and pulque as he was, and in two hours had

had his way with three of the women. By the time Crazy Knife had slept off his drunk, along with his gratified lusts, and was large and hard again, all the women, including the one he hadn't taken, had succumbed to the violence of the Kiowas' lustful attacks. Fifteen braves, some repeating several times, had been too much for four women to manage, Crazy Knife mused as he watched and waited to be sure the one below in the narrow valley was alone.

Mexican women, unlike Kiowa women, he thought, were weak anyway. He remembered with a fiendish chuckle the six braves raiding, looting, and burning the simple *jacals* where the people lived. There they had come across an old blind woman, her face as pinched and wrinkled as the puckered, shriveled, ironlike hide inside an old scalp.

In drunken revelry, they mounted the old woman on dares, banging into her until she went senseless. Then they burned the dry old *jacal* around her. They shrieked in inebriated glee over her screams as the flames returned her awareness with no means of escape in the darkness of her sightless eyes.

He studied the wagons below him as the sun seemed to hang suspended throughout the long, hot noontime. Still he had seen no other men, and the pair that had wandered away had not reappeared. There would be time to take her, the one below, and maybe even ride off with her to serve him through the night. If she lived, he'd take her as a prize for Crooked Leg.

His power had grown, a strong medicine, stronger than it had been at the Mexican village.

The midafternoon sun already threw long shadows as Holten rode the hills and hollows of the vast, high plateau of eastern Colorado back toward the Santa Fe Trail. Secured to his saddle hung the carefully butchered hindquarters of an antelope for roasts and stew. He'd insist that the four of them eat plenty before it spoiled. It was anyone's guess what the condition of the game ahead on this rarely traveled portion of the trail might be.

Eli guided Sonny to quarter across to the northwest from his hunting trip, hoping by angling to come upon the trail at about the point he would find Giselle and the wagons. Deep ravines crisscrossed the plateau and the trail followed them in the line of least resistance.

An old animal path took him in the direction he wanted to go. Unused for a long time, the narrow rut had nearly grown over by brush, though it was still distinct. His tracking senses alerted, an alarm speared through him some twenty minutes later.

Faint dust still hung in the air and the disturbed earth in the rut told him that someone on horseback had passed this way an hour or two before him. The animal had not been shod. That little observation made the hackles rise on Holten's neck. Ahead, the sun slowly slid toward the western ridge he sought. The angry orb lingered with a hot, brassy flare of light that spun gold out of the dried wisps of grass. Holten urged Sonny with blunted spur rowels and approached the trail cautiously, keeping his anxieties in check.

His first true indication of alarm was the sight of an Indian pony alongside the old game trail, obediently standing with reins dropped. The markings on its chest and flanks indicated Kiowa. For all his concern for his charges, he had to proceed cautiously. He, too, ground-reined his mount and edged up to the rim of the slope. Beyond it, he looked down on the wasted remnants of the Santa Fe Trail.

A spurt of fury lanced through Eli Holten. Down there, alongside Colette's wagon, Giselle struggled silently with an Indian in the first moments of a sexual attack. The Kiowa had her caught up from behind, with one hand over her mouth, her arms pinioned. His corded muscles bulged in the effort to drag her down. Holten felt a stab of alarm, his first impulse to run screaming the several hundred yards to the wagons. Wisdom from his many encounters with hostiles kept him in place. His pause allowed fury to rise in him like a fiery tide. Anger replaced alarm. Primed for action, he did not move impulsively. Carefully he gathered his icy fury in his gut.

In the heat of his struggle to rape the woman, the Kiowa would be oblivious to action around him, Holten reasoned. He quietly raced back, swung up on Sonny, and hit a gallop over the ridge. He rampaged down through sage and tall grass, to throw dust and pebbles in all directions. He couldn't shoot for fear of harming Giselle. Eli's only hope lay in the Kiowa's not being aware of him until he fell upon him. By then the Kiowa had Giselle on the ground. He hovered over her, trying to fight his way into the leather divided skirt, still holding a grimy hand over her mouth.

Plummeting toward them in a cloud of dust, Holten wasn't certain what happened next. Either Sonny stumbled over a gopher hole or veered to avoid a rock and lost his stride. Inertia sent Holten pitching over his mount's neck. He landed on his head and partly on one shoulder. Light burst like an explosion in his brain before everything went black.

Instantly on the alert, the Kiowa gave up his attack on Giselle. Absently he dropped her beside Colette's wagon in a trembling, terrified heap. He darted to the unconscious intruder only a few racing steps away.

Forgetting the six-guns strapped to his hips, Crazy Knife jerked out his Bowie as he ran. Intent on taking the blond scalp of the dead or disabled enemy who had interrupted his pleasure with the woman, he ignored all else around him.

Holten lay face down in the dust and gravel of the trail. With a cry of counting coup, Crazy Knife leaped on the dazed scout. He pulled Eli's head up by his hair and brought the knife up to slash away the scalp. Holten, numbed by the fall, and only partly aware of what went on, lay powerless to react.

A hurled chunk of sharp-edged, wedge-shaped granite bounced off the side of Crazy Knife's head. It stunned him momentarily. He left off the scalping to leap up with the maddened howl of a wounded bear to determine the cause of the sudden agony in his head.

At once the little man in black pants, boots, and white shirt who had thrown the rock rushed toward him, obviously bent on ripping Crazy Knife apart with his bare hands. Behind the enraged little fellow, his woman companion appeared around the end of a wagon. Crazy Knife rubbed his head and faced the onrushing little powerhouse. Quickly he calculated the odds. The fallen white man already struggled to get up. He might be dying but Crazy Knife couldn't chance it. Two to one. Not good.

Then the little man caught up to him. Although he held a thin-bladed knife, like a child's toy Crazy Knife thought, the furious fellow bewildered and brought considerable pain to his adversary in a baffling way. He didn't fight with his hands. He used his feet.

He whirled, jumped, and yelled, one foot, then the other lashing out to crack agonizingly into Crazy Knife's knees, groin, and belly. One high kick struck the side of his head. Impulsively, Crazy Knife turned and sprinted away up the grassy hill to his horse, hopeful someone wouldn't unleash a rifle and wing one at him while he was fully exposed.

Eli Holten lay for long moments while he returned

141

to his senses. Giselle, Colette, and Hugh huddled over him, concern traced in their expressions.

Giselle's calico blouse had been torn and her heavy black hair formed a tangled mess around her terror-blanched face that, only now, began to get back some of its color. Drops of blood from lips rudely bruised by the Indian's coarse hand, dried at one corner of her mouth.

"Wha' happened?" Holten mumbled.

"The horse," Colette offered. "She throw you."

Holten stared at her, his senses returning now on swift wings, and brightened. "Look again," he suggested. "She's a he. So I got thrown. I know that. The Indian? What happened?"

"Gone," Giselle stated simply. "Ran away. Tried to cut off your hair with the big knife."

"Who stopped him?"

"Hugh," she told him. "The apache." She pronounced it "a-posh."

"That was a Kiowa, not an Apache."

Giselle laughed, a tinkle of euphoric relief that her attacker had been run off and that Holten was all right. "No, Eli. 'A-posh' in French is the same as your Apache, said different, but means tough street fighter. Hugh D'Arcy, A-posh. Tough little guy."

"He used his feet," Colette informed Eli.

"He . . . what?"

"*La savatte,*" Giselle explained. "It is a—how you say?—method of fighting with one's feet."

"Well, I'll be damned," Holten gasped.

D'Arcy grinned from ear to ear at him as Holten tried to sit up. "I also 'ave," D'Arcy said, "'ow you say, good chicken weeng."

Colette spoke up again. "He threw the stone from way over there by the wagon and hit the Indian in the head before he could cut your hair, Eli."

D'Arcy still beamed. "I live once in New Jersey for

two year. Could not speak the English, but I learn to play baseball, and was good pitcher. They say I 'ave weeng like zee chicken. Once I make a, what is it, no-hitter.''

Holten shook his head, groaned, and came to his feet. "Time we be moving," he advised.

12

Scowling, Maj. Randall Covington looked up from the words he had just penned in his journal. Their progress had been remarkably slow. That damned Adams had to be plotting against him. He and Locke. The men moved too slowly, they would be late reaching Bent's Fort. All a part of some grand plan to discredit him with his superiors. The troops needed something to motivate them.

For a few days following the flogging, every one of the malingering misfits had performed with alacrity. They stepped lively and exercised extreme care to military courtesy and the ritual of daily routine. Then, slowly, the improvement began to erode away. What could he do?

Inspiration came when a stray breeze flickered the flame of a kerosene lantern and brought with it the aroma of the evening meal. Covington savored his idea, licking thin, bloodless lips. Yes, it would be perfect. Without rising, he put a hand to his mouth and bellowed.

"Orderly!"

"Sir, yes, sir," a nervous rookie blurted when he entered.

"I'll have Sergeant Major Adams here at once."

"Yes, sir."

Harry Adams arrived three minutes later. He saluted properly and reported himself. Covington feigned reading from his journal for a while, compelling Adams to hold his hand to his kepi brim. At last Covington looked up, returned the salute.

"Stand at ease, Sergeant Major."

"Thank you, sir." Adams waited in a silence induced by Covington's reticence. "You, ah, sent for me, sir?"

"Yes—yes, Sergeant Major Adams. Effective to-morrow morning, the troops and horses are to go on half rations. The same for water."

In spite of his best efforts, Harry Adams sucked in a great draught of air. This was the most insane of a lot of unsound orders. "Sir, begging the Major's pardon, sir, but field rations are sparse enough. The horses are showing wear, sir. Reducing rations for either will not be to the benefit of anyone, sir."

Gimlet-eyed, Covington glowered at his leading N.C.O. "I've warned you before about questioning my orders, Sergeant Major. You are dangerously close to the most flagrant insubordination. I am not required to explain myself to you; however, I shall."

Covington rose and began to pace, hands clasped behind his back. "We will not be able to resupply until we reach Fort Union in New Mexico. The added miles the War Department so brilliantly saddled us with to and from Bent's Old Fort and the Cimarron Cutoff only exacerbates this situation. Better to have the men a little hungry all of the time than to be starving the last few days. Don't you think so, Sergeant Major?"

"With all due respect, sir, I can detail hunting parties to take fresh meat, which will augment our rations, sir. There are antelope, elk, bison aplenty."

"Food for savages," Covington dismissed airily, "not fit for civilized men. My order stands. That will be all, Sergeant Major. So inform the commissary sergeant and the men charged with squad mess duty. Oh, and the men and their equipment are to be searched to uncover any individual hoarding that might be going on."

"Now, sir, that is entirely uncalled for. It will create disorder in the ranks, threaten open revolt."

"Mutinous soldiers are shot," Covington snapped. "Keep that in mind, Sergeant Major. Dis-missed."

While they got ready to ride on one morning two days after the Kiowa's attack, Holten found Giselle securing last-minute bundles and bags in her wagon. The news he brought was hardly what she wanted to hear. Yet, to be warned was the start of being prepared for the worst. The air hung heavily around them, the sky gray and cold.

"Storming up in the hills," Holten pointed out. "Pretty black up there. We'll get a good wetting before this day's over."

Giselle's sharp, dark eyes grew instantly alert. She scanned the sullen clouds over the distant range and the sky to the southwest. She turned tense, her eyes filled with alarm, though she was in control of her wits.

"Won't be the first time either of us has been wet, Eli. It rains in my native France all the time."

"Not like this," he observed. "This one's going to be what they call a real frog-drownder." Woops, he thought, he hadn't meant that like it sounded. Giselle missed the slang reference some Americans, of English descent, gave French people.

"Do we stay here, Eli? Or ride it out in the wagons?"

"Might as well keep movin'. Long as we can, at least." A light wind with a chill to it made ground dust rise and rattled in the sparse spears of grass and chaparral. Eli motioned to Colette and Hugh to start

146

and stepped up into Sonny's saddle. "There's no place out here to shelter from it anyway."

The dark cloud that moved toward them hung like an ebon blanket and from it Holten could see ribbonlike tendrils of distant downpour. A gleaming vein of silver forked down out of the black mass to the south and before he could count five, thunder rumbled in the valley. The mules twitched their ears in nervousness. With Holten leading out, the three wagons creaked into motion.

Around them the firmament grew close, with tatters of rain clouds scudding toward them as though picking the wagons as special targets for their fury. On the wings of the wind came a fine, thin, chill rain.

Holten waved them to a halt. "Time for slickers," he yelled at Giselle. "All hell's getting ready to bust loose."

He climbed down and put on his voluminous "fish," noticing that without being bidden, Colette and Hugh did the same. Getting back up on Sonny, Holten made sure to screw his hat down tight on his brow. He might even have to tie it in place with his bandanna, he thought, as the sagebrush bowed before the wind, long branches flailing each other.

The fine mist that had accompanied the earlier breezes now turned into buckshot pellets driven slantwise by the rising wind. Out of concern for the safety of the wagons and their passengers, Holten kept the pace slow with the world walled off from him by a torrent of rain that now poured down like a mighty cascade. It went on for half an hour. Then the wind moved on to conduct its nasty business elsewhere.

His concern was for their approach to the Santa Fe Trail's ford at the north fork of the Cimarron River which, in this stuff, would be formidable to cross. If the downpour continued too long they wouldn't be able to cross for several days. His vision obscured by the wall of water around him, Holten let himself be guided by the broad, age-rounded track of the old trail.

At least when they reached the Cimarron the wide, shallow river's fringe of cottonwoods would provide some windbreak from the elements. Anything was preferable to being drenched and pounded as they were now. Holten could find only one consolation in the madd ning rain which in this country could keep up for hours, sometimes days.

If Crooked Leg's band was abroad in this territory —a fact well confirmed by the incident two days before—he'd be bogged down somewhere on the rimrock, his fiery lust for blood and booty thoroughly quenched by the downpour. Be thankful for small favors. Holten tipped his head down and a cascade poured off his hat brim onto the saddle horn, drenching his hand on the reins as well.

Around them along the trail small ponds began to form in the low pockets of tiny hollows. As the rain poured in to fill these, runoff from the surrounding slopes added to their measure and some of the small puddles joined, growing estuaries into big ones. The land was being flooded. One of them, a great gray oval of pearl water tinged with mud, directly blocked the trail and spanned a good twenty-five yards across and a hundred long. No telling how deep. Holten threw up his hand for a halt and rode back to Giselle's wagon.

He reined up alongside the driver's seat. He didn't comment, but she looked like a drowned beaver. Surprisingly the drowned beaver grinned impishly.

"Everything okay back here?" he called up to her over the roar of the rain. Her spunk showed in her gritty nod of assent. "Whatta ya think of these here apples?" he yelled. "Remember I told you it wouldn't be all sweetness and light on the Santa Fe Trail."

Her grin turned into a broad smile. "I love it, Eli. What an adventure."

Struck dumb, Holten had half expected her to say she wished she'd stayed in Dodge. Her traveling companions, too, were probably thinking they'd like to get down from the wagons and go off somewhere to make *le grand amour* in the mud. Then, to his complete surprise, through the drumming rain, he could hear a faint song.

A man's song, sung from the farthest wagon. The damned little dandy, Hugh D'Arcy, sat back there, soaked to the hide and miserable, chirping his fool head off. A moment later he heard Colette's lyrical alto join Hugh in a lilting carol to life or love or something beautiful. Certainly not to mud and rain. Eli grinned up at Giselle, who had also heard.

"And I thought I'd have to be nursemaid on this trip. They're sure full of sand and fightin' tallow, those two."

"'Ow is that, Eli?" she asked. Then the sense of his words hit her. "I told you," she shouted. The rain still streamed off her hat and poured down her bright yellow slicker.

"You're no slouch either, mam'selle."

"Can we get over that lake, Eli?" she asked, her voice pitched higher in apprehension as she yelled above the rain's incessant roar.

"You've got high wheels," he shouted back. "Depends on the condition of the roadbed under there. Not much choice. We've got to keep going or we mire down. Move 'em out. I'll stay close. I'll ride back and tell Colette and Hugh not to start crossing until the wagon ahead is on the other side. Get your mules going fast so you can keep the momentum."

Holten rode back to the other wagons, vague outlines against sheets of falling water. Giselle shouted French obscenities at the mules and let fly her bullwhip to crack over their ears. It urged them ahead at a fast trot. Eli stopped to watch, holding up his hand for Colette not to move.

Giselle's wagon picked up speed, gathered assisting force on the downslope, and careened into the pond. The mules hit the water at a high run. The wagon lumbered easily behind them. A high geyser of sprayed water went up as the mules and wagon negotiated the pool at a fast clip.

In the middle the water reached to the axles and no higher. Giselle handled her teams like a champion. As the wagon began to decelerate with the tug of water and mud, out again went the crackling whip and the shrill, demanding French words of displeasure cut through the din of rain.

Inspired by fear of the shrieking, fishwife voice behind them, the mules doubled their energetic thrust into the collars, and in moments the leaders found solid footing. Haunches churning, they trudged through the shallows and headed upslope from the bank. Behind them, the wagon too rose out of the water and soon rested on solid, though not dry, ground.

Colette hadn't such good fortune, nor was she so skilled. The mud had been compressed so she had deeper ooze to contend with. Holten urged Sonny out to her bogged wagon. Giselle had pulled her teams up ahead to allow the next wagon plenty of room to emerge from the sump. She walked back to stand in the downpour and study the progress.

"Don't worry, Colette," Holten called. "Have you out in a shake."

Like Giselle, the spunky little coquette smiled with water streaming over her babylike features. "Me worry, Eli Holten is so close? Ah-ha-ha," she laughed that same French devil-may-care chuckle he'd heard from Giselle that night outside Dodge City.

Holten figured he only needed to double the team on Colette's wagon and she'd be out. Giselle's mules would more frazzled after their run, so he rode back to Hugh's wagon for his team and his help.

"Time to stop singing and thinking about pussy, Hugh old boy," he called, not caring if the little jasper understood every word or not. "Need your team to pull your lovemate out of the mud."

Together they unhitched and led the mules up, waded out, and snapped the trace chains into the doubletree of Colette's lead pair. Hugh got up beside Colette and after first kissing her, grabbed the reins. Holten, on Sonny, held the headstall of the lead mule and between them they walked the fractious animals and the wagon almost effortlessly out of the bog.

Holten and Hugh took his team back across and hitched up. This time Holten advised D'Arcy to go out onto the flats and skirt the pond. Giselle and Colette had already begun moving down the trail. Eli rode Sonny ahead to spot hazards and in minutes he and Hugh had to busily try to catch up with the women.

Miles and hours away, although battered by the same storm, Maj. Randall Covington had near chaos on his hands. Around the long column of horsemen riding in twos, who prevented a total soaking with their tentlike blue issue ponchos, the rain hurtled like gravel grains. Whipped up by a restless wind it came in lashing gusts for over three hours before taking a notion to ease off. The fury of the weather, coupled with a troop that had grown sullenly defiant, became maddening to Randall Covington.

He'd spent his days nursing a self-generated fury. After the punishment of Private Cate, Sgt. Maj. Harry Adams had resorted to a grudging compliance wiht Covington's orders; obedient but keeping his opinions to himself. Then, when the order to reduce rations had been issued, Adams nearly placed himself

151

in open revolt. Covington now began to distrust Cpl. Joe Locke and the five-trooper cadre even more. All of them seemed to take their cue from the hateful Adams and offered little more than dutiful subservience to Covington's direct commands.

Covington's rage at the abysmal weather and the troop's attitude impaired his limited abilities at command. The manual must have instructions for inclement field conditions of this sort. Yet he couldn't recall them. In this rain, he knew of nothing to do but slog ahead. Around him, his command plodded like dumb beasts. The depression of lousy weather and scant rations totally washed away any semblance of a military unit. They only looked like cavalrymen. He also knew the clearly evident bad blood between him and their beloved Sergeant Major Adams disturbed them.

Covington had reacted to the troop's daily degeneration in morale after the Cate incident, and his alienation from Adams, by bearing down even more harshly. Their near-mutinous response to having food issue cut by half brought them close to violence. If he couldn't get willing obedience, he ruminated, then by God, he'd get blind obedience. But he *would* get obedience.

Two mornings after the loss of Cate's horse, Covington could see his control slipping. He'd ordered Adams to get the men up that morning in time for a formation and inspection after breakfast, and to do so in time that the column could be in the saddle and moving out at full daylight. He gave Adams the orders from his tent, erected for him nightly.

"As the Major directs, sir," Adams said, his voice sounding tired and whipped.

"You don't seem to agree, Sergeant Major, that some good, sound military discipline is what this troop needs to restore its fighting spirit and its faith in command."

"Sir, it is not my place to question orders. My duty is to carry them out."

"You are not behaving like a high-ranking noncommissioned officer, Adams."

"Sir, I will carry out your orders to the best of my ability."

Covington's anger-glistening eyes narrowed. "You're still nursing a hurt that I didn't let your precious little Private Cate off, aren't you?"

"Sir, I overstepped my bounds. It was not my place to question your authority."

Covington produced a droll expression. "Some change in you from the fire-eater you were that day, Sergeant Major."

"Will that be all, sir?"

"You threatened to make a report of your side of the incident when we get to Arizona, Adams. Do you still intend to?"

"Is that an order, sir?"

"Is what an order?"

"To reveal my intentions, sir."

"Damn you, Adams. You are patronizing me. Yes, that's an order. Do you or do you not propose to report the incident and my actions?"

"I do, sir."

"And jeopardize thirty years of loyal service to the army? Very well, Sergeant Major. You know best. We shall see who comes out on top. My intention is to ride into Arizona from this trip and field exercise with a first-class fighting cavalry troop to put the lie to your accusations. Formation and inspection at six a.m. or at first light, and prepared to ride immediately thereafter. We'll see, Sergeant Major Harry Adams, whose word and whose authority speaks louder from here on out."

"Will that be all, sir?"

"Yes, Sergeant. Dismissed."

153

Adams saluted crisply, about-faced, and departed Covington's tent.

Ten days later, Covington had persuaded himself his experiment had worked. He drove the troop and horses until nearly dark each day and had Adams rouse the men before daylight. Even the horses had begun to look haggard. He had only one recourse: to push them harder. Beat their incompetence and their indifference out of them, he believed, and fighting men—one fused, ferocious fighting machine—would emerge. If a pipsqueak like Autie Custer could do it with the Seventh, so could he.

At night, after the troop's long hours in the saddle and with infrequent rest stops, Sergeant Major Adams, unobserved by Covington, slipped away into the night with Private Cate. In the dark away from the resting troop, Adams replaced the dressings of the whip's slash wounds across Cate's back. Adams gently and tenderly applied soothing balms, covered the welts again with clean pads. Cate's healing progressed rapidly under Adams's competent care.

The men of C Troop knew it was going on. They also knew that Major Covington would take terrible reprisals if he knew. Now, as Covington rode off to the side, midway in the column slogging along the rain-pummeled Santa Fe Trail, his eyes made out the figure of Sergeant Major Adams's horse sloshing back to him through mud clear to the fetlocks. Adams rode up and saluted with exaggerated formality that bordered on insolence.

"Sergeant Major?"

"With the Major's permission, sir, the men have been in the saddle four hours. Considering the severity of the weather, sir, don't you think a rest is called for?"

"I do not."

"Forgive me, sir, if I again sound insubordinate. The demands made upon these men, and they're all

154

green recruits, sir, fresh from training, not to mention the short rations, is accomplishing little to achieve your goals or to reestablish esprit de corps." Sensing he had failed to reach the officer, Adams added, "Then there's the horses, of course. As government property, their condition and well-being are of primary importance."

"Sergeant Major, I thought the subject of half rations was closed." Then, ignoring the sarcasm in the sergeant's voice for once, Covington fumbled under his poncho for his watch. "Sergeant Major Adams, in an hour, at one p.m., you may call a halt for twenty minutes for the men to attend to bodily needs and look to the condition of their horses. I hope you are making sure each man carries field rations for midday."

"They are, sir," Adams answered tightly. Not that one could consider a single hardtack biscuit and four ounces of cold pickled pork adequate fare. "Sir, would there be anything wrong with calling the halt now? The man and horses will thus be better refreshed for the afternoon's march to night camp."

"Are you seeking to countermand explicit instructions, Sergeant Major?"

"No, sir, only . . ."

"That will be all, Sergeant Major Adams. Dismissed."

Adams sighed, whipped a salute to the soggy brim of his sodden kepi, and turned as if to leave with no further comment.

"Oh, Sergeant Major," Covington cracked like a parade ground command.

Adams stopped abruptly, wheeled his horse, and rode back close to the major. "Sir."

"There is another thing I wish to speak with you about."

"Sir?"

Covington's eyes had a vague look, and Adams

searched them for a clue. "This is not the appropriate time. Come to my tent after mess this evening."

"Yes, sir."

"On second thought, Sergeant Major Adams. Don't report to my tent. I'll seek you out."

Adams was puzzled, even fearful of the major's intentions. "As the Major wishes, sir."

"And call the halt in an hour, Sergeant Major. Dismissed."

"Thank you, sir." Adams did not salute as he rode away.

13

Although by mealtime that evening it no longer rained forcefully, the land around the resting cavalry troop wept with moisture and the mud made life disagreeable for men and horses. Night fires for warmth and cooking had been hard to start and keep going. The buffalo chips gathered earlier for fuel, and carried in a sling under the commissary wagon, had drawn moisture and tended to smolder and smell terrible. Yet somehow the cavalrymen made it through the disagreeable evening. Attitudes had grown about as sullen as the weather.

Since he had been ordered to wait until Covington came to him, Adams crouched apprehensively by a fire with some of the troopers. They vainly tried to find warmth in the blaze and to dry clothing soaked by the day's exposure. Suddenly Covington clumped out of the darkness and Adams could feel the men tense around him.

They all sprang to attention beside the fire, including Adams. "At ease. As you were," Covington called and they relaxed, though remained standing.

"Good evening, men," the major called out as he walked up to where RSM Adams stood by the smoking dung fire with a circle of enlisted men. "You all did well today. You're a credit to C Troop."

There came obedient, gratuitous mumbles of acknowledgment among those around the fire and others close by enough to hear. "Sergeant Major Adams."

"Sir?"

"Where is Trooper Cate?"

"I don't know, sir. Shall I send someone to fetch him?"

"No, Sergeant Major, it's you I desire to speak with, and I believe the men should hear this."

Puzzled, Adams responded quietly, "Sir?"

"Sergeant Major, I believe as a man in your position, you fraternize too freely with the enlisted men."

Adams was astonished. "Sir?"

"You and Corporal Locke are the ranking non-commissioned officers on this detail and henceforth you and Corporal Locke will make camp together, exclusive of the rank-and-file troops. This is established practice in a disciplined unit, and I am doing everything in my power to create such out of this troop during our travels and field exercise before reporting for duty in Arizona."

No other field commander Adams had ever served under had made such an idiotic order. To the contrary, men slept by squads and platoons, with their noncoms right there at hand. It facilitated command and control in the event of a surprise attack. Harry Adams also knew from sad experience with Randall Covington that to question the order was equally idiotic.

"As the Major wishes, sir." Adams burned with being humiliated so openly before the men.

"That will also mean no further contacts with Private Cate, except as they pertain to the duties of this military detail."

"Sir!" Adams bit off the question he wanted to ask.

"Adams, last evening while taking a stroll in the

158

night, I had occasion to observe you out away from the assembled troop with Private Cate. The medical care of Private Cate is not within your military purview, and your touching of his naked body is highly suspect."

Harry Adams recoiled as though he had received a physical blow. He could not comprehend such an unconscionable statement. Filled with rage at his abject degradation before the men of his troop, Adams could only stand, slack-jawed, and shake with fury, no proper words coming to his defense.

"That will be all, Sergeant Major Adams. Good night, men."

Major Covington spun and walked away. His boots made sucking sounds as he yanked them savagely from the mud. Rain began to fall again, and the sky turned pitch black with thick rain clouds totally obscuring the stars. Several of the troopers, avoiding eye contact with the sergeant major, walked away also. Adams stood by the fire, which sputtered in dying gasps as the rain settled in, apparently for the night.

Deeply troubled, Adams walked away into the prairie darkness to try to regulate his heartbeat and his thinking. The word "desertion" even entered into his jumbled thoughts. He immediately dismissed that. One thing for certain, Covington intended to thoroughly discredit him with the men. The bad part, Adams acknowledged, was that for the life of him he couldn't think of a way to deal with that.

At least not one that didn't involve the imminent demise of Maj. Randall Covington.

No railroad served the fifty miles between Dancerville and Plymouth, Colorado. Out of Plymouth it was only twelve miles farther north to a whistle-stop railhead on the Santa Fe in either direction. To remedy this transportation problem for the folks in Dancerville with business in Plymouth or a need to get somewhere on the Santa Fe, old Finn Hennessy went to work. He restored to full use an abandoned Abbott-Downing four-seat Concord coach that had been slowly giving way to decay and dry rot in a field outside Dancerville for twelve years that he could remember.

Now, once a week, he'd get old Dad Briggs dried out long enough to ride shotgun for him, on the two-day haul to Plymouth, with his lever-action Winchester. Because it was only the two of them, Finn, who had always had a good hand at lettering, got some gilt paint and, after he'd given his refurbished coach a coat of sparkling red, lettered "Hennessy & Briggs Stage Line" in the narrow panel over the door and below the roof line on each side. Here and there the gilt had dripped and on one side the word "Line" had to be scrunched up for want of space. Generally, folks thought Finn Hennessy had done a right proper job with his lettering.

"Rain held up the run two days, Dad. But things have dried off," Finn said to Briggs as they readied for the Plymouth run. "Question is, you dried out enough to take a ride today?"

Dad Briggs shot him a scowl. "I can count and I know the schedule same as you, Finn," he snapped, chin hair waggling.

Both men had bushy, gray-shot whiskers and wore grimy, sun-bleached whipcords and calico shirts. There were those in Dancerville who said the pair was too long in the tooth for such a demanding business. Both of the old-timers laughed about it all the way from point to point.

It was fifty miles, and since neither Finn nor Dad were spring chickens, they provided themselves a midway stopover with a good cabin for them and their passengers to rest overnight. The cabin sat in a dusty country where even the sage grew sparse and wood was wanting. They made their cook fires from buffalo chips, which made a hot, short blaze, leaving nothing but a fine gray ash. This day, four passengers showed up to fill the coach.

Normally Finn and Dad averaged two, at the most three. They had a sack of mail for the post office in Plymouth, and would bring the Dancerville mail back with them.

Dad Briggs's whiskers fairly bristled with Finn's implication that he couldn't hold his cargo. "I'll tell you something, Finn Hennessy," he growled. "Just you toss up a two-bit piece an' Ol' Spunky here'll bore 'er dead center 'fore she hits the ground." He gestured with his Winchester.

"Hit the ground!" Finn howled in high hilarity. "I see the time you were so drunk you couldn't hit the ground with your hat in three throws."

"You got a lot of mouth, Finn. Most of the gents climbin' in this trip appeared to be heeled. Couple of 'em with lever-actions. I see a scattergun toted in too. That gives me ease."

"How come? The Hennessy an' Briggs Stage Line ain't had no holdups. Ain't nothin' to hold up."

"They's stories around there's some Kio-ways on the warpath. Way west of here, to hear tell it. You wouldn't know this stuff, Finn, 'cause you don't hang around the saloon and hear the news."

"No, I don't. Besides, you do well enough holding up that end of the bidness for Hennessy and Briggs anyway, Dad."

"Renegades off the reservation down in the Nations," Briggs went on, ignoring the jibe. "Fella was in town 'tother day, knew all about it. 'Bout ten of them heathen savages rode roughshod over a little Mexican town. Killed about fifty people and a bunch of children, then just raised jubilacious hell with their womenfolk."

"Meskins don't know how to defend theirselves," Finn dismissed, expertly catching the reins to the nigh leader and wheeler between the fingers of his left hand and the off-leader and wheeler, as well as the whip, in his right, ready to move. "They think God almighty in His infinite mercy will protect 'em from all harm. Irresponsible, that's what it is. They all in back there?"

"I allow," Dad said.

"You, Molly!" Finn shouted at the nigh leader. "Up, Whistler!" His short buggy whip creaked over his head, sufficient noise to get the four-horse team shouldering into the collars. The Hennessy & Briggs stage, its axles well greased, rolled and creaked on Finn's new leather throughbraces out of Dancerville. Their departures had become so commonplace that folks rarely came down to see them off. More met their arrivals from Plymouth, hoping to have a letter in the mail.

Twenty miles out of Dancerville, Crazy Knife had been scouting a well-used road that along here followed the twists and turns of a river, which ran roughly parallel with the northern border of Indian Territory to the south. It took the path of least resistance past a tawny bluff dotted with rocky outcroppings. What trees survived on the rimrock grew twisted from the cracks in the rock, leaning away to the northeast, bowed and crochety-looking as old men from the weight of persistent wind and years. The furious, though cooling, rain of several days before was only a memory; the morning promised to heat up to a regular scorcher.

Crazy Knife leaned down to the stream to slake a sun-dried thirst. The water flowed cool and sweet over his lips. He could see pebbles on the bottom through the wavery stream as clear as though through air. So far the white men had not come to break the sod, erode the ground, and turn the pure water brown. Crazy Knife liked that. It was the way things were supposed to be. He became alerted to the sounds of something moving along the riverbank road, coming his way.

Wheels sucked in the soft sand and rolled over harder ground with more clatter, growing closer. Yet it came slowly as though the driver was in no hurry. Horses' heads appeared over a low swell.

Crazy Knife's eyes grew big as the four horses pulled the first big red covered wagon he'd ever seen past where he hid among the rocks and willows along the river's bank, flanking the road. The two men on top, one driving and one holding a rifle, had the white hair of the man killed before the Kiowas attacked the Mexican wagon train. Yet Crazy Knife knew them to be old men.

When the vehicle had passed and the land around Crazy Knife grew quiet again, he hunted down his horse with his prized rifle in the saddle boot and set off through the morning that grew hotter by the minute. He wanted to make contact with Crooked Leg's band.

Crazy Knife still served as Crooked Leg's advance scout. More and more braves heard about the adventures of those who had left the imprisonment of the white man's reservation. Such tales persuaded them to ride out to join Crooked Leg. The red wagon would interest Crazy Knife's chief.

He also wanted to get back to report the three wagons moving west, surely loaded with riches, and with two thoroughly comely women ripe for Kiowa plucking. Crazy Knife still didn't understand what had hit his head to cause such extreme pain as he made to scalp the big man killed in the fall from his horse. He only knew he was frightened by the mystery of how he had been hurt with no one standing near and no one holding a gun.

He was also astonished and partly panicked by the little black-haired white-eye in funny clothing, the likes of which he had never seen white men wear. The kicking that the little man used to fight was a humiliation Crazy Knife preferred to forget. He was disappointed that he could not take the white woman captive to Crooked Leg. But now he could promise there'd be two of them.

Crazy Knife squinted in anticipation of spilling the blood of the two white-haired men on the red wagon. If he could get them, he would then have three white-haired scalps, and no Kiowa that he knew of had so much as even seen one. Finding his horse, he leaped into the saddle to track down Crooked Leg to report the results of his four-day scouting mission into the prairie to the northeast and the promise of plunder and women.

He couldn't know that at that very moment Crooked Leg's braves busily looted the Hennessy & Briggs way station looking for treasures and whiskey. They found neither. Crooked Leg called a council of his two head men, Broken Tail and Bignose.

"We wait here in the hills," Crooked Leg decided. "White man lives here. He come back. We get rifles, horses, scalps when they do."

"White-eyes who build this lodge and not live here all the time have much riches to have more than one lodge to live in," commented Broken Tail.

"Foolish to wait here for white man," Bignose opined. "Travel to where the sun rises. Find more white-eyes lodges. Many scalps and women." Both had joined Crooked Leg from the Fort Sill agency recently and were disappointed they had missed the revelry at the little village.

Crooked Leg felt blind without Crazy Knife serving as his eyes. He had other young braves now to scout, yet didn't trust their abilities as trackers and observers like Crazy Knife. Crazy Knife would know what to do.

Now he brought his hands together for a glancing clap of decision. "We stay here in the hills one day to rest the horses and watch for white-eyes to return to the empty lodge. If not, then we ride east to find white scalps and women, much riches." He glanced at Broken Tail and Bignose. Eyes doubting, they grunted gutturally in reluctant assent.

Making excellent time from Dancerville, the Hennessy & Briggs coach rolled into the yard of the way station at a little after three o'clock. Finn Hennessy had brought some fresh groceries and canned goods for the way station's larder, as well as four bottles of whiskey to reprovision the place. He and Dad got down, preparing to release the team and turn them out for the night in the corral.

The passengers climbed out, stretched legs and muscles kinked and cramped by more than twenty miles over rough roads. The Concord, jouncing easily on its cradle of leather throughbraces, offered a good deal softer ride than almost any other conveyance. While Dad started ahead to attend to the unhitching, Finn went around where the rear boot contained his fresh provisions. The passengers strolled away to find private places to empty bladders suffering varying degrees of fullness.

An alarmed shout shattered the stillness of the dead-silent afternoon. "Oh, shit! Injuns!"

Finn and Dad and the others looked in all directions to see Kiowas stalking them out of the brush. Straight-backed and swarthy, many carried rifles. Finn Hennessy thought fast. The Kiowas were afoot, and all his provisions were on the coach, with no time to unload them.

"Back on the stage," he shouted, electing to make a

run for it.

With no time to argue, the passengers sprinted for the coach, carrying what weapons they'd brought. Three of them made it before Kiowa guns started chewing up the hot afternoon with their chopping blasts and bullet-whines.

The fourth, terrorized and tardy, appeared out of a dense stand of scrub trees, awkwardly yanking his britches up over bare shanks as he scooted for the departing stage.

"Come on, Bob," a passenger yelled, a frantic, shrill pitch in his voice.

From somewhere, a Kiowa rifle cracked and the running Bob jerked in full tilt, cartwheeled, thudded to the ground, and lay still. Finn raised his whip while Dad methodically levered rounds through his Winchester, to kill or wound a Kiowa with each shot.

"Bob," the same voice inside yelled. "Jesus, I got to go to 'im."

"Stay in the coach," Finn commanded. "We're movin'." He had already set the reins in his fingers and the big wheels started to roll.

"But 'e's my brother," the man lamented in a terrified tenor.

"He ain't no more," Dad yelled back emphatically. He might be an old man, but in his time, before his nose got stuck in a jug, he'd been a hell of an Indian fighter.

Behind the hurtling coach, as it roared out the rutted trail toward Plymouth, Dad could see Kiowas scurrying for their horses. "Good call," he yelled at Finn Hennessy over the rush of wind in their faces. "We're better runnin' for it. You got some brains after all. They'd of had us dead to rights in that damned shack."

Conditioned by years to be cool under fire, Dad turned and yelled back at the passengers, a memorable line that none would remember or recount.

"Paint for war! Make sure the only widders an' orphans an' grievin' mothers tonight is in a Kio-way lodge."

Then out of the billowing clouds of dust churned up by the hurtling Concord's wheels, the horsemen emerged. Fearsome faces craned around horses' heads for an opportunity for a shot but conserving their ammunition for the clear kill. From out of chaparral-bound gullies and coulees beside the headlong-plunging stage, more Kiowas rode into sight, dark and grim-visaged like demons boiling up out of Hades itself. These at the sides did pop random rifle shots at the rolling, rumbling coach.

Dad Briggs worked his shots from side to side. To his left, he made telling hits on men and horses. Then he swung the muzzle high, furiously ejecting a spent round and jacking in a fresh cartridge. Shooting from roof level to the right behind Hennessy's head he accounted for two more Kiowas.

Those inside battled for their lives as well. Rifles, the shotgun, and now and then a short gun poked out briefly to blast from the open coach windows. For long minutes the thundering blaze and blast of gunfire sounded like election day in Juarez. Beside Dad Briggs, Finn Hennessy took a solid round from the right that shattered his upper arm. It plowed big splinters of bone and lead fragments into his heart and lungs. Dad turned in firing to see Finn slump, great gushes and gulps of blood pumping out his gaping mouth. Finn's sagging body rolled away from Dad to tumble from sight into the dust as the coach dashed helter-skelter over the road.

Dad leaned right again to fire, too busy to worry about Finn or to try to control the driverless, stampeding teams. He cranked a round point-blank at a Kiowa preparing to leap for the stage from his horse. Stopped by a head-shot from Dad's Winchester, the Indian missed his leap, thumped against the side of the coach and fell under it, his bones crunching like chicken eggs as the heavily burdened wheels rolled over him.

A stunning force, like a mule kick, immobilized Dad's left side. A bullet had entered his back and quartered up through his gut, exiting just below the rib cage. He tried to hold the Winchester in a left hand instantly numbed, and drew his six-gun with his right. With it, he slammed another Kiowa about to board the rolling stage from Dad's left side. Another bullet whacked through the meat of Dad's left shoulder, driving great wedges of fire into an already torn and battered upper torso. From inside the stage, only one gun seemed to be continuing the battle.

With his right side still functional, Dad emptied his six-gun. The Winchester's forestock welded into the paralyzed claw of his left hand, he lost contact with reality and tipped off into the swirl of dust churned up by wheels and hoofs alongside the plummeting, rumbling coach. Leaping and prancing, the teams thundered on.

Quickly the Kiowas surrounded the coach and halted the panicked teams. A passenger, his face spotty with crimson from exertion and fury, bolted out of the coach and fired his .45 Colt into the face of the nearest Kiowa. The slug carried away most of the side of the man's head.

"That's one for Bob, you red heathen son of a bitch!" he screamed.

Five Kiowa guns opened up at the same moment. Hot lead slammed Bob's brother from several directions at once.

A Kiowa near the coach leaped down to count coup on such a courageous man and to take his scalp. Others swarmed into the Concord where two un-scalped bodies were piled on the floor like logs. A short, fat warrior swaggered to the big leather boot

168

cover at the back and slashed it with his knife. A pair joined him in search of whiskey. A yell from Crooked Leg startled and stopped them. Their attention was directed back down the trail in the direction the chief pointed.

Above the carpet of chaparral the old man who had fired the rifle from beside the driver climbed the steep, tawny slope slowly dragging one foot after the other. He used his rifle to lean on whenever he paused for more strength. The Kiowa war party gaped in wonderment and amazement. Several made signs to ward off such powerful medicine. They had been certain that the old man had been dead when he fell off the coach.

Now they watched his progress with the intense stares of a hunter who follows his gut-shot prey as it attempts to crawl away while it slowly and painfully bleeds to death. The minutes lagged slowly in passing. For some reason, none of the warriors moved to finish off the old man.

When the angle of bluff shielded Dad Briggs from their view, they remained still until at last he appeared on a ledge of rimrock over them. There he came, a dark and bent, gun-toting silhouette, backlit by the waning yellow of the setting sun. An exhausted, dying old man, barely able to stay on his feet, his hairy and leathered face held a trace of its fierce vitality as he paused up there in defiance of them.

From his aerie, the old wounded eagle wobbled and stared down with dimming eyes at the gathered Kiowas and the scene of carnage around the coach. Weakly, though abruptly, Dad Briggs brought up his right fist, the middle finger rigidly extended, and jerked it derisively at them as he bellered insane, bullyragging war cries.

Astonished by his gesture, the Kiowas howled as they mounted and urged their ponies up the dun-colored bluff. In awe of the insulting, arrogant old man and his willingness to die standing up, they closed in on him.

They quickly surrounded old Briggs, who postured defiantly and tried to crank cartridges from an empty Winchester tube magazine, the forestock cupped weakly in an all-but-useless left hand. He was blood soaked. They all knew he should be dead.

"Fuck you and the horses you rode here on," Dad Briggs shouted at them.

While the old man screamed obscenities at his tormentors, the Kiowas began to ride a circle around him on the bluff top until they came in lance range. They tightened their hooting, shrieking loop around him, letting his life out in small spurts with their lance tips.

At last Dad Briggs fell, the massacre's final victim, punctured and bleeding from a score of stab wounds. He dropped to his knees dying, though able to hold the position long enough to swivel his white-haired head for all to see. His teeth gritted in a scowl and his eyes still flashed defiance.

Then Dad Briggs went over headfirst into the dust, bitterly grasping the tail end of consciousness.

14

Crazy Knife found the Hennessy & Briggs way station deserted and eerily silent. The ground had been trampled by stamping horses and marked by the wheels of the big red coach. Disappointment filled him as he read the signs of an attempted Kiowa attack on foot and the start of a mounted chase. An unscalped man in a business suit, dead from a bullet, lay near the rude pole corral. Crazy Knife was puzzled by the man's bare buttocks gleaming white in the late afternoon sun, the belt line of his britches barely covering his thighs.

"Had my brothers killed him, he would have been stripped *and* scalped," he said aloud in puzzlement.

He poked around until he found a fresh pile of smelly man droppings and some scraps of white paper behind a thin stand of scrubby trees. Crazy Knife concluded that the dead man had been surprised in voiding himself. The big wagon might have been gone by the time he ran to the corral. Then he went back and took the dead man's scalp of short-cropped chestnut hair. He put little value on the previous owner nor on the circumstances that allowed him to take it.

Crazy Knife followed the twin ruts of white man's road, read the sign of the chase, and smelled faintly the still-churned fine dust and wisps of gunpowder smoke that hung over the trail. He heard sounds of celebration ahead at the same time he found the naked, battered, and bloody remains of the white-haired one he had seen driving the big red wagon. The dead man's hat was parked aslant of his face-down head.

Crazy Knife got down and lifted the hat to find out why. A ragged circle of bloody skull lay buried in the long, thick, white hair. Someone had come back for the trophy and replaced his hat. Silently, yet with eagerness growing in him to join the festivities up the trail, Crazy Knife moved on, kicking his horse into a lope.

When he arrived, the wildly cavorting braves had thrown the two bodies killed away from the coach up on top of the pair of corpses inside and set fire to the vehicle. Black smoke rolled skyward like an inky cloak. Despite the heat radiating from the burning coach to add to the sun's already unrelenting fury, frenzied, inebriated Kiowas danced around it and chanted drunkenly and loudly about their victory. Several braves shrieked gleefully and brandished their five scalps.

The sweet, burnt-grease stink of roasting flesh reminded Crazy Knife of the day they burned the blind old Mexican woman and in his remembering came the soaring emotion of being a Kiowa warrior. It called to him the need to dance and shout in wild abandon when the enemy's topknot was off at last. Even the small boy, Little Elk, toed his steps with studied care and yelped with the rest. At the side, stoically apart from the boisterous, deafening display, Crooked Leg squatted to talk with Broken Tail and Bignose.

A brave howled recognition of Crazy Knife and leaped to him with a half-full bottle of white man's amber whiskey. Crazy Knife tipped its bottom skyward and let a huge gulp run down his eager throat.

Its scalding fire seared his gullet and stomach and bounced immediately into his system. He felt himself filled with new vigor and power. No wonder, he thought, that they called it brave-maker. Another gulp like that and he might be moved to race back alone and scalp the full head of the hateful little intruder in the fancy clothes and violate both women at the three wagons in quick turns with searing thrusts of his manhood.

Instead, he walked proudly and boldly to where Crooked Leg hunkered down with the others. They solemnly passed around their own glass-flask of the spirit-renewing whiskey. Crooked Leg offered it and Crazy Knife squatted beside them to enjoy another hefty swig. He could feel its magnificent power clear into his toes.

"My son," Crooked Leg said huskily. "You now have missed two good fights. When we killed the men with the little thick-furred goats and now the chase of the big red wagon you were away being my eyes."

"My duties for the bearer of the war pipe kept me away, it is true." He smiled shyly. "I saw this battle making up and nearly reached you in time. Now I have happy words for you from my scouting."

Crooked Leg looked about him and his lips curled. "These warriors will become like old women in the morning from white man's whiskey," he said scornfully. "They need to leave off the white poison and purify themselves with many sweats and brave deeds in battle. That way they grow strong again like the Kiowas of the old trails. Then they can mount many women and drain the good medicine from their loins to make more warriors."

Nodding agreement, while taking another gulp of the "white poison," Crazy Knife spoke up. "These are my words from the days of my scout. Back toward the rising sun, maybe two sleeps, on the big trail from white man's country to the Sundown people, there are three wagons heavily loaded with treasures and pulled by many of the long-eared horses. Much plunder awaits the Kiowas."

"It is good," Bignose interrupted, already eager.

"Women," Broken Tail spoke softly. "Are there women?"

Crazy Knife had saved the best until last. "Two of the white man's women, more pleasant to look upon than even those in the lodge of the dead black robe."

"How many men protect them, my son?" Crooked Leg asked.

"One was killed when he fell off his horse chasing me. He was a big man, bigger even than the largest Kiowa. But he is dead and only a little boy of a man in funny clothes now watches over the two women and their wagonloads of useful things." He carefully omitted any reference to the humiliation he had endured being hit from nowhere and then kicked by the little man.

Crooked Leg picked up the bottle of thick blue glass and examined its amber contents. Then he hurled the vessel from him with such violence that a stream of whiskey sprayed from the mouth. It struck a rock and produced a sparkling shower of liquid and shards. He searched the faces of those around him with his eyes. Satisfied, he grunted and slapped his hands together with a glancing blow.

"Hear me! We will drink no more of the white man's whiskey for it is not our way. The falling-down fort where the white pony soldiers camp is near. We must be careful, but we are now strong and many. Crazy Knife will again scout the wagons of the two women. When the time is right, we will attack. We will take the women captive and save them for the enjoyment of our brothers still not willing to join us on the war trail. This will show them the rightness of

174

our quest. We will share these riches with them so that Crooked Leg may build a mighty band to drive the white men to the north and the cringing Spaniard in the south from our rightful lands. Crooked Leg has spoken."

Eli Holten rode up alongside Giselle's lead wagon after they'd crossed Big Sandy Creek and were on the last leg of the trip to Bent's Old Fort. Because of the proximity and ever-present movement of troops out of Fort Union to the south in New Mexico, and from bases northward in Colorado, Holten felt the threat from the Kiowas in this vicinity to be minimal. In light of it, he decided upon a little diversion.

"Ever seen wild horse?" he asked, swinging Sonny up close to the driver's seat of the big Conestoga.

"No. I would love to," Giselle told him. "I admire the horse and to see some in the wild state would be quite thrilling. A nice thing to add to our adventure in the West."

"Saw a small herd to the south a few miles this morning. Beautiful. They've an interesting history, too. How they came to be here, and how they've developed. We're still ahead of schedule. Not a bad time to take an afternoon off. We could stop along here for night camp, give everybody a breather, rest the mules and you and I could take a ride."

Her horse, along with those of Colette and Hugh, had throughout the trip tagged along behind the wagons, their reins hitched to the tailgates. When the caravan halted, Eli set about saddling Giselle's, while Hugh unharnessed the mules and Colette began to set up camp. With all in readiness, Holten led the bay gelding to Giselle.

They made appropriate apologies to, and received knowing looks from, Colette and Hugh. Holten and Giselle mounted up and headed off into the immense, trackless hill country to the south. What an enormous world, Holten thought, relaxed with the woman at his side. A world of monotony and yet one of thrilling contrasts. A place of heights and depths and distances that overwhelmed the imagination. They rode close together, enjoying each other's company in a setting of relinquished responsibility.

"Such a beautiful afternoon, Eli," Giselle remarked. "So much you've done to make these days on the trail for me ones to remember."

"One more coming up," he said. "There's a pleasant valley ahead. A stream cuts it. Big rocks and trees. Like a scene from a painting. I think you'll like the place. The horse herd has it for its base. Plenty of graze and close to water."

In a half hour they had found the stream and rode into the moist density of its broad tree-fringe. "Let's tie up our horses here in the shade," Eli suggested, "and walk."

To pick their way through the small forest of aspens and cottonwoods they veered away from the creek from time to time, then came back to it. Suddenly, upstream from them, they spied a band of small, lean mustangs standing shoulder to shoulder placidly guzzling the crystal purity of the spring-fed stream. One or two stood midstream of the little freshet to slake their thirsts. Taking her cue from Holten, Giselle moved easily and slowly for a better view, staying close to the cover of trees.

"They'll probably not spook," Eli said quietly. "Although it's just as well not to disturb them."

Roans and buckskins and a little brown-spotted white pinto made up the small group at the water's edge. While they watched, Holten explained wild horses to her in guarded tones, holding her hand.

"Domesticated horses were first brought to Mexico by the Spanish. Only a few with Cortez, Coronado's expedition scattered runaways from Texas clear up into Kansas. Then over the years these multiplied into the thousands. By a hundred years later, the Spaniards had introduced the horse into New Mexico. Some of these broke away and turned wild. Others were run off by marauding Indians. As these strays grew into herds, they expanded to the north, west, and east.''

"They're magnificent beasts," Giselle breathed.

"Lacking grain, they are smaller and stockier than most horses domestically bred. They also have less stamina. In this well-grassed, but sparsely watered country, they developed into an itinerant, wiry, sinewy, and athletic little impish breed. They call 'em mustangs, and some say of them they are the 'bronco of the plains.'''

They watched the small herd finish its watering and drift away toward the grassy valley above where the two riders stood. Holten added that another band, out of Mexico, moved into California.

"There, less affected by thirst and hunger, they became heavier in build and more muscularly filled-out than their leaner cousins on the Great Plains. As they migrated into the Pacific Northwest, they were somewhat domesticated by the Cayuse Indians, to the point that 'cayuse' became a nickname for the horse and the name eventually migrated down into the Great Plains and south as far as Texas, where 'cayuse' is used almost more than 'horse.'''

Giselle listened with rapt attention and fascination gleamed in her eyes for the seemingly endless store of knowledge possessed by the blond giant at her side. They had drifted on afoot, following the horses who had drunk their fill and now made their way back to the main mustang herd.

Hand in hand they strolled into the benevolent sunlight from the cool, dank air of the wooded area that followed the stream. They found the immense pastoral valley—flat, with mild undulations for miles—hemmed in by rising low ridges, whiskered by the sparse growth of small pines. The wind blew in this country most of the time, even more so than in Kansas, sometimes wild, other times sad, squeezed out of the canyons to sweep down into broad pastures such as this. Now the wind moderated, which added to the glory of the day and their mood of total relaxation.

Around them, companions to the grass, wildflowers of all imaginable colors, predominated by yellows, reds, and purples, nodded drowsily under the warm sun and balmy breeze, as though unaware that fall lay not far ahead. A short distance from them more mustangs, the component of the wild herd with even more colors represented, grazed. They sneezed, snorted, and whickered in a companionable way. Like the wildflowers they nibbled, and like the two human intruders, they basked in the serenity of the afternoon.

Bays, browns, sorrels, grays—the dappled ones Holten referred to as "flea-bitten"—whites, blacks, buckskins, roans, and piebalds were the color schemes. Those of variegated colors, Holten explained, were piebalds or, from the Spanish word meaning "paint," were called pintos.

"Eli," Giselle remarked with obvious admiration, "you know so much about horses, about . . . everything. Always what to do, what to say. And the lover *extraordinaire.*"

"Not like that stud over there," Holten observed.

His extended finger pointed out a great black stallion with a roughly diamond-shaped white blaze above his eyes, the herd's monarch. A giant black wand swayed under his belly as he approached a little white mare. With much prancing, head shaking, and

178

shrill neighing of lust, he deftly lifted himself into a rampant, hind-legged stand and moved in to find easy, waiting access. In a few bold strokes of that polelike device he inseminated the small mare.

Then the magnificent stallion, larger than the runty mustangs and probably crossed with an eastern breed, intoxicated with gratification, raced away from the herd in a heel-kicking gallop, out across the sun-swept valley. He trumpeted his supremacy as he tore through the thick grass. In the distance he stopped, grazed a bit, then looked pensively back at the herd, probably picking his next target.

"Oh, Eli," Giselle cooed. "That makes me eager, too." With her right hand holding his, she reached across to find his manhood growing erect, restrained down the side of his buckskin pants leg.

His own emotions and need rose in him. Holten reached across similarly with hand and flexing fingers to manipulate the short spread between her thighs, feeling her gulf of delights even through the thick material of her riding trousers.

Still fondling, they turned to face each other for a kiss, long, ardent, and wet. Their hot tongues fought to savor the warm, moist eagerness of each other's mouth.

Giselle broke from the erotic kiss and with her cheek against his, velvety lips devouring his ear, skillfully worked free the buckskin fly buttons and slid her hand in to gratify her early longings with a fevered stroke of the smooth, responsive, bone-hard member it had become.

"Take me, Eli," she moaned, her whisper like a shout as her mouth encased his ear. "Take me like the stallion takes the mare."

"Get out of those pants," he whispered into her ear, close to his own lips. "Horse fashion. Usually call it something else, but for now that's most

179

appropriate. Not as fast as that stallion, though. Of course, he has a field of mares to breed. I have only one."

"Lucky me," she hissed. "No share with other mare."

"Love your poetry, lady," Eli said.

Giselle stepped away from him and with her eyes riveted in promise and fevered anticipation on his, plucked free her buttons, worked out of her boots, and slid the tight pants legs down and away. She stood before him fetchingly, the long swallowtail of her blue calico shirt swept down to cloak Holten's target for the afternoon. Her bare thighs revealed below the shirttail sent Holten's already-tantalized emotions soaring.

When his own britches slid off, he had none of that advantage. The open front of his shirt swept around his engorged limb of eager, up-curved manhood like a stream splits around a large sandbar.

"Let me show you the place," she coaxed, flopping on hands and knees on the carpet of wildflowers, shoving her buttocks in the air, in imitation of a mare. She reached her hands back to spread the saucy, waiting lips.

With little more by way of preamble, Holten dropped to his knees and, like a supplication to Eros, allowed his member to introduce itself to Giselle's waiting hands still thrust behind herself. Feeling the awesome presence, she grasped it and guided it to entry.

"Uh-God!" she grunted as she tried to crane her head back to look at Holten as he knelt over her from behind. "He's magnificent, Eli," she cooed.

"Only because you are," he said softly. He rallied to the ease with which her anticipation and his allowed the fleshy shaft to be impelled to penetration. He stroked easily and slowly, felt the gradual rise of his desire to take her more brutally.

180

He kept himself above it for her sake. To reach the heights of ecstasy, Holten closed his eyes on the world around him, centered on the sensations of the constricting, totally damp sleeve into which he pumped.

"Oh, Eli," Giselle moaned. "Oh, it's magnificent." And then, "But look!"

Holten, in his supreme arousal, allowed his eyes to flicker open. Near them in the herd, as Holten pumped into Giselle's responsive passage, the great black stallion had come back and girded himself for the mounting of a nervous bay on the fringe of the herd, closest to him.

Holten watched fascinated as, like him, the mighty, shrill-neighing stallion lifted himself on hind hooves, braced his forelegs on the mare's back, and pranced into position behind the meek, waiting filly.

In some strange, ethereal oblivion, hypnotic in its hold on him, Eli bored into Giselle as if she were his mare, his eyes fixed on the great beast performing before him. He matched the animal's plowing beats, the periphery of his vision misty and hazy, focused only on the stallion's point of contact.

In this rare, magnificent trance, Holten continued thudding into Giselle, himself now half-man, half-horse servicing a beautiful and willing woman-horse of his harem. Giselle bucked against him, matching his deep, hard thrusts until he yelled with the force of his powerful climax.

15

Tranquility and triumph fled the moment Eli and Giselle rode back over the bluff and down to the wagons. Hugh and Colette were agog with big news for them. Gleaning scraps of intelligence from the mixed garble of French and English, Holten figured they had been interrupted in one of their *le grand amour* sessions in one of the wagons.

"*Les soldats chevaliers,*" Hugh chattered excitedly, "more than it was hard to count. We, Colette and I, hear many horses coming and the sound, the clank, of maybe rifles and swords *et object militaire* on these horses. We are afraid and take up our weapons. We go to look out the back of the wagon." There he paused and actually managed a blush. "They are come from the way we come."

Holten pondered. A moving unit. No doubt Covington and Adams with C Troop en route to Bent's Old Fort. Only one, at the most two sleeps distant.

"They come first over that hill back there. Two riders, one with the little red-and-white flag on a spear with two crossed swords on it. Beside him was *un soldat ancient*, older than him and the others for sure, with many yellow stripes on the sleeve."

Eli Holten grinned in recognition. No better description could be had of his old friend, Sgt. Maj. Harry Adams and his guidon bearer riding at the head of a column.

"This soldier, like Hugh says, he stop over there. . . ." Colette pointed down the trail a short distance. "He stop there and wait on his horse—a fine picture for the artist—and the soldiers keep coming two by two and I think the whole army of *les États Unis* will ride by Hugh and me. A man comes riding beside the soldiers, in clothes that look like the officer, maybe in charge, and they talk, this officer and the man who waited. After a while, that man leaves the officer and comes to us to see if we are all right."

Hugh piped up. "We tell him we *très bon*. He says we are only a day or two from the Bent's Fort. And the officer tell him we can come behind with the soldiers and be safe at the fort."

"He tells us," Colette said with a faint smile, "the Indians, how you say? Kiowa? Around here some place and not safe to be alone here. We tell him our guide and lady come soon back and maybe we go again in the morning."

"Did you tell him my name?" Holten asked.

Colette and Hugh looked at each other, trying to remember. "I think, no," she replied.

"Just as well," Holten opined. "What happened then?"

"Nothing," Hugh responded. "He tell us to get to Bent's as soon as we can where it is safe. He wish us well on the trail, says maybe he will see us again at the Bent's Fort."

"Then he ride away," Colette interrupted. "I think maybe this man and the officer not good friends."

Holten was puzzled by her observation. "How so?"

"They have words, like argue. But the man we saw

183

first can't argue," Hugh explained. "He has to listen to what the officer tells him. Then he says something more and the officer like barked at him, loud words and the first man can do nothing. I think maybe the first man want to protect us by having us go to the fort with them but the officer does not think so. But then he comes to say we can ride after the soldiers. He acts like maybe sad, that he should do more for us, but the officer will not let him."

Holten grunted. Surely sounded like Adams and Covington. One a splendid soldier and noncommissioned officer and the other with oak leaves through family influence and hardly competent to command a detail of manure shovelers. And it sounded like the two were on the outs about something.

"How long ago did they pass?"

"Hour," Hugh said. "Maybe a little more."

Holten studied the sky. At this time of year there were still three or four good hours of daylight left. If they set out at once, they might catch up with the column. He had questions that needed answers if something was going on between Adams and Covington. Also it would ensure the safety of Giselle and the others, if Crooked Leg indeed was on the rampage in these parts.

He considered it further. Moving as fast as they could, they'd probably reach the troop before nightfall. Covington would have to go into night camp soon anyway, a check of the hour on his thick-cased Hambleton hunter's watch showed him. It would probably be safe enough for him to push on alone to make contact with the column, get a reading on conditions. Deciding, he spoke to Giselle.

"I suggest we push off at once and try to regain contact with the column. They're not that far ahead, so I don't think there's even the slightest chance of an Indian attack so long as there are troops in the

184

vicinity. I'd like to ride out ahead and learn what I can. Bring the wagons up as fast as possible."

"We will be safe, we will be fine, Eli," Giselle assured him, still aglow from their fantastic loving. "We will come *alles vite* behind you."

"The sooner I get going, the sooner I can reach the troops and return. Keep them moving and if anything should happen, get the teams at a gallop. Don't stop. Not for anything. And shoot a lot. The troops will hear it and we'll get back to you."

"Nothing will happen, *mon amour*, Eli," she urged him. "We are French. We are survivors."

"See you soon," Eli yelled, giving spur to Sonny. Behind him the wagons soon creaked into action and swung out into the trail again.

For perhaps half an hour, Holten traveled, alternating trot with lope, so that in the main his pace remained swift. Then, coming down a low slope, he saw the column in the distance, a blue centipede on a multitude of legs, inching over the slopes and valleys of southeast Colorado bound for Bent's.

"Forty miles a day on beans and hay" was more than a song for the U.S. Cavalry. It took another quarter of an hour at a brisk canter to catch up with the troop's rear guard. Holten cut off to the side, to pass it at a trot. They looked weary and trail-worn, which he might expect from troops under Covington's command. He'd believed them to be some distance behind him. Covington had to be driving them like a demon.

Holten caught sight of Randall Covington midway in the long queuelike formation, riding at the side. Eli swerved Sonny wide of the column to come up a few rods away from the major. As he did, Covington stiffened in recognition. Holten waved cheerily and set the biggest fake smile he could muster, then reined closer.

"Major Covington."

"Holten! I should have guessed. I assumed as much. I gather you're the guide assigned to take us on into Arizona."

"Correct, sir. May we stop for a palaver?"

"I have duties with the troop. Our rendezvous is set for Bent's Fort."

"So we meet a little early. There's a slight complication. I'm guiding the wagon train you passed a couple of hours ago."

"You're the one? I saw a pretty woman and heard there was a scout. I could have figured a great womanizer would be close by. Only you would qualify for both."

Holten winced. Only been with the man two minutes and already the insults had started. "I understand Harry Adams is your ranking noncom," Eli deftly changed the subject. "That, in itself, should make a troop commander's life easier in the field."

Covington merely grunted. "Very well, Holten. This is as good a time as any to set some ground rules." Covington swung away from the column and they veered off into a wide arroyo.

"When your column passed the wagons back there," Holten said, "you apparently gave Adams permission to let them tag along, at least to Bent's."

"Grudgingly, Holten. In a weak moment. This is a military expedition to transport troops. I have no authority to commit my command to the safety and welfare of civilians wandering aimlessly through these foothills."

"That's a logical point of view, Major, and I, for one, appreciate your consideration. Nobody's asking you to risk your command in their behalf. Being in the proximity of a military formation decreases the chances they'd be perturbed by Mr. Crooked Leg."

Covington's cold stare stabbed at Holten. "You're glib, Holten. Along with all your other legendary skills and your hidden talents, you also think you can get what you want with hot air."

"Perhaps, Major," Holten forced a smile. "Perhaps. I really only proposed to state the case for the civilians I'm guiding to Bent's Old Fort. There I was to meet you and begin my official assignment. My understanding with Miss Robideaux is that she will retain another guide at Bent's for the balance of her trip, and my responsibilities with her are concluded."

"Very well, Holten. I'd already this afternoon offered the sanctuary of my command for the safety of your people. They may accompany the column to Bent's and no farther."

"Thank you, Major Covington."

"And . . . Holten . . ."

"Sir?"

"I said I had a hunch you were the one picked by General Crook for this detail. Colonel Granville Scott, who gave me my marching orders, was vague and evasive. You would definitely not have been my pick. The incident two years ago of the newspapers' exaggerations and inflammatory editorials on my criticisms of General Crook were, I'm sure, contributed to or supported by yourself."

This shit was getting old fast. Holten answered flatly. "That, of course, is also gross exaggeration."

"Come now, Holten. And what of your dastardly desertion with three Apache scouts? You certainly wield incredible power in high places to have gotten off from that one unscathed." Covington grinned a humorless grin of taunting challenge.

"However it appeared, Major, may I remind you that that action was based on specific orders, which

187

originated with the commanding generals of two military departments."

Covington cupped his chin with one hand thoughtfully. "I often wonder, Holten, what skeleton lurks in George Crook's closet that you know of that persuades him to continue you as his personal scout. Before you showed up in Arizona, Tom Horn held that distinction. What hold have you on him?"

"Sir, if you were a civilian, I'd thrash you for that insinuation."

"That's your answer to everything, isn't it, Holten? When the truth pinches, kick the daylights out of the accuser. I heard that after I, ah, reported to Washington you murdered Lane Stafford."

Scarlet fury flooded Holten's face. *Lane Stafford.* Another of Covington's cronies, he recalled now. A particular bit of slime who sold rifles and whiskey to the Apaches, cheated the Navajo and Hopi on their trade goods, and generally had a reputation as a cheat and liar. He'd used two children to force a confrontation with Holten, with every intention of killing them afterward. He had a gun, no, actually two, in his hands, blazing, when Holten shot him full of holes.

"You son of a—" Holten cut off the expletive before he worsened the situation. It was time for a subject change. "I thank you, sir, for granting my wagon train sanctuary with the column. I think it best after all if we wait until we arrive at Bent's Fort for further discussions."

"No, Mr. Holten, this will essentially conclude our deliberations. Do your job properly and restrict your reports directly to me on conditions and hazards of our route in the field and its perimeters, and we'll get along just fine." Covington made as if to leave.

"Oh, by the way, Holten," he went on. "It will also be unnecessary for you to have any contact with members of my troop. Stay away from the command, and especially do not attempt to confer with Sergeant Major Adams."

"Sir, in the field and in the conduct of my assignment, ninety percent of my work is with the ranking noncom. You know that's standard procedure."

Icy bile covered Covington's words. "Unless for some reason I am incapacitated, Mr. Holten, you *will* report to and take orders from me directly during this assignment. There will be no need for you having any contact with the troop."

"Officially, I suppose you can order that. In the off-hours, I reserve the right to socialize with whomever I please."

Covington took a deep breath. Holten had him there. "Holten, because of your performances where I have been involved, and insofar as I am concerned, you are on probation during the course of this military exercise."

Holten had had enough. "I've no obligation to you, you pompous son of a bitch," he snapped. "According to the condition of my employment, I am responsible to and take orders exclusively from General George Crook. I am here as a courtesy from him to you. As such, you will do nothing to rewrite the terms of my contract."

"You'll do as I say, goddamn you!" Covington thundered. Recovering himself, his tone became cold again, menacing. "Believe me, sir, I am fully capable of going over General Crook's head, even Corrington's, to the War Department, and your scouting days will be over."

Holten sighed with resignation. Covington could do it, *would* do it. So much the advantage of bought political influence and power. Without another word, Eli moved as to leave. As he did, he spied

Giselle's wagon breaking the crest of the rolling hill to the east, Colette right behind her. Holten fought back his rage.

"Major Covington, could we set aside our differences long enough to ride as gentlemen to pay our respects to Miss Robideaux and her companions?"

Covington glanced at the approaching wagons. "Very well," he said with ill grace. They mounted and together rode back up the trail.

Giselle halted as they approached. "Mam'selle Robideaux, I have the pleasure of introducing Major Randall Covington, commanding the column on the road ahead of us. He has graciously consented to allow your wagons to travel with the column to Bent's."

Covington rode forward, obviously impressed with Giselle's beauty and apparent charms. In a grand gesture, he reached out and kissed her hand.

"*Enchanté, mademoiselle. À vôtre service.*"

"*C'est merveileux. Vous parlez français,*" Giselle squeaked in delight.

"*Oui, un peu. Je ne parle pas bien français.*" To Holten, Covington's voice sounded uncommonly apologetic.

"You speak much more than you admit to, I think," Giselle answered teasingly.

Covington cleared his throat to hide embarrassment over this discovery. "Rather than coming behind the column in the morning, I'd suggest that your greatest security will be in the center of the troop. In this manner, we will escort your entourage to Bent's Old Fort."

The disagreeable old bastard was puffed up like a pouter pigeon, Holten thought as they set out to join the column.

*   *   *

190

A modest breeze that had toyed with the foothills through the day died with the moon-bleached night. A hot spell had been threatening for days and the balminess of the night portended a blistering sun on the morrow. By lantern light on the rear gate of Hugh's wagon, Hugh and Holten played gin rummy. Colette and Giselle were in Giselle's wagon after supper making woman talk.

Under a night sky shot full of stars, a figure trudged up the trail from the vicinity of the troop's encampment. Maj. Randall Covington, in full dress uniform, complete to red sash under his pistol belt, marched out of the darkness into the dim visibility of the lamplight emanating from Giselle's wagon cover. Hearing the women's voices, Covington halooed and rapped on the wagon's side. He ignored Holten's peering face illuminated by Hugh's lamp.

Giselle responded by parting a curtain at the back of the wagon and poking her head out. "Major Covington," she greeted courteously. "What a pleasant surprise."

Holten admired her ladylike qualities.

"I come to inquire, Mam'selle Robideaux, if you would care to take a short stroll with me into the chaparral to enjoy the beautiful evening."

"Major, I would be delighted. Give me a minute to fetch a wrap."

In a few moments, the two strolled east along the ruts of the Santa Fe Trail.

"Holten," Covington acknowledged smugly as they passed, touching his kepi bill with a short riding crop he carried like a swagger stick.

"Major," Eli responded. Instead of being made jealous, Holten was mildly amused by Randall Covington.

*   *   *

191

The area around Bent's Old Fort lay deserted, aside from the nearby camp of an old mountain man Holten knew went by the name of Wood Fenton. Fenton, who spent more of his time these days with a jug than he did with knife and fork, was a tall, gaunt individual with several days' stubble on cheeks splotched with ringworm or some other infestation, grimy with roadbed dust and patently down on his luck. Fenton, Holten decided, wasn't fit to guide a sick Indian to an outhouse.

Though nothing had been said, Holten believed that Giselle had politely, but demurely, spurned Covington's advance on the plains two nights before, while at the same time tactfully not totally defusing his wick. She was smart enough to realize that Covington made the decisions and could withdraw his invitation of the troop's protection to Bent's on a whim.

Now Eli faced a dilemma. Giselle, Colette, and company could not be abandoned at Bent's and her presence with the column moving south into New Mexico could only add fuel to what he could clearly see was an already volatile situation. He had also seen Harry Adams only long enough to inform him of Covington's decree against their communicating, but assured Adams their chance would come.

Confronted with Giselle's quandary, Covington reversed his previous posture and flatly insisted that the wagons accompany the column to Arizona. When Covington was around Giselle, Holten could see a studlike gleam in the major's usually flinty eyes. Trouble, Holten thought, hurried at them on the double.

To complicate matters, Harry Adams slipped Holten a long letter detailing, in chapter and verse, dates and times, Covington's ruthless behavior in the field since the troops had left Jefferson Barracks. In it, Adams cited violations of standing regulations and even of the Articles of War. He also expressed fear for his own life, stemming from his threats to expose Covington's almost sadistic treatment of the command.

Reading the communication, Holten was astonished, then disgusted, particularly with the circumstances leading to the illegal flogging of Private Cate. The entire affair had, indeed, been a rape of honor. Instead of destroying the letter, as Adams urged, Holten preserved it, burying the pages deep in his belongings on Sonny's back. It was, so far, the only written evidence to strap Randall Covington's hide to the main gate.

16

"Holten, I've come to the conclusion that the War Department simply didn't know what it was doing," Randall Covington informed the scout early the next morning.

"How's that, sir?" Holten asked warily.

"This nonsense about backtracking to the confluence of the Cimarron's two forks in order to take the cutoff. Had we taken it to begin with, it would have saved time. As it is, it only prolongs the journey."

"You may not believe it, but I agree with you entirely," Holten answered.

"Humph! Be that as it may. I have reached a decision. I want you to scout ahead along the old Becknell route through the Raton Pass. We'll take that way and get in all the training exercises the desk soldiers could ever dream of."

"I'm . . . relieved, Major. I meant what I said. Backtracking did not make sense. And, with the wagons along . . ."

"Yes, of course, the wagons," Covington dismissed briskly. "I want you to set out a day ahead of us, mark the trail clearly, and scout at least as far as the lower ramparts of the Rocky Mountains."

"I'll leave in the morning."

"Fine. Do that. It should take you no more than two days, after which I want you to start back in our direction. We'll rendezvous at the night camp location for the second day."

"As you wish, Major," Holten concluded the discussion, eager to be off and on his own.

Three days out of Bent's Fort, headed southwesterly toward Raton Pass, Holten scouted the perimeters in a gray morning fog. Abruptly, he came upon a scene that chilled his blood. In country where the rolling hills began to be cut by steep, rocky gorges and abrupt, rather than undulating, changes in the terrain, he spotted, from hiding, an incredibly strong force of Indians. From the distance, they appeared to be predominantly Kiowas, reinforced now by a strong contingent of Comanches.

Across the rugged valley from Holten's hidden vantage point on the windswept rimrock, the Indians moved down a narrow trail afforded by a downthrust ledge of the canyon wall opposite him. Holten had little doubt it was Crooked Leg's agency jumpers, augmented now by more reservation-quitting Kiowas and Comanches. They would have been lured by the magnet of the war chief's escapades over the past few weeks. He wished he had a spyglass.

Eli felt certain he could identify the Kiowa who had attacked Giselle, riding in the vanguard. All rode grimly, as if bent on more nefarious deeds. As the party advanced single file down the ledge, the leaders disappeared well into the canyon before the end of the file had come off the ridge and onto the trail. Holten gasped. More than two hundred.

And the column, with its precious companion wagons, headed right into the area where Crooked Leg would be operating. Holten had approved of Covington's decision to take the more difficult, though remote, way through the pass. Now, seeing the powerful war band, he had to exercise all his limited stock of forbearance to keep from riding back to the column and relieving Covington for "willful disobedience."

Quickly he eased to Sonny and urged him into a mile-eating lope that would get him back to Covington in the least amount of time. He stayed wary of scouting outriders of the giant band he had observed. Arriving at the column at the midday meal break, he sought out Major Covington for his ominous report.

"They looked like they're headed for this branch of the Santa Fe Trail. Probably figure to raid Mexican villages through Raton Pass and down the east slopes of the Sangre de Cristo Mountains."

Covington's eyes glistened. "Perfect. We'll catch Crooked Leg red-handed and drive his heathen butchers back to their rightful place in the Nations."

"Major, four days ago, you argued for violating orders and taking this route as being the best course to avoid contact with hostiles," Holten challenged.

"That was then, this is now," Covington answered smugly. "The commander in the field has the best understanding of conditions."

"I submit, sir, that you haven't the least idea of the hostiles' disposition," Holten snapped.

"Then enlighten me, Scout. That is your duty."

Holten sighed. "Major, by all indications, from the relaxed appearance of their pace, they are not aware of a cavalry column in this area. In other words, you're not the target as far as I could tell."

"Then the element of surprise will be in our favor."

Holten's gray eyes spat fire. "Major Covington, my scouting report suggests that Crooked Leg outnumbers you on the order of two to one, if not greater, based on the Indians I did not see, as well as those in the canyon. My advice is to return to Bent's Fort and not risk a confrontation. There you could

196

get word to some of the Colorado units up north to reinforce you. Or, I could try to slip south through to Fort Union in New Mexico.''

"Nonsense!" Covington barked. "In the delay, we'd lose contact with him completely. These men of mine are now trail-seasoned. They'll fight like wildcats.''

"On the contrary. From my limited observation, they are demoralized and exhausted the way you've driven them. You don't stand a chance against highly motivated warriors—and they're desperate now—of two of the toughest, fiercest, most warlike tribes on the plains.''

Covington spoke smugly. "And any American cavalry trooper is superior to twice his number.''

"Custer said something like that. . . ." Eli couldn't resist the barb.

"Custer," Covington interjected with the finality of personal conviction, "was a contemptible, impetuous pipsqueak.''

Look, Holten thought fleetingly, at the pot calling the kettle—.

"He'll ride you down in fifteen minutes, as Crazy Horse did Custer. There are too few defensible positions in this canyon country up ahead. You're either on the ridgeline and exposed, or in a canyon where they can mass above you and take you like shooting ducks with a punt gun.''

Covington's voice came in a snarl. "Quite to the contrary, Holten, my good fellow. *We* will catch Crooked Leg on the ridgeline, or we shall trap *him* in a canyon and reduce his force like fish in a barrel.''

"Then, sir, I request permission to return to Bent's Fort with Miss Robideaux and her wagons.''

"Permission denied," Covington snapped. "You are now the duly contracted scout on this mission, Holten. You'll not be able to desert as you did before with those cowardly Apache scouts. As for Miss

197

Robideaux, she went into this with her eyes open. She, too, is committed. You'll recall it was against my better judgment in allowing her to join the column in the first place."

Before your balls started talking louder than your brain that is, Holten thought bitterly. Covington could change colors faster than a chameleon.

"Then, since that is your position, Major, may I suggest that we explore our immediate area, determine a defensible position, fortify, and prepare for a siege?"

"And sit there until next winter? No, sir, by gad! Crooked Leg is, from what you tell me, moving south into Raton Pass. We will move out, pursue him, harass his rear guard, and hope to put *him* in the indefensible position."

Holten and Covington exchanged a long glance. Each probed the other's thoughts and suspicions. Neither favored the other, yet in this instance, Covington held the upper hand. Not a muscle of Holten's face betrayed him. He remained impassive as a tombstone.

"As soon as he scouts your position, he'll set a trap for you that'll be another Little Big Horn."

Covington narrowed his eyes in contempt at the insinuation. Holten knew he had despised Custer. He continued to peer at Holten. "We'll be prepared for that as well. Resume your scout, Holten. Make certain Crooked Leg's scouts don't discover our presence. Sergeant Major Adams and Corporal Locke will be forward spotting for the troop. I will be prepared for defensive or evasive action and tactical deployment of the troop if engaged. All right?"

It wasn't all right, not by a wagon load, Holten thought. "This runs deep, Covington, a lot deeper than it looks. Crooked Leg will read you like a book. Forget the forward position. Crooked Leg will know of your presence before sundown. He'll attack your flank, your most vulnerable side, and slam into your hind end like a freight train.''

"And we'll be ready," Covington gloated. "My front and rear will be commanded to sweep around and encircle him. We'll send him and his heathen brethren to the happy hunting ground."

"I wish I had your reckless confidence."

"That will be quite enough, Mr. Holten. Move out, and remember, any communication with Sergeant Major Adams will be done through me. Likewise, you will confine all of your intelligence to me.''

Stung, and furious at Covington's apparent stupidity, Holten abandoned caution. "You're signing C Troop's death warrant, Major. Together, Adams and I have a chance of pulling your ass out of this in one piece. For God's sake, don't shackle us with that kind of order. Hell, I wouldn't obey it anyway. Under the circumstances, all petty personal difference should be set aside. Life or death hangs in the balance.''

"You sound like a dime novel, Holten."

"And if I *don't* comply?"

"You have your assignment, Mr. Holten. This is a military engagement, now bound to make contact with and round up a band of renegade hostiles. I have the authority to shoot in sight anyone guilty of openly defying my orders!" Wiping a froth of spittle from the corners of his mouth, Covington called to a passing trooper. "Ride ahead and summon Sergeant Major Adams, Corporal Locke, and their cadre to report here."

Gigging his mount, the trooper dusted off toward the head of the column. The day, like those before, had heated up. As Holten rode away, he could clearly see that both soldiers and their mounts were in no condition to ride into a pitched battle, which this definitely would become. He pitied them . . . and

Randall Covington's blind ambition.

In an hour, Holten reached the area where he had first seen the Indian force. The craggy ridge and downthrust ledge of tawny granite partly shielded by stunted aspens was deserted. All lay quiet. Holten probed ahead warily, eyes alert and darting for glimpses of Indian outriders. Now his tracking of the Indian force led him back toward the long-unused trace of the old Santa Fe Trail as it meandered into the jumbled drop-offs and other hazards that led to Raton Pass.

Stopping Sonny below the crest of a rise, he looked downslope to find the assembled Indians in a broad, rocky valley. Not the "fish in a barrel" position Covington postulated. They had plenty of boulders for individual cover. Lookouts crouched out on the bluffs, and tactically, Crooked Leg had the perimeter of his main force well guarded by a circling ring of determined, mounted braves. The Kiowa leader, at this point, left nothing to chance. From the activity Holten observed, it could be that Crooked Leg's scouts had by now spotted the vanguard of the small cavalry unit. Holten's intuition told him that the Indians' attack plan had already been hatched.

He knew full well that Covington had little chance when, on command, about a score of mounted braves rode off in a northerly direction, toward the Santa Fe Trail.

Half those remaining headed off to the south, while the other portion moved out toward the east. Crooked Leg's strategy grew painfully clear. Make a feint attack on the column's front, taunt them into a chase of the small band, and then hit Covington forcefully from the sides and rear and close in on him like bringing the blades of shears together. With little effort, the Kiowas would cut through the fragile fabric of C Troop. By all indications, the hostiles had put on war paint, gathered in their best homicidal lusts, and were taking out after the troop as a matter of stern principle.

If only, Eli thought, he could get back to Covington in time. The man had to be persuaded of Crooked Leg's tactic. He leaped to Sonny, painfully aware of the hostiles and that the lives of a hundred fifty individuals depended on his getting through before Covington got himself sucked into the trap Holten had so accurately predicted.

His ride back was uneventful, though Holten had scanned every rock and bush for signs of danger. Riding into the troop's position, Holten's breath caught. Everything was wrong. Covington had formed the troop into five ranks of twenty troopers, two behind him as he led out. The troop's supply wagons and Giselle's three wagons in two ranks came next, surrounded by twenty more soldiers. The rear guard consisted of another line of twenty-four troopers. Indians, Eli had learned from painful experience, couldn't be fought with Civil War tactics. And that, precisely, was what Covington attempted with his idiotic formation. More worrisome, Holten couldn't see the guidon or recognize Harry Adams among the lead troopers.

He rode up, took a position alongside Covington, and cantered forward. The major's eyes had widened in uncharacteristic zeal. There burned in them also a glistening, wild look, one of near-dementia.

"We have them on the run, Holten!" Covington enthused. "They unfortunately debauched onto the trail ahead, a small band, and I sent Sergeant Major Adams and Corporal Locke with the cadre to polish them off. Huzzah!"

Once more it was Holten's turn to be horrified. This was Fetterman on the Bozeman and Custer at the Greasy Grass reprised. "'Debauched'?" he quoted nastily. "It may have looked like you caught them unaware, but Great God, man. That was the feint I warned you of. Command the wagons to circle right here, corral the horses inside, and use the wagons as breastworks. It's your only hope. The Kiowas at this moment are flanking you and moving up on your rear guard. For God's sake, Covington, use your head. Now.''

Covington looked at him, the derangement now a glitter of sinister glee in his wide eyes. "No, by God,'' he shrieked, a trickle of drool at one corner of his mouth. "Now we'll beat the incompetence and indifference out of them.''

Before Holten could figure out that one, Covington yanked his saber out of the scabbard, its sliding hiss ominous as a death rattle, arced it forward and took off at a gallop.

"Take arms and follow me!'' he screamed back at the troop. "Charge, at the gallop, yoooooo!''

The five ranks of green recruits blindly and dutifully pressed close behind. Between the fifth rank and rear guard, the lumbering wagons and their escort were obliged to participate in the charge or be left behind. Holten found himself with no recourse but to join the ludicrously unmilitary—at least tactically unsound—charge.

He knew that somewhere Crooked Leg gloated and poised to operate the fulcrum of his tongs of death. In the distance ahead, Holten could hear the rattling crack of Indian lever-action Henrys and Winchesters against the throaty boom of cavalry Springfield carbines. Adams's detail had doubtlessly been surrounded and it was only a matter of minutes before it would be wiped out.

Holten dropped back to be close to Giselle to protect her to the last. With a bullet, if need be, to save her from a lingering, brutal death at the Kiowas' hands. The roar of more than a hundred and thirty mounted soldiers and the rumble of wagons assaulted his ears.

"Keep going," he yelled at Giselle, whose expression told him she found no adventurous thrills in the desperate situation. "Do your best with the team, but watch for me. I'm going to try to get you out of this."

Eli knew the battle had been joined when a Kiowa bullet cracked over his head like a banjo string. They were out there, invisible wraiths pumping lead, tightening the net around C Troop. He realized he had only one way out, if only to save his own neck and that of the civilian party. He moved boldly with his decision.

A wagon circle would force Covington to at least fight from its scant cover. Bullets of converging Kiowas and Comanches slit the air with sizzling cracks overhead and beside him. Through the dust and smoke, he caught Giselle's eye and signaled her to start circling. Colette, always obedient, followed, and Hugh picked up the trend. The two troop teamsters fell into line and when the circle was executed, Holten signed for a halt. The creaking vehicles ended up a span of their wagon tongues apart.

He rode Sonny to Giselle's wagon, hoping to get down soon and make himself a smaller target. The trooper escort quickly bunched inside the quasi-protection of the corral.

"Take the team inside the circle. Have Colette serve as horse holder. Get Hugh up here with his rifle. There won't be much room for all the horses and teams, and the troop fighting from here, but it's all we've got."

Biting her lip, plucky Giselle got busy unhitching. Bullets from unseen positions in the hills and coulees smacked around her. Colette and Hugh leaped to follow suit, and the army teamsters got the message. Across a short distance Holten saw that the troop had already lost its ragged military formation and, panicked, fought without command. He couldn't see

Covington, but imagined the major had lost all control of the men. Some of the troopers saw the safety in the wagon corral. They fell back to its dubious cover, better than full exposure on the field. Others began to ride a brave circle outside the wagon corral, picking out exposed hostiles and firing. At least, Holten thought, they'd learned a little from Harry Adams during their sojourn at Jeff Barracks.

Every third trooper inside the wagon ring stepped to the job of horse holder as trained. Holten handed Sonny to one of them. As he did, he slid his Winchester Express out of the left hand saddle boot. This would be a job for long-range shooting. He wasn't exactly happy with the defense perimeter, although it was better than Covington's alternative.

At the moment Holten concluded Covington might have bought an early Kiowa round, the major appeared on horseback out of the dust clouds of battle at the gallop. Jumping his horse over a downed wagon tongue and into the corral, he skidded to a halt. Covington found a horse holder and headed for Holten, who had taken up a position beside Giselle's wagon, eyes searching for a potential target.

Crooked Leg's braves used available cover to excellent advantage. Bullets seemed to come from nowhere. The weathered butt of Holten's .45-70 Express swung quick and snug to his shoulder. The hammer clicked back. With the sureness of habit, the squint of his right eye caught the sights in line, to traverse and search to make dead meat. While he centered on his sight picture, his peripheral vision scanned for movement, ready to swing up and fire like a shotgunner after ducks.

With their prey contained, the Indians fought on foot now and one—in Covington's words—"debauched," to move from a far rock toward one closer. Holten instinctively caught the running man in his zone of fire, sighted on the skunk head–covered topknot as he calculated the bullet's drop at the distance. The big Express rifle thundered. Holten's 600-grain slug took the Kiowa in the throat. Blood sprayed as the dying warrior made a grab at himself in that direction and toppled backward.

Twice Holten dodged shots aimed at him and triggered rounds in response. Flashes spat from the hillsides and the air boomed with the sudden discharge of exploding cartridges. A rifle whammed viciously somewhere near him and Eli glanced over to see Giselle lever a fresh round into the .44 Winchester upon which she had trained "at Mr. Winchester's establishment in Connecticut."

She grinned at him out of the grime coating her face. A beautiful, thrilling sight, Holten noticed fleetingly. Then he pointed his attention out into the blazing afternoon sunlight. He saw a running brave on the hillside, probably a Comanche from his high moccasins. He jerked a thumb at her to indicate it was her target. Giselle acknowledged by swinging the Winchester to the right and pumping forth a round. Impact and undirected nerves sent the hostile cartwheeling.

Holten made a triumphant circle with his thumb and forefinger and wagged it at her. An instant later he went back to his own sights, seeking quarry.

For a crazy, curious moment he wondered how it would be to make love to her under fire. Suddenly his reverie and his sight taking got intruded upon by a throaty growl behind him. He turned to come almost nose to nose with a furious, red-faced Randall Covington.

17

"Leave it to you, Holten," the berserk officer shrieked, "to totally destroy a perfectly tuned military tactic. You called this wagon formation against my strict orders."

"Fuck your order!" Holten shouted back before he turned away and pressed cheek to rifle stock. His voice came muffled. "Lives now need to be saved." The scout banged a noisy round at a moving figure on the hillside.

Covington's soft, pudgy hand clapped surprisingly firm on Holten's shoulder. "I'll have you shot for this," the frenzied officer railed as he attempted to yank Holten around.

Eli came about at his own pace, cold now, resigned to what he must do. "You will like hell. My appointment to General Crook gives me a brevet rank of lieutenant colonel. As such, I relieve you of command for incompetence in the face of the enemy."

Major Covington's crimson features washed livid. He screwed his mouth into a hateful twist. White foam appeared at the corners of his mouth and he sprayed the air with spittle.

"You can't do that!" he wailed, his expression that of a spoiled child.

"I already have," Eli Holten told him icily.

Covington's body trembled with rage and humiliation. He started to raise his saber as if to strike the scout. Then he went rigid with supernatural control.

"I'll deal with you later," Covington shouted over the roar of cavalry carbines that now barked from the cover of the wagons. Then, almost as abruptly as he had appeared, Major Covington vanished into the chaos of combat.

Alerted to something strange on the hillside at an oblique angle to the south, Holten crouched by the wagon watching, trying to read the sign, the Winchester at the ready. An odd popping of rifles came from that sector, yet no bullets seemed directed at the troop's defenses. Two quick shots from the Kiowas roared in the distance.

Holten whipped a round that way. At that range he expected to only disable or perturb an Indian into keeping his head down. A moment later he saw the cause of the odd situation. Grinning, Holten realized his hunch had been right.

On the hillside, in the midst of the Kiowa horde, Harry Adams materialized out of the ground to scramble ahead to a hummock of gravel. Holten, without conscious thought, leaped from behind the wagon and sprinted over open ground toward where Adams had appeared.

He gained cover behind a rock the size of a small pony. The Kiowas went wild. A reckless bombardment of lead peppered his position, the dust cuffed and kicked all around him. Holten could see several of the Kiowas, counted at least three crouched close to the land near Adams. They took what cover they could as they crept forward, shooting toward Adams as he squatted against the protection of the hump of rock.

To relieve the pressure on Adams, Holten loosed a nerve-shattering Sioux war cry, followed by the insulting taunt, *"Hu ihpeya wicayapo!"*

Eli jumped up, fully exposed to hostile fire, and furiously cranked rounds through the Winchester at the Kiowas threatening Adams. Smoke rolled back from Holten's busy gun muzzle. That did it for the Kiowas.

Their startled faces snapped around at the war cry and saw an apparently battle-crazed giant who sprinted toward them. Several warriors broke and ran. Adams grabbed his chance and came leaping like a wild man out from behind cover. He brandished his empty, issue Springfield carbine overhead like a club, intent now not on sanctuary but on killing Kiowas.

When Adams burst from the mound he seemed all arms and legs, each doing triple duty. He bounced his carbine stock on one brave's head in a vertical butt stroke, kicked the feet from under another, and as if with a bayonet thrust, punched the thick muzzle into the groin of a third.

At once Holten piled out from another rock he'd taken cover behind and continued his race to Adams's side. He slung an underhanded, poorly aimed shot at one of the Kiowas who had regained his feet. A bullet splintered the air over Eli's head and knocked his hat askew.

Holten fired again and his targeted Kiowa went down, probably for good. Boosting himself to his feet, a Kiowa went after the gritty Adams now in a hand-to-hand melee. Another warrior started for Adams's exposed back, ready to plunge a huge, gleaming trade knife up to the Green River trademark. A .45-70-600 round from the rifle of the sprinting Holten sent him spinning away and down, to end his scalp-taking days. For a moment that loosened up the fight in that sector.

"What kept you?" Adams barked in good humor.

"Sorry," Holten answered in like vein. "My dance

card was full.''

Adams strode toward the approaching Holten, a wry grin on his lips and relief in his eyes. His face and hands were smudged with the ebony of spent black powder, his fingers nervously and lightly drummed on the stock of his carbine. A bullet sent Holten's hat sailing. It reminded them they were still in the midst of a gore-hungry mob of furious hostiles. Holten made a grab for the twirling hat, caught it in midair as the two hit the dirt side by side against a protecting boulder.

"He'd've shot me if I'd disobeyed,'' Adams gritted, his head close to Holten's as they lay behind the rock's refuge. "I had to take 'em out even though I knew we were doomed. Kiowas got 'em all, Locke and all those other brave boys.''

"You got out, Harry. That's what's important. Right now, we've got to figure how to get ourselves back to the troop. I've relieved Covington and we may have a chance now.''

"Good. You should have shot the bastard,'' Adams opined.

Eli glanced over the more than a hundred yards that separated them from sanctuary. More than seventy troopers remained alive. Some had shot their horses and used them to fill the gaps between the five wagons. Giselle and Hugh fought closest to his and Adams's position. He stuck his hat on his carbine muzzle and waved it above the rock, hoping to get one of the French traveler's attention. Surprisingly, it worked.

Hugh's hat poked out from behind a wagon on his Winchester barrel in acknowledgment. He had seen, and understood, Holten's need for the cover of heavy rifle fire. A heartbeat later their barrage began to pepper the hillside around the pair. It created a clear avenue for a sprint to safety.

"Got your wind back, Harry? Ready? Time to go.''

Adams grinned through gritted teeth. "I was born ready. Let's go! Loser buys the drinks."

"Get your money ready. Now!" Holten shouted.

Holten and Adams sprang up and legged it through the scant chaparral. Their boots plowed granite dust and pebbles as they gained momentum on the gradual downslope. Holten decided to lose this race to Adams and turned several times to lay a deadly fire at anything in the area they left. Between his barrages and that from the smoking muzzles of Giselle and Hugh, the hostiles in the vicinity wisely hunted their holes. Adams closed on the circled wagons and dived over a downed tongue to somersault into safety.

Holten lost the race by a good ten yards.

Covington's C Troopers made a good accounting of themselves. Unfortunately Holten could quickly see it wouldn't be good enough. Better than half of the men were out of action, dead or wounded. From their flimsy defensive cover, they laid down a withering fire into the enemy's main line, which proved frustratingly impossible to penetrate. The land before them was marked by blocky granite boulders, hummocks, and natural depressions that provided perfect cover for Crooked Leg's attackers. The siege settled in with the Indians creeping up closer.

They found holes, made themselves comfortable for the duration, and picked their targets. From the troop's vantage point, there simply wasn't anything showing to shoot at. The slowed pace gave Holten opportunity to consider what had happened so far.

Eli knew from bitter experience there'd be no reasoning with Randall Covington. Instead of wisely conserving and concentrating their shots, the C.O. had kept the troop blazing away, firing at anything.

Holten needed to inform the rookies that the incompetent officer had been relieved of command. Chances were he'd have to have Covington restrained, which would take valuable men off the firing line. He needed every gun because, he knew too well, they faced a catastrophe.

From the enemy now came only a sporadic round. The shrewd Crooked Leg had his force save its ammunition for the ready target, the clear shot. C Troopers dropped all around the stockade. It gave Holten cause to consider which side was being commanded by a heathen barbarian. It seemed to the scout that he alone was in charge of the only effective combat team in the engagement. And, for the time being, he was helpless to change it. A dozen troopers, along with Giselle, Hugh, and Colette, fought valiantly, stayed cool, and, taking their cues from Holten, fired only when an apparent target presented itself. Even the saucy little French handmaiden, the last person Holten would have tagged as a steel-nerved fighter, stood her ground like a feisty terrier. She picked her shots and laid them in with calm, telling effect.

Likewise, the little dandy from Montmartre had risen to the occasion like a champion. Hugh's normally impeccable black hair had become a tangled mop, his white shirt was torn and dirty, his tight black riding britches similarly smudged. Grinning whitely through a mask of powder grime, D'Arcy hugged the back of his wagon.

Carefully he shoved out the side of his head to scan the countryside for prey. Then, agile as a fox, he swung out the Winchester to take off another Kiowa. Over the incessant roar of cavalry Springfields and answering barks of Kiowa Winchesters, D'Arcy abruptly began singing the jaunty, spirited "Le Marseilles" at the top of his lungs as he fought grimly. His melodic, bold baritone was unrattled by

211

fear. His aplomb served as an inspiration to the soldiers around him who could hear.

No fiery "Dixie," nor Custer's brassy "Garry-owen," not fifteen hundred pipers nasally wailing "Scotland the Brave" could have spurred the courage of the embattled troopers better. When the undaunted Giselle and Colette took up the anthem in their crystal altos, even Holten felt a renewed vigor and vengeance pump through his system. Totally ignorant of French, Holten launched into the song as well, "la-de-dah-dah-ing" his way through the words in a high shout with his companions so that troops and attackers alike could hear. One to be emboldened, one to be cowed. Abruptly he felt his spirit doubled to batter his way out of the trap.

Though nearby, Harry Adams didn't join in. Prone in the gravel under Giselle's wagon, his .45-70 cartridge supply replenished, Adams kept busy pouring round after round into the hostiles with telling effect. His accuracy significantly reduced the odds against C Troop. Above the din and rattle of gunfire and his own preoccupation with picking targets and accurately laying his sights, Holten subliminally grew aware that Covington stood in the protective cover of the wagon over Adams's prone position and screamed curses at his sergeant major.

Holten, occupied with his own battle for survival, fought with hellish fury. He gave little heed to the encounter between the sergeant major and the troop's former leader. Kiowa marksmen kept him from acting on his determination to confine Covington where the major could do no more harm. He kept his rifle busy on the occasional exposed figure on hillside and flats, and Covington's recruits seemed to be firing with greater control and renewed energy. Maybe the Frenchies' song had driven them to new heights of valor and a renewed zest for combat.

Meanwhile, Kiowa bullets smacked uselessly into

the thick wood of the wagons around Eli or occasionally twanged away into infinity with a shrill whine when they glanced off a thick iron strapping or a forged wheel rim. Slugs thudded into the dirt up and down the line of entrenched recruits. The troopers' big Springfield .45-70s spat jets of flame when a Kiowa revealed himself on the hillside. Holten squinted along his Express rifle sights, his trigger finger half-tensed against the sinister half-moon curve as he anticipated a clean shot.

Turning orange, the sun slanted close now to the skyline. In an hour it would be lowering into sundown and then twilight. If darkness came before the Kiowas became discouraged, those trapped inside the wagon corral would be at the mercy of the treacherous, wraithlike nightfighters. Unlike some superstitious tribes, Kiowas, especially Crooked Leg's bloodthirsty braves, had few qualms about killing after dark.

Fight to the death, no survivors, scalps before scruples; these seemed to be Crooked Leg's watchwords. Holten grinned mirthlessly into the sunbaked landscape before him. An hour, two hours at the most, and the fight would close in. Stealth, and sharp knives or war hawks, would replace deafening muzzle flashes. Holten mentally inventoried his remaining cartridges and his lips thinned to a hard line. A new alternative goaded his battle-weary mind.

The cover of darkness might also give him an opportunity to slip Giselle and her companions away to some sort of security. It would be the least he could do. Near him, Holten heard the distinctive whump of a handgun round, peculiar to ears accustomed by the day-long fight to the big-bore belches of cavalry carbines.

A quick twist of his head and out of the corner of his eye he caught the figure of Maj. Randall

213

Covington standing close to Harry Adams's defensive position under the wagon. He'd seen the major, fleetingly, like that before, Holten remembered.

Covington was wild-eyed, apparently staring out across the land at the Kiowas, his service Colt single-action dropped to his side. A tendril of thin smoke lifted from the muzzle. White puffs of spittle gathered at the corners of Covington's downturned mouth. Holten could see little of Adams aside from legs and boots, projecting from the wagon's undercarriage.

His attention was pulled back to the battle as a slug homed in on the spot where he had stood seconds before. He could see a puff of gunsmoke high on the hillside, much too far for such accuracy from the typical Indian weapon. While he pondered it, a weak call for him from Adams alerted Eli.

Pain rang in the name the sergeant major rasped out. Was he hit? Holten leaped to him. At the same time, a muffled cadence of thumps caused Holten to wheel around. Stark astonishment froze him when he saw the retreating figure.

Maj. Randall Covington had taken out on the high lope, to disappear into the confusion of battle around them. Holten wasted no time on useless imprecations. Quickly he knelt beside his friend.

Adams lay face down in the dirt, arms still extended in his prone, carbine-firing posture. What sent a spurt of shock through Holten's system was a red-and-black-rimmed hole in the middle of the back of Adams's dark blue shell jacket. He crouched further to crawl under the wagon, to get closer to his friend of many campaigns, who was obviously dying. Holten's brain, muzzy from the intensity of the fighting, didn't quickly come to grips with what had happened.

"Harry," he blurted, turning Adams over. "Harry. Awh, damnit, Harry."

Adams's face was twisted and white. "Eli," he

214

whispered. "He did it. Backshot me. He sent me out to die this morning. Cover his track. Couldn't stand it that I made it back. Did it himself."

How close to death Adams had drifted Holten had no way of telling. The vital force in the old face remained undiminished. Sgt. Maj. Harry Adams seemed determined to die like the hard-bitten campaigner he was.

"God, what an animal," Holten growled, a bright, burning fury in him now to hunt down and kill Randall Covington himself to avenge the mindless shooting of his friend.

The sergeant major's voice ground down to a whisper. "Remember what was in the letter, Eli. See him drummed out of the army. It's too good for the likes of . . ." Adams gagged and choked, as a harsh spasm of deep-chested hacking racked his body.

Holten impulsively grabbed him, hugged Adams to his chest to try to make the difficult moments of dying easier for a man of dauntless courage. The roar and crunch of battle around them momentarily faded from his consciousness.

The coughing wound down, and Adams's voice came weaker. "He's mean, vicious, Eli. Watch him."

"Don't worry, Harry," Holten whispered. "I kept the letter."

"Huh?" Adams grunted. A thin smile set into his lips, though his voice weakened more. "That eases me. Get him. Always thought . . . I'd take one head on . . . standing up. So I get it in . . . the back, lying down. This is funny." Harry Adams died with his words.

"Yeah, pardner," Holten choked out. Burning tears slowly dripped down his cheeks. "But face to the enemy, and that's what's important." Shit, he thought, they didn't make them any better than Harry Adams.

He released Adams's limp form and slid out from

under the wagon. Sad as Harry's death might be, they still had a fight to be won, lives to be spared. Pushing away the brutal assassination until he could quietly deal with it in his heart, Holten dashed back to his station behind the wagon and pressed fresh .45-70 rounds through the spring-loaded door of his Winchester's side plate into the tube magazine.

Fighting to forget Adams for the moment, Holten fixed his attention on the hillside where the sniper had again gone to work picking off troopers at his leisure from his vantage point high above the embattled wagon circle. A Kiowa appeared on an intermediate ridge, perhaps overconfident by the lack of accuracy from the raw recruits.

Abruptly, Holten whipped his rifle to his shoulder, lined his sights on instinct, and squeezed the trigger. The exposed figure on the hillside slumped, probably gut-shot; the echoes of his death chant rose. Still the harassment continued from the superior sniper.

Late afternoon shadows streamed like thick syrup down the hillside above Holten. He watched for muzzle flashes from the Kiowa sniper. Then his sharp eyes spotted the man. At that distance, the Kiowa marksman had to gauge his target and bracket the scope-sight before shooting. All the time he remained out from under cover, and that took a few seconds.

That was all the time Holten required. Now he knew where to look. The sharpshooter's rifle muzzle appeared first over the boulder and that fast, Holten had his sights lined on the area. He considered it a hell of a ways up that hill. Two seventy-five, maybe three hundred yards. He had the rifle to do it with, though. He'd have to shoot high, almost lob it in like a mortar round, near to the maximum range for the Express rifle.

Now the black-haired, dusky head rose over the boulder and the muzzle of the precision rifle inclined

216

toward the troop. Holten adjusted his elevation and the Winchester bucked against his shoulder.

A wild yell between an Indian war cry and the wail of a moon-sick coyote rode down the hillside. The rifleman who had menaced the troop for a terrible two hours or more rose into the air and jackknifed out over his protective ridge. It would have gratified Holten to know that Crazy Knife, the brave who nearly scalped him alive, had died.

Catching fire from Holten's classic shot, the rookies began to deliver a withering fire into the flats and hillsides at the Kiowas. The brush popped and trembled as the attackers sought new shelters. Out the corner of his eye, Holten caught sight of a trooper, crouched for safety, dragging his carbine as he made his careful way to the beleaguered wagons. The young man's face was grimy and seamed.

"Mr. Holten," he called, coming erect behind the protective cover of a wagon. "Private Cate, sir."

Holten took time out from the fighting to face the young soldier. "I know of you, Cate, from Sergeant Major Adams, and you needn't call me sir."

"I think Sergeant Major Adams is dead, Mr. Holten. He's not moving under there."

"I know, Cate," Holten answered grimly.

"He was good to me. Fair. Tough, but fair. I came to say I think you're in charge now. Major Covington is gone."

"A Kiowa bullet? He bought it?"

"No, sir, he beat it."

At any other time, Holten would have been amused by that bit of repartee. "Deserted his command?"

"The enemy fire's being concentrated in your sector here, Mr. Holten. Probably you didn't know. Seem to be centering their force this direction. I guess the major saw a chance to get out the back way." Cate's words rang with urgency, uttered breathlessly.

"Did he go on horseback?"

"Yes, sir. So did about five others. There are only about eleven of us left from the troop holding the line, Mr. Holten."

Holten pondered it. Sacrificed his troop to save his own stinking hide. Left them to die like dogs, and the greenhorns, looking to save their own skins. Hell. As vicious a commander as Covington would still have those who'd see advantages in toadying to the man in power. If fortune favored fools, as it assuredly did in Randall Covington's charmed life, the major and his cohort of poltroons would get through. But, by God, Covington would be alive to taste the bitterness of Holten's revenge.

"Son of a bitch," he cursed, then recovered himself. "You're right about my being in command. Shortly before the major's cowardly act, I relieved him. I, ah, rank as a lieutenant colonel, under General Crook's direction. Now, let's get the situation clear."

"Yes, sir," Cate answered, drawing himself up.

"All the rest dead, Cate?"

"Or badly hurt, sir. Nothing we can do for them. I'd best get back."

"Hold them off as long as you can, Cate. You're second in command now. I'll also need your testimony when we get out. Got it? I'll see to it you get a couple of chevrons on your sleeve for all this."

Cate brightened. He snapped a jaunty salute and turned away to get back to his place. He wanted to keep improving their odds as best he could. As Cate, crouching, passed across the gap in the wagons, a bullet audibly smacked him in the temple and he spun, staggered, and went down in a heap.

"Shit!" Holten roared. "God damn to eternal hellfire that stupid, cowardly bastard, Randall Covington." Shocked at his uncharacteristic outburst, Holten gritted his teeth. Had to keep it together . . . he *had to*.

A flaming Kiowa arrow, a Roman candle in the deepening twilight, muttered ominously as it soared its arcing course to embed with a thud in the canvas of one of Giselle's wagons. Instantly, the impregnated waterproofing compounds took fire with a thundering whoof of combustion. Roaring fingers of sinister flame probed into the dusk.

Holten reacted with calm. Crooked Leg now meant to breach the defenders' line at that point, massacre the few survivors, and claim title to scalps, guns and anything else of value. There'd be a great dance by the light of burning wagons in the dark when all the scalp locks were off. And they had to know that women had ridden with the troop. Urgently, he beckoned to Giselle, Colette, and Hugh.

They raced to him and bent close. Silently they studied his eyes for instructions. "We're going out of here. They'll all try to come pouring in that way after the wagon's burned. Now, when the wolf's at the front door, it's time to duck out the back. We're going to take advantage of the confusion. One at a time, try to get into the wagons for extra ammunition and as much food as you can carry. Get ready. When I give the signal, pick a horse and follow me.

"Meanwhile, the troopers that are left and I will pour everything we've got into that area in front of the burning wagon. Want to make them think there are a lot of fighters left in here. As you finish collecting, join us. Got it?" His gutsy foreign companions, aware of their desperate situation, nodded. "Colette, you go first to dig up some stuff. Giselle next, and Hugh, then me after that. Go!"

In minutes, between carrying out their orders and getting back to keep gun barrels hot and muzzles smoking, the four girded for the escape. Three of the troopers, although wounded, managed to put up a good show. One by one they died, riddled by Kiowa bullets and arrows. Holten grew aware that the only firing came from the four of them. With all the troopers dead, they hadn't a second to spare. Life was for the living, and the strong. There was nothing Holten could do to change the situation.

Darkness lay in a thick blanket over them, the sky lighted by the furiously burning Conestoga. A nerve-shattering call rose out of the stygian night in front of the four survivors. Many throats picked it up. The Kiowas screeched their victory chant. Rising, they laid a heavy fire as they raced on foot toward the circle. Painted bodies massed to break through at the burning wagon. Holten had read the Kiowa mind right. Crooked Leg had sent them in, reckless now, for the coup de grace.

Eli screamed at the others, "Now!"

Keeping in mind the driving need to save Harry Adams's letter, Eli raced back to find Sonny in the milling, circling herd of panicked horses. In the dimness of his vision, he could see the women hunting theirs.

Everyone's mount secured, Holten shouted and punched rumps to drive the pitching, prancing herd toward the gap in the circle approached by howling Kiowas. That diversion, he reckoned, would help shield their escape. Following the leaders, and scattering Kiowas, the troop's remuda thundered away into the night.

Leading a skittish Sonny, Eli raced into the dark toward the far rim of the wagon circle, aware of the others behind him. Across the wagon tongue and into the dark and cool of the vast plain, they melted out of sight. All stayed quiet, as Holten had calculated. He soundlessly mounted and led them out, letting Sonny carefully pick his way through the dark.

Minutes later, they rested on a ridge to let their

breathing and hearts settle. Below them, the scene became stark, howling chaos. As each wagon was looted, warriors burned it. Shrieking Kiowas and Comanches raced helter-skelter to take scalps, clothing, and weapons, whooping as they went. The victors' blood-frenzied festival had begun.

18

Harold Sinclair, U.S. marshal in Dimmick, Colorado, had just yawned on his badge, polished it against his sleeve, and repinned it to his vest when out his side office window he spied the clot of tired-looking riders plodding down Main Street from the north. His sharp eyes quickly picked out tarnished brass buttons and the blue of army uniforms.

"Soldier suits," he said out loud to the big, fat tabby sprawled in the center of his desk. "What d'ya suppose is going on now?"

With a final clatter of hooves, the small squad drew up in front of Sinclair's office and he heard the leader command the others to get down and relax. A moment later, the unseen man's boots stumped across the board sidewalk. Sinclair stayed in his leaned-back position in an oak swivel chair, his feet on the desktop. Without knocking, an officer in a badly soiled and wrinkled uniform swirled in.

"I take it from the sign outside you might be Marshal Sinclair."

"Might be, and am. Who might I be addressing, Major?"

"Covington, Randall H., commanding C Troop—all that's left of it—First U.S. Cavalry, out of

Jefferson Barracks, Missouri, bound for Arizona."

Though Sinclair was alerted and already reading volumes between the lines, they shook hands with Sinclair's boots still propped on his desk. "Indians?" he asked.

"Been riding all night. Hit us yesterday morning about thirty miles north on the old Santa Fe Trail. The men out there with me are all that survived out of a company."

"Crooked Leg's Kiowas or I'm a shoat. Wiped out a stageload of folks up northeast of here a week ago, I've been told. Was them, they figure, killed a gang of greasers herdin' a bunch of them woolies out south across the line even earlier. And a couple of days after that plumb rubbed a Mezkin village clear off the map. We been hopin' they wouldn't hit here. But we're ready for 'em."

"At present, Marshal, I'm more concerned with the tragedy that befell my command. The civilian contract scout assigned to me defied me at every turn. Blindly led me into the Indian trap, then against my direct orders and while I had the situation well in hand, in an act of the most craven cowardice and insubordination took it upon himself to appropriate my wagons and make an absolute shambles of a well-planned, well-timed military maneuver against the hostiles."

"Huh!" Sinclair grunted. It sounded more like this one was rehearsing to cover his ass in front of a court-martial than making a report. "Who was this guy?"

"Eli Holten."

"Never heard of him."

"That's not the least of it. When my sergeant major confronted him for his gross dereliction in the face of an enemy who was exploiting the disadvantageous position in which this Holten had placed us, Holten shot him down in cold blood."

Something still didn't ring quite true. Sinclair shrugged it off. "That's serious. Where's this guy now?"

Covington continued his preplanned story, ignoring Sinclair. "In total defiance of standard procedure, he teamed up with a Frenchman and two women and insisted they be given the protection of my troop to Arizona. I had to take them in. My superiors in Washington would take a dim view of my leaving vulnerable, ill-equipped foreign nationals on the plains at the mercy of the hostiles and the elements. However, I am well persuaded they are in fact agents of some sort of international conspiracy and this Holten is in league with them."

Sinclair frowned, his dark brown eyes hidden behind narrowed lids. "That does make the cheese more binding. Do you want to wire Washington?"

"Er, ah, no, not at the moment," Covington stammered.

"Well, where do you think this Holten is? Did he get out of the Indian trap?"

"I'm sure he did. If he didn't I'll need confirmation. If he did, then I feel certain he'll find a way to get himself and his coconspirators safely away. He must be hunted down and shot. He is extremely dangerous."

"And these French people?"

"Er—aaah, they must be handled with extreme delicacy if we should find them. Guests of the government and all that. No questions, no interrogation. An international incident must be avoided at all costs. And they must not be listened to. They'll support this Holten against me with every lie in the book."

"I guess what you're asking me is to mount a posse and go hunting this Holten."

"Precisely. When can you leave?"

"Now, Major, this is all sort of high level for a

plain old U.S. marshal," Sinclair attempted to slow down the rush toward civilian involvement with what he saw as a military matter.

"Marshal Sinclair, my normal post of duties is in Washington and I am only occasionally assigned such vital field responsibilities," Covington lied smoothly. "Like me, you are an employee of the federal government. I am well connected in the Capitol, the War Department, the Justice Department, and the Cabinet. Help me execute this mad dog, Holten, and discreetly and politely confine his French agent friends, and your cooperation won't go unnoticed."

"Whatever happened to 'innocent until proven guilty'? And 'a speedy and public trial'?" Sinclair asked, goading.

"When I return east, I will be in a position to assure your comfortable future in the government service," Covington evaded.

"And if I sit here and do nothing?"

Covington drew himself up haughtily. "Exactly what was going to happen anyway. You'll rot away in that chair the rest of your days, petting that perfidious cat."

"You make the choices rather clear, Major Covington. I wish I had that in writing."

"Come, come, Marshal. We're gentlemen, aren't we? And as such, aren't we men of our word? You'll help me bring in Holten over his saddle?"

"And if we run up there and find him among the dead where you were attacked?"

"A deal, my friend, is a deal. The day I see that man's grave is the day your valorous deeds will be on their way into the Congressional Record."

Sinclair swung his feet off the desk. "I'll get you and your men put up at the Dimmick House for some rest, a bath, and a hot meal. Gordon down at the livery stable will pick out fresh mounts and rub down and grain your horses. After you've refreshed, maybe slept in a clean bed for a night, we can start out."

"I had hoped, Marshal, that you could mount a civilian reconnoiter sooner," Covington said coldly.

"Huh? You run a hard bargain, Major Covington. Our little town here faces a real emergency with these marauding Kiowas in our midst. Yet, you want me to go skallyhootin' off on some wild goose chase. I got about fifteen men deputized, I guess, on call to help me run things if them heathen Kiowas was to show up here. They're reasonably ready to ride. Still, it'll take three, four hours to be mobilized at best. Banjo Price, my regular deputy, could handle things, mobilize a larger home guard if we were away and anything was to happen around here."

"You're well organized, I'll say that for you. My men desperately do need rest and recuperation. I fully intend to start out with them myself after Holten. Perhaps first thing in the morning will be good enough. Can you ride today, this afternoon?"

"I suppose it could be done."

"I'd like my report to include the efficient, lightning-quick reaction time of United States Marshal Harold Sinclair," Covington said glowingly.

"I guess that can be arranged. At least five, six of us. How will I know this hombre?"

"Tall, blond, too damned handsome for his own good, and I don't mean that facetiously. The French operatives, two women and a man, most likely will be with him."

Holten's little band of survivors found a small, hidden valley beside a chattering crystal stream to spend a day recovering themselves and their horses. Hot food, the first in two days, went a long way toward reviving the humans. Out of cigars, Eli

226

chewed on a pungent pine needle and sipped coffee while he reflected on their journey from the massacre to this point.

In their flight from the dreadful scene of carnage he'd seen signs of vague trails that verged on wagon ruts which led to well-traveled roads. He continued following them south, aware that somewhere in the distance was a town. Dimmick, he knew, was in the area somewhere, close by the upper entrance to Raton Pass, though he'd never been there. By daylight, he also cut the sign several times of a half-dozen cavalry mounts moving in the direction of where he judged Dimmick to be.

With the coming of dusk, after he managed to snatch six hours' sleep during the day, Eli made a decision. He left his companions for a look-see at Dimmick and to learn what he could. Now, aided by the cover of darkness, he stopped Sonny on the rim of a mesa, his eyes defining a cluster of buildings in the distance. He made out a clot of dark, blocky shapes with here and there a lighted window casting a yellow rectangle into the night. Alongside the town, moonlight glinted on the course of a broad, shallow river. That had to be Dimmick. Though too far for smells and sounds, the air around Eli carried the hints of human habitation up to his keen senses.

Another sensation also rode on the air to Holten. Danger lurked down there as well. He played a perilous game, risky from more than one angle.

Covington had made his cowardly escape and the signs said he came here. He could have told any kind of story and filed any sort of fictitious report to General Crook at Fort McDowell. There'd be wrongs that needed righting, and without doubt by force. His long-barreled Remington cap-and-ball conversion, he knew, was loaded, yet he unsheathed it and, despite the low light level, assured himself of the brass cartridges in the cylinders. He replaced the weapon and rode slowly down the hill.

Sonny, not fully recovered from the rigors of the past several days, bobbed his head and watched the trail for hazards while at the same time trying to keep his bearing nobly erect. Sonny, Holten mused into a night sky that resembled the high color of flour-gold against black sand in a prospector's pan, had enough thoroughbred in his bloodlines to go until he dropped.

At the foot of the bluff, nearing the fringes of the settlement, he halted Sonny again. Through the dense night, he could make out the lateral rails of the town corral fence and the black blotch of horses standing there. He'd give odds they were the matched bays of C Troop. Covington and his few blindly loyal henchmen in blue were there. Probably still spreading lies about him and possibly even implicating him in the death of Harry Adams.

The deck had been heavily stacked against him. Once more, Eli Holten was about to be thrust into a situation where the whole world would be after his scalp. The easy thing would be to turn tail and vamoose, to hell with it all. Yet, times came, he knew, when a man simply had to fight—even a sometimes cynical and hard-bitten loner who played his skills and his guns like some men played cards, with the same sardonic eye to gain. There were also times like these, when profit lost its significance and a man stepped out to do battle for the old gods of decency and integrity . . . and honor.

His mind occupied with such thoughts, Holten dismounted, leaving Sonny tethered under an ancient pine, and began his reconnoiter of Dimmick. Himself culpable and knowing Holten to be the only witness, Covington would be certain to brand the scout as the cat's-paw. Angry as Holten became at this prospect, and still fired with a white-hot need to avenge the murder of Harry Adams, he still kept on his guard against acting impulsively. Seconds later, silently making his way along a path from the corral into the town, he heard a sharp sound that drifted back to him from ahead. Holten identified the distinctive screech of chair feet rasping against a board sidewalk as someone sat or changed his position.

He picked out a darkened alley between the blacksmithy and another building and ghosted forward on tiptoe. A soft drone of male voices penetrated the night ahead. To hear better, Holten slipped to the end of the alley and slid the side of his head past the building. He saw two figures not ten feet away in oak armchairs, taking their nighttime ease. Orange cigarette tips glowed in the dark like cat eyes. The larger, bulkier man passed a pint bottle to his companion.

"Been in the cavalry long?" he asked as the slighter and younger man took a long sip and gasped at the potency.

"Eleven weeks. Most of that out on that damned Santa Fe Trail. You like wearin' a badge, mister?"

"Me? Yeah. I'm Marshal Sinclair's *segundo,* his chief deputy. Name's Price, by the way. First name's a mouthful. Benjamin Joseph. Somehow, in my cowboyin' days, they bobbed 'er down to Banjo and Banjo it's been ever since. Got nothin' to do with music."

"Mine's Thomas. Oliver Thomas. Private."

"Like you got two first names." Price chuckled in the dark. "Mr. Sinclair taken a bunch of men out lookin' for this Holten jasper. More'n he figgered would go on short notice. So I'm in charge while he's away. This Holten won't dare come around here. You see him shoot this Adams?"

"No, sir. Only what Major Covington already said. When we saw the major mounting up out there, I and the other boys figured a retreat had been called and

229

we followed him."

"Have another drink, Mr. Thomas. I take it this Holten had words with your Sergeant Adams. About Holten's messing up Major Covington's plans to give the Indians what-for. They say Holten went for his hogleg and it was Katie Bar the Door."

"Something like that."

"Well, anyway, Mr. Sinclair's out there with eight fellers to catch this hombre and there ain't going to be no questions when they get their dally around his neck. Just goin' to by God blast his black soul to boot hill."

"I don't know as that's right, though they ain't asked my say-so. Major Covington's putting us back in the field in the morning to help hunt for Holten ourselves."

"Mr. Sinclair told me about it," Price advised him.

Holten slipped back down into the dark of the alley. He'd heard enough. Maybe if he could talk to this Price and show him Adams's letter he might possibly enlist some support in Dimmick. Get Covington contained and he felt sure the handful of troopers would be no particular problem. Decided on that, he doubled back and slipped around the other side of the livery stable. With a hitch of his gunbelt, he stepped out of the shadows and strode down the street tall and straight and icy cold toward Price and Thomas with a confident, swinging walk.

"Somebody's coming," he heard Private Thomas blurt in surprise.

"Halooo," Holten called.

Price came to his feet that fast. "Who's that? State your business."

"It's . . . " Thomas called. "It's Holten!"

"I need to talk with somebody," Holten began, moving closer to the boardwalk where the two now stood.

"You'll do your talkin' in jail, mister," a surprised

Price yelled as he launched his bulk off the boardwalk. He came on to confront Holten in a menacing way. "Come gentle and I'll go easy on ya."

"I'm not going to jail. I've got evidence that'll clear my name."

Price made a grab for Holten and the scout could suddenly see he'd been mistaken in thinking he could deal with Price. Now he'd have to fight his way out of this one. He hoped he could do it without gunplay.

Eli sidestepped Price's lunge and caught him a good blow below the breastbone and the bigger man folded over his arm. Both went down while, out of the corner of his eye, Holten saw Thomas leap for his carbine. Quick as a monkey, Thomas snatched up the Springfield and had its stock on the way to his shoulder when Holten jumped to his feet, unlimbered his Remington, and fired.

The rifle changed ends, the shock and sting temporarily paralyzing the trooper. Before the Springfield landed, Thomas had beaten it to the ground, diving for the cover of the alley mouth. Peeking around the corner of the building, crouched below the level of the boardwalk, Thomas's eyes lighted on the carbine. Its stock had been split by Holten's bullet, yet he judged it would still shoot. Still, the sight of Holten standing with a long-barreled Remington leveled at him put an end to any of Thomas's notions.

Hopeful no more shooting would be necessary, Holten sheathed the .44 quickly and turned to Price, on his feet now and coming toward Holten.

"I said you're goin' to jail," Price screamed, lunging at Holten.

"I am like hell," Holten countered. He made a lightning move as he gave his answer. His right fist boomed against Price's jaw with a flat, wet smack.

Price topped him by several inches and considerably outweighed him as well. That might be an advantage. Holten ducked Price's blow, which only seemed to whisper over his head. Recovering, Price waded back in, swinging.

The slender Holten kept to lightning moves of feet, torso, and fists. He never went where Price figured he should be and many terrific blows got wasted.

Holten lifted him from each miss with a thudding uppercut. A gash opened over Price's eyes and blood blurred his vision, his breath whistling through his set teeth.

Price's bloodied eye now gave Holten the advantage. He started pounding the giant Price again. Price lunged, but this time it was not a wild advance. He remembered that despite his lean, lithe body, Holten proved a hard man to handle.

Holten continued to sidestep intended blows and slashed with a fist that jarred bone. He delivered another smack on Price's jaw. Eli ducked under three more blows and came up with his right haymaker.

Holten battled Price to his knees and waited, only for Price to sway to his feet and rush in as fiercely as ever. A thoroughly terrified Oliver Thomas stayed out of it.

Eli kept snapping in blows, delivering them on the move. Price bore in more desperately and Holten slammed another fist to his eye. Price's vision, already greatly impaired, worsened as each blow puffed the skin higher and loosened fresh blood. The big man's punches became erratic. Not seriously injured, he could barely see. Realizing Holten had the advantage maddened him and, infuriated, he raised his great hams of fists to charge again.

By then Holten was aware of Price's dimming sight and began settling on his heels to bring up a blow. His panther-quick speed was no longer necessary to deliver the final blow. Price hung there and then leaned forward to fall on his face and lie still.

Holten swayed back and looked around at the empty street. He gulped for air, his legs none too steady. Assuming Price to be whipped, Eli started to walk away, then stiffened as he sensed a breath of movement behind him. He spun to see Price feebly bringing up a revolver, the barrel weaving as he fought with weakened arms and faulty vision to control it.

"Oh, why must you be such a dratted damn-fool?" Holten grumbled as he skinned the Remington. He blasted the Colt out of Price's hand without more than bruising him.

At once, Holten spun on his heel and strode down the alley past the cowering Private Thomas and beyond the corral to where Sonny was tied. Trying to state his case in Dimmick had been a waste of time.

Behind Holten, the sounds of a town coming alert rode to his ears. Price was evidently rounding up a gang to come after him. Thomas would surely find Covington to report Holten's presence in the vicinity. The world had started to crash down around Eli Holten's ears.

19

Carefully Eli Holten slipped through the darkness. To the right stood the long, black buildings of Dimmick's business places and to his left ran the corral. He took a chance on the moonlight and made it to the shadow of the corral fence.

He moved away from it in the direction of the sandy bluff that jutted beyond the town like a great, slanted shelf. Holten followed the fence, kept to its shadow. He angled away from it as soon as he could, circled around the corral, and sprinted to Sonny. He swung into the saddle and headed out of town, riding hard. His slate eyes had gone cold and bleak, his mouth twisted into a bitter, hard line.

Shortly he came upon the path he had ridden in on as it rose abruptly and angled up the broken face of the bluff. He urged Sonny on to climb the bank opposite the town and the horse began to follow the main trail as if it knew where it was going. The path led him to a ledge of loose rock and sand. Above it reared the blunt crest of the mesa. There he reined off and drew Sonny to a halt. Holten looked back at Dimmick, strung along the moonlight-silvered spread of the broad river. Downstream he could make out the black outlines of the hotel and saloon and the restless noises of cattle penned outside town for shipment. He could also discern the movement of shadowy figures in the town making ready for pursuit.

The outskirts remained empty of any following riders and Holten nudged Sonny along. When he came to a faint, weed-grown branch of the trail he paused again, this time under the shadow of a white oak, and watched for signs of pursuit. His hope now was to elude Price's stalkers and somehow find Sinclair. If he could get the drop on the posse, he would plead his case before somebody came along to gun him down.

Holten went on to follow the ledge upward as the trail bent around the face of the bluff and out onto the flat tableland. Sinclair would be somewhere north, probably on the way to the vicinity of the massacre site, probing that way for a sign of Holten's party. He suddenly grew hopeful they would not blunder into the blissful little valley where he had left Giselle, Colette, and Hugh.

Across the broad, hard-baked plateau, Holten made his easy way through the night. He moved as fast as prudence would allow. He knew that behind him Price, reinforced by Covington's crew of turn-coats, would be fast coming up on him. He had to find Sinclair before Price did.

An owl's hoot softly broke the quiet of the night and from behind him the sound of horses came with a swelling rush. Holten pulled into the comforting density of a cluster of scrubby aspen. He waited and watched, holding his breath and patting Sonny to ease him and keep him quiet. Out on the trail across the mesa they came.

Moving fast and all together, they made no effort to hide their presence. He could make out loud talk and a shod horse struck sparks into the night from a road pebble. Leather squealed and the rasp of hard-breathing horses came to his ears. Like black, ominous ghosts they drifted past within a few feet of where Holten waited apprehensively. They remained blithely unaware of him crouched in the dark.

When the quiet of night returned around him, Holten rode back out to the trail to begin following them. Price and Covington, probably hoping to squeeze Holten between them and Sinclair's posse, would find the marshal's band first. It would double the dangers he'd face in trying to get Sinclair's attention long enough to produce Harry Adams's letter. At least until then, he could ride easily.

While he rode, Holten read the story in the moonlit road. The track of the second band of pursuers superimposed over the hoof-scars of the posse that had first set out to track him down. It led a winding course northward along the trail that meandered over packed ground and soft sand, to cut across land sparsely carpeted with desert weeds and scrub growth. Riding tired horses all through the night, after the dash from town after Holten, they had circled and backtracked as they tried to cut the fugitive's sign, using all the wiles at their disposal to run the culprit to ground. They little realized their quarry came up behind them. It held one advantage for Holten. That tactic would prevent them for some while from catching up with Sinclair.

Dawn broke with no sign of shadowy riders ahead of him. He kept watching the skyline for a glimpse of Price and Covington, though none showed. They moved fast once more, and by all appearances would lead him directly to Sinclair.

Their trail took him over a long roll of sand dune, and he pulled up at the sight that greeted him on the other side. Holten swayed to a halt at the distinct thud of hooves in the distance. The early morning sun slanted its warming rays on a dozen horsemen ahead now jogging slowly along the plain line of the trail. They sought Holten's sign while at the same

236

time keeping alert for the whereabouts of the Sinclair posse.

Holten watched, hidden by the lip of the rising dune, as they made their way ahead of him. The kepis and blue shirts of Covington's troopers were mute evidence of their presence with Price. It would be a risky play, standing off the combined posses single-handedly, yet it seemed the only alternative he had left. Abruptly, the picture changed and the odds reversed in Holten's favor.

From his higher vantage point, the scout watched over the vast distance as Price and Covington led their band, looking like a cluster of ants, bleak and hard pressed. They rode to the east of a tall knife-edged upthrust of rocky ridge, following a broad canyon off to the northeast.

To the west of the great granitic sawtooth, fully hidden from sight of the Price-Covington posse, Holten could see a pall of gray smoke clinging to the tops of a line of cottonwoods tracing a small stream. With any kind of luck, Harold Sinclair was over there fixing his breakfast. Eli Holten had gained the advantage he looked for.

While he rode that way, Holten scouted Sinclair's position carefully for outriders or concealed sentries. Observing none, he moved cautiously toward where he calculated the posse's encampment to be. This would take stealth and daring. He'd have to get close to them without being apprehended and suddenly appear among them as though he had just risen up out of the ground.

He tied Sonny some distance from the tree-lined streambank and proceeded on foot. Sinclair was obviously confident of his superior force and no sentries inhibited Holten's easy stalk of the camp. From hiding in the low scrub growth, he could see the breakfasting posse and the bustle of the camp getting ready for the day's ride. He counted eight men clustered around, and spied the individual he assumed was U.S. Marshal Harold Sinclair crouching by the fire with a cup of after-breakfast coffee and chewing an unlit cigar.

Harold Sinclair was short, bull necked, with graying black hair. He wore a long, off-white linen duster over his black broadcloth suit of clothes. Almost out of place in this setting, he wore a white shirt and black four-in-hand tie. His suit trousers were crammed into knee-length stovepipe black boots with high heels.

Sinclair continued to chew on the unlit cigar that still had its red-and-gold paper band in place. His neck and jaws were clean shaven and red as a new brick, as was the rest of his face.

Holten stood up and stepped out into the clearing that was the posse's campsite. For a moment no one gave him much attention. Then someone shouted. "Stranger comin' in, Mr. Sinclair."

The butt of a gun barely poked out from its holster behind the fringe of Holten's shabby buckskin jacket as he sauntered lazily ahead. Sinclair narrowed his quick gaze at it.

"Don't anybody make a play for a gun," Holten cautioned loudly, now walking resolutely toward the fire. "No call to find out who's fastest."

"Take it easy, boys," Sinclair yelled. "I intend to take you all back to town in one piece." Sinclair still squatted comfortably down on his heels. He tipped his hat back and gazed up at the coldly gleaming eyes of the scout he knew was wanted for murder.

"You'll have to be Holten," he said plainly.

"And I take it you're Sinclair. You tell these men, Mr. Sinclair, and particularly those behind me, that if I hear a hammer go click there'll be one less U.S. marshal in Colorado, and very likely two or three fewer of its citizens voting in the next election."

Sinclair's eyes still probed Holten's. There was no

238

question he meant business. If he'd sneaked into the lawman's camp, Holten had obviously also heard they, too, were there for serious business.

"Listen to him, boys," Sinclair called loudly. "How'd you find out, Holten? You even know me by name."

"I was in town last night."

"You met Banjo Price?"

"Not only did I meet him, I had to kick the shit out of the stubborn mule."

"That took some doing. Banjo's a first-class brawler."

"Granted," Holten allowed. "But not much of a tracker. He and Covington and a gang of civilians and troopers rode east of yonder ridge when your trail down this side was as easy to read as a newspaper."

"Damn him!" Sinclair fumed. "He was under orders to stay in town and look after things. Covington probably lit one of his damned fires under Banjo."

"I think it's more a case that Price is of a mind to be the one to settle my hash himself . . . if his six-gun's working. I shot it out of his hand last night when he tried to backshoot me. He'll be nursing a bruised hand and a pretty sore eye this morning, too. I'm here to make a dicker with you, Sinclair."

"Things must've been hot in town last night. I'd like to've seen that fight. What's your deal, Holten?"

Tired of looking down at Sinclair, Eli crouched to hunker close to him. "I can shoot just as well from here, too."

"Don't remind me," Sinclair said.

"Tell me when I'm wrong. Covington told you I was primarily responsible for the massacre, right?"

"So far."

"And I was also responsible for the death of Sergeant Major Adams."

Sinclair bit his lip in thought. "Uh-huh."

"He also probably told you that if you played ball with him, he'd help your cause along with his influence in Washington."

"You're pretty shrewd, Holten."

"Not really. I just know Covington. And try this one on for size. He wants me shut up and he fingered you to put a window in my skull."

"I own up to that and you'll drill me anyway," Sinclair protested.

"Not until I've spoken my piece," Holten allowed.

"Let's get to that."

"Covington's own orders tripped him up. He treated the troop miserably on the trail, even had a man flogged, in total violation of regulations. He himself shot Harry Adams in cold blood to stop his mouth. But not before he had ordered me to have no conversations with Adams. I got to Adams long enough to let him know that. Adams feared for his own life, so he wrote me a letter detailing Covington's behavior. I have that letter."

"Could be a forgery."

"Harry Adams's handwriting will be on file in reports and such. That's real easy to check, given a little time."

"Then maybe you two conspired."

"My performance as a contract civilian scout and his as a thirty-year soldier are matters of record. Nothing in them would indicate that either of us could ever be even remotely guilty of such a charge."

"You got that letter with you?"

"Mr. Sinclair, that letter is my ticket to a long life. You think I'm just going to hand it over to you after Covington's promised you heaven and earth when I'm dead and gone? I'm not easily double-crossed."

Sinclair eyed him, an eyebrow cocked. "If you're tellin' it straight, Covington sure's hell managed."

"Covington's a bastard."

"Okay, maybe I'm the one guilty of conspiracy.

240

Covington gave me two clear-cut choices, and one of them would leave me high and dry."

Holten nodded in acknowledgment. Covington was also an animal. "Here's my deal. You and I walk out to where I've got that letter hidden. Meanwhile, your men throw all their guns in a pile and stand back away from them thirty feet. And stay away until after we get back. Any of them try anything sneaky, you're dead meat. I may be, too, but your hide's the one you're worried about. You read the letter and if you're persuaded I'm talking straight, we'll ride out and find Covington and Price. They're not that far."

"And if I'm not persuaded?"

"One thing's sure, I won't shoot you. So rest easy on that score. I'll probably take you hostage for a ways. Then I'll let you down easy and you can walk back to camp while I put a few miles between us. The next time you're in my vicinity, I *will* be gunning for you. And it won't mean a tinker's damn to me if I take you down from ambush."

"Tough talk."

"It's a tough business."

"Let's have a look at that letter. You heard him, boys. Pile up the artillery and stand away like the man said. We'll be right back."

A quarter of an hour later they returned to Sinclair's breakfast fire. The lawman had read only two paragraphs before he announced, "I want to read all of this to my posse."

Holten watched closely as Sinclair gathered his men and read aloud the contents of the letter with charged emotion. By now he'd pegged Sinclair as a decent man but even ordinarily decent men could be swayed by the high-sounding promises of a sweet-talker like Randall Covington. Still, he was ready to drill Sinclair without thinking if he made a false move with the letter. With the possemen's guns stacked, Holten knew that now he held the lion's share of the chips.

". . . and so, I'm trusting this account to you, old friend, in hopes it survives me to the detriment of that madman, Randall Covington." Sinclair concluded Harry Adams's testament. He carefully and thoughtfully folded the letter as Holten had presented it to him and handed it back.

"That letter puts things in an entirely different light, Holten. I don't think you can blame me, though, if Covington did, indeed, hoodwink me in a big way."

"He's got a way of doing that until he's burned someone for the first time. After that it's a different matter."

"What'll we do?"

"I'll need to get him corraled and I'm hoping I can depend on your help and that of these riders of yours. I'll probably take him and the troopers that skedaddled with him on to Fort McDowell in Arizona and let the army deal with them."

"You'll have your hands full."

Holten sized up Sinclair. He was not that bad a sort. "It'll be tough without some help, that's for sure."

"After all this, do I hear an invite, Mr. Holten?"

Holten grinned at Sinclair, who returned a white smile and suddenly Eli knew that everything would be all right. "Consider it an invitation, Mr. Sinclair. Now let's get your men armed again and start riding. May I buy you a drink when we get back to town?"

"Only if you let me buy the second round."

The soft sounds of gunfire from a considerable distance drifted down the wind through the cottonwoods around them. The muffled barks were sporadic at first, then increased in their intensity. Sinclair and Holten looked apprehensively at each other.

242

"East by north," Sinclair announced, a matter-of-fact tone in his voice. "Price is up there." He was, Holten discovered, cool in a crisis, a characteristic that boosted his esteem in the scout's eyes.

"I think he's getting the fight he was worried about in Dimmick," Holten opined. "Maybe they blundered back into Crooked Leg. Let's ride up there and see what we can do to prevent another bloodbath, Mr.—you go by Harold?"

"Good friends call me Hal, Eli."

"You ready to ride, Hal?"

"Damn betcha. I got a bone to pick with our Major Covington for hoodwinking me."

"That's nothing against the score I've got to settle."

"Then let's ride!" the lawman boomed.

20

With fatigued horses pushed as fast as they could, their ride around the north tip of the ridge and south through the valley to the relief of Covington and Price took an hour. Startled coveys of quail and mountain grouse whirred out of their path and a darkening sky added another touch of drama. Holten grew increasingly anxious that all he'd find would be a baker's dozen of scalped, lifeless bodies.

Eli took little note of the land around him, only peering ahead, eager to close the miles faster. The sounds of gunfire in the distance grew louder and more urgent as they raced toward the battle. Plowing through a shallow stream, kicking up great sprays of water, Holten shot up his hand for a halt in a screen of cottonwoods along the bank. Sinclair reined up beside him.

"Jesus and my Aunt Tillie," the marshal said softly. "Crooked Leg's got him by the balls like Crazy Horse had Yellow Hair."

The action went on less than a mile away, up the slope of the barren ridge. Like Custer, Covington had been driven into a tactically indefensible and vulnerable hillside position. Their view was clear to the battle site where the little force of troopers and civilians fought from behind a ring of dead horses, shot for breastworks. Eli didn't know whether Covington or Price had had the presence of mind to order the hasty fortification. He rather imagined it was Price.

The Kiowas, probably with some of the surviving Comanches from the wagon fight, safely crouched behind hillside rocks and poured in the lead whenever one of the embattled posse raised his head for a shot. Holten figured it to be only a matter of time before Crooked Leg would have the scalps he looked for.

He noted another reality with grim satisfaction. The fight three days ago had significantly thinned Crooked Leg's ranks.

"What do we do, Eli?" Sinclair asked. "Charge their line?"

"Naturally. Only if we go in together, all horns and rattles, up to Covington, they'll quickly fill the gap and we'll be stuck there with him. No good."

"So?" the lawman queried.

"Hit 'em in two places, divide their force, break their communications link. But we've got to get into the zone of fire before they know we're here. Element of surprise."

"Split up? That's spreading it pretty thin, Eli."

"All we got. I'll take half the men up topside, on that ledge yonder. You take the rest and circle out in the valley, follow the screen of these trees. When you see me start down the slope, you come at 'em from below, bellering like banshees. And pick your targets. Fire into the air a little for effect if you want. No random shooting. Isn't any point in our catching each other, or Covington and Price, in the crossfire."

"Got ya."

"They're in a ring, surrounding those jaspers up there. Ride a half-moon formation and stick to it. Drive as many as you can ahead of you. That'll make easier targets for you, and the fellers trapped up there.

Maybe Covington and Price will get the ones you miss. Don't worry about getting to them up there. Just kill Indians."

The men around them heard the plan and began checking their weapons. Sinclair waved a line separating their group. "All you to my right ride with me. The rest of you follow Holten."

"See you in church, Hal," Holten quipped.

"At somebody else's funeral," Sinclair said.

"Let's hop to it, then. Those boys up there ain't going to hold out forever."

Holten led his group quickly back through the screen of trees toward the start of a canted rocky ledge up the slope of the ridge of tawny granite. "That ledge looks wide," he called to his part of the force. "Stay away from the edge, single file, out of sight as much as possible. When we go down over the side, ride like hell and zigzag if you can to make a poor target. Stay spread out and keep the half-circle formation. And I want to hear a howl that'll carry all the way back to Dimmick."

Holten marked the gutsy grins on the grimy, whiskered faces of the townsmen and ranchers around him. Damned if he didn't sound like a general pep-talking the troops. "Okay. Let's go."

They picked their way quickly up the angled shelf, hearing the roar, though not seeing the fight, on the hillside below. The lip of the ledge screened their movements from enemy eyes downslope. At last Holten reached a point he calculated to be directly above Covington's position.

He dismounted briefly to scoot to the edge and reconnoiter. He ducked back again when a bullet sang past his head.

"Somebody's seen us. Up and at 'em."

Over they went with a cry, to slide down the steep slope in frantic haste. Loosened slope rubble churned up and slid around them. Great clouds of dust billowed to nearly obscure the riders. It masked their true numbers and added to the terrifying effect of their surprise charge. Holten threw back his head and let go a piercing Sioux war cry and the spirit was picked up as Holten's four men plummeted down the slope.

The old Rebel Yell came from the throat of a Dimmick merchant beside him, shivering the air: *"Woh-who-ey! Who-ey! Who-ey!"*

His reins draped over the saddle horn, Holten levered a few rounds at the sky through the Winchester and filled his lungs again for another heart-stopping bellow. He felt its wild, frenzied power fill his frame.

Huka hey! Huka hey! Maka kin le, mitawa ca!"

He did feel like he owned the earth. Bullets whizzed past him and for the moment, as Sonny propelled him at breakneck speed down the rocky incline, the wind whistled in his face and he felt invincible. No, he was *not* afraid, and he *did* own the earth. Lord, the thought suddenly occurred to him, how he did love to fight.

Far below him, through the dust and with eyes damp from the grit, Holten could see Sinclair's band hitting the gallop across the flats and starting up the sides of the hill toward Covington. Their charge, too, was punctuated with battle cries and puffs of rifle smoke, Holten's and Sinclair's little bands had become powers to be reckoned with.

Beneath him, and growing closer by the second, a dozen or so Kiowas, afoot, showed on the hillside. They leaped up and scampered from one shielding rock to another, to be trapped between the guns of the charging riflemen on horseback and the beleaguered fighters behind the horse breastworks. Covington and Price had their men up now, firing as astonished Kiowas wavered and broke into panicked flight, although doomed, with nowhere to go.

As they neared the trapped townsmen and troopers, the two salient ends of Holten's group fanned away, shooting down fleeing Indians as they tried to race away to sanctuary on the opposite sides of their now-broken circle. Holten's surprise charge had its desired effect. From inside the circle of dead horses, men now picked up the spirit to leap out and charge to help finish off the exposed Indian force.

Out of the corner of his eye and to his left, Holten saw a mounted Indian, long gray hair flowing in the wind, gallop out of the action, headed for the valley floor. Crooked Leg.

He swung Sonny to sweep past the ring of dead horseflesh, and quartered downslope in pursuit. At last he churned through the hard-baked gravel of the valley floor, impeded only by low scrubby chaparral. Anything was better than those hillside rocks. The others stayed committed on the slopes.

Now leaderless, the Kiowas and Comanches became fair game for the nearly two dozen grim fighters under Sinclair, Price, and Covington. Holten gave them a backward glance for assurance and prodded Sonny to greater speed.

Crooked Leg hit the main trail at a high gallop a hundred yards ahead of Holten. Now it would be a contest between horses. Holten let Sonny find his pace, knowing the Kiowa chief's stocky, short-legged mustang would be no match for the sleek Morgan.

Desperate, Crooked Leg pushed the pony for all it was worth. The little beast had heart, Holten mused, he'd give it that. It wouldn't be enough. Even though Sonny wasn't running at his peak, he gained inches with every step. At last the Indian pony visibly began to slow.

All of Crooked Leg's quirting and kicking ribs with heels did nothing to urge the little horse past its endurance. Abruptly, Crooked Leg swung off the trail and without reining up, flung a knee off the animal to hit the ground running.

He had no place to hide and for an old man, he raced like an antelope. That fast, Holten dropped off Sonny and, leaving his reins trailing, started at the run after Crooked Leg. Now the chase became more equal. Riding boots were less adapted to running than soft Indian moccasins. Crooked Leg kept his head as he raced through the distant chaparral. Yet he carried more age than his pursuer and gradually his stamina dwindled. Holten began to gain an advantage.

At last Crooked Leg slid to a stop and wheeled. He bounded back toward Holten, gripping a broad, gleaming Bowie almost as long as his lower arm.

In Lakota, Holten shouted, "I am Tall Bear of the True Oglala, a member of the Raven Owners' Society. You are a woman, a woman who wants to use a knife like a man."

"I know words of the Cutthroat tongue, enough to understand," Crooked Leg replied in the same tongue. "I am Crooked Leg of the Tis-windee-ki Kiowa, bearer of the sacred arrow bundle and war chief. When I'm through, I'll make a woman of you, Tall Bear." Although old, Crooked Leg was as gritty and determined as the granite hills that surrounded them.

Holten reached behind his right hip to whip out his own knife, a coffin-handle Bowie shorter than Crooked Leg's by two inches. Still, it was a formidable weapon. Crooked Leg's rheumy, glinting eyes and pinched features showed no sign of defeat or surrender as he continued to pound toward Holten, knife hand back for the first thrust. For a second, a smile curved his lips. Holten crouched to meet the attack.

He sidestepped as the Indian's blade, intended for his vitals, whistled past his left arm. With the miss, Crooked Leg caught himself, leaped, and whirled, then came back at Holten as the scout wheeled. Eli Holten planted his widespread feet and defensively brought up his own blade.

This time Holten ducked as Crooked Leg's gleaming Bowie scribed an arc over his head. He heard the Kiowa's grunt of exertion as he strove for a death cut. Holten's blade sliced the blousy bottom of Crooked Leg's shirt, but failed to touch flesh.

Again they passed and spun around to resume the combat, hearing each other's rasping breath. Crooked Leg came at him, backhanded the Bowie to cut Holten in half at the waist. As the razor edge swiped toward him, Holten leaped backward, sucked in his gut, felt the shock of it along his pistol belt. It glanced off the buckle.

At once Crooked Leg charged, carrying the Bowie like a saber to make a chop at Holten's neck or shoulders. Holten made to parry the thrust. His right leg snapped forward and struck . . . to slide on sundried grass. As he went off balance and forward, a line of fire erupted at the base of his neck.

Cold steel bit into heated flesh. Holten felt a hot spurt of blood and reacted instantly. He dropped down and away from the knife that sought to claim his life. Pain came now as he tucked his shoulders for the roll. Holten let it wash through him a moment before shutting out the most intense agony.

He came to his feet, facing Crooked Leg. Immediately, sensing victory, goaded by taking first blood, the war chief lunged at his kneeling opponent. Thinking fast, Holten flipped his knife into the air, caught it by the tip and in one quick overhead flex of his arm, sent it whizzing hilt-first at Crooked Leg.

Eli's knife made one lazy half-loop in the air and, lancelike, impaled the Kiowa war chief in the brisket with an audible slushy thud. Biting back his discomfort Holten came to his feet, hand reaching for the Remington at his hip.

250

Crooked Leg dropped his knife and for a long moment stood staring with crazed fascination at the brass guard and worn stag hilt that projected from his gut. His eyes gradually inched up to lock on Holten's as his mouth began to form the notes of his death song. Holten stood transfixed, watching the dying man.

His life's blood and vital juices pouring into his abdominal cavity, Crooked Leg continued his wailing, lifting cry as he stared at Holten. The shrill, high-pitched notes came as screeches on the scout's ears. The final tones of the chant trailed off.

Crooked Leg buckled and fell forward, which levered the keen knife edge on an angle into his heart and lungs as he landed face first in the gritty soil. At last Holten could move and, his breath coming in rasping gasps, he knelt and rolled Crooked Leg over. With great difficulty he pried loose his blade, wedged in the man's chest. He wiped the knife clean on the sleeve of the dead chief's grimy shirt.

"I would take your scalp to honor your great fighting spirit, grandfather," he told the corpse. His words came as choked hisses. "But Covington would use it to make me the barbarian."

Holten stuffed a bandanna under his buckskin hunting shirt to stop the bleeding. Biting his lip against the discomfort, he went to find their horses to take the Kiowa chief's remains back to the battle site.

"There he is, Marshal. That's the man," Randall Covington shouted when the scout rode back to the scene of the major's latest debacle. "Arrest him!"

"Shut your mouth, Covington," the scout growled.

"Looks like you got the old troublemaker, Eli," Hal Sinclair observed at sight of the body draped over a Kiowa war pony.

"He nearly got me, Hal," Holten offered.

"Eli? Hal? I see it now. Oh, yes, I see it clearly. Another conspiracy against me, that's what it is. You two. You—you'll not get away with it," Covington raved, eyes wild and glazed, spittle foaming at the corners of his ugly, twisted mouth.

Covington snatched a rifle, loosely held by a posseman, and started forward. He halted abruptly when Eli Holten rammed the muzzle of his Remington forcefully under the crazed major's chin.

"Put . . . it . . . down," Eli commanded. "Or I water the grass with your brains. I'd like to, you know. For Harry Adams."

Hal Sinclair took the Winchester out of Randall Covington's hands. "What do we do with him, Eli?"

"Like I said before. The army takes care of its own. I'd like someone to take a look at this shoulder. Old Crooked Leg put a cut on me. Then we can noon here and start back for Dimmick."

Sinclair nodded. "Put him and his fellow deserters in irons," the lawman instructed one of the posse.

"Holten! You can't do this to me, Hol—tennnnnn!" Covington wailed pitifully as the scout walked away.

With Covington and his deserters-under-fire secure in Harold Sinclair's jail in Dimmick, Holten and the marshal locked the fourteen remaining Kiowa and Comanche captives in the livery stable upstairs haymow. They would await escort back to Fort Sill and the justice of martial law. Holten wired succinct details to Frank Corrington and General Crook and received the expected response to take the errant major on to Fort McDowell in Arizona Territory to await a military tribunal to judge his actions.

Banjo Price, ordered by Sinclair to apologize to Holten, went around with them to the Dimmick Dry Gulch Saloon for their long-awaited evening of victory drinks and robust, happy man-talk. Sinclair, having gained approval from his superiors, and a proper contingent of his deputized townsmen—all of whom basked in the glory of being triumphant Indian fighters—would accompany Holten on the journey.

Price good-naturedly promised not to charge out on any more wild goose chases. He would see to the law keeping in Dimmick in Sinclair's absence. From Price, Holten learned it had been he who ordered the dead-horse barricades.

"I had to do something, Holten. Major Covington lost all his composure and sense of command at Crooked Leg's first attack. Yellow bastard started babblin' about how we had to make a run for it. When any fool could see we weren't gonna get off that hillside. So I had the boys shoot the horses and we forted up."

"You saved a lot of lives that way," Holten observed.

"Not as many as I'd liked to. 'Fore it was over we lost three men and five wounded. But the Kiowas are done with their nastiness, so I suppose it was worth it."

His respect for Sinclair's *segundo* having done an about-face, Holten felt he had two staunch allies if trouble ever struck him in this country. The trio passed the late hours getting mildly drunk. Holten only slightly regretted that Giselle had declined his invitation to join them.

Her small party had been found safe and eager to press on to Dimmick with the victorious posse. From the moment of their reunion, Holten had sensed a change in the lovely Frenchwoman. He vowed to find out the cause.

The next evening, with the spreading of a balmy dusk and wine-rich air along the river as pleasant to the senses as fine brandy, Holten and Giselle strolled its banks through the deepening night. A twilight breeze wafted up the river valley, heady and strong with the pungency of water, sage, and piñon. Fireflies warmed up the darkness and cicadas tuned their chitinous instruments. Near a huge boulder that protruded into the stream they halted.

A cloud passed over Giselle's face, dimmed her smile, and seemed to fill her eyes with the same purple haze that settled into the valley. As the last of the afterglow dimmed the splendor of the western sky and the first weird howling chant of coyotes trembled across the silence of the enfolding hills, the girl shivered and drew close to Holten. For all her defensive posture, her voice sounded resolute.

"I won't be going on to Arizona with you, Eli," she stated finally. She again lapsed into silence, though Holten could read the depths of her emotions by the stiffness of her body and the tempo of her breathing.

"I had so wanted to see it, and maybe one day I will. The loss of my wagons and teams and my possessions make it necessary for me to return east where I have friends."

"I understand," Eli said, already feeling a keen sense of loss and wanting to fight it. "If it's money you need, maybe I can help."

Giselle's soft laughter startled the night. "There is much I have not told you, dear man," she began wistfully. "Money is not the problem. Without my things lost in the wagons, it's impossible for me to continue in the manner to which I am accustomed."

"Maybe you'd reoutfit and come back. We'll stay in touch."

"Perhaps," she answered absently, eyes holding a distant look. "You see there is more to me—to my name, than I have told you. I am Adrian Marie Giselle Robideaux, la comtesse de Triveaux, now exiled from my beloved France with the deposing of *l'Emperor*, Louis Napoleon." She gave Eli an appealing glance. "Those contemptible rabble and

254

their Commune of Paris. I was but a small girl at the time. However, we Robideaux managed to preserve our fortune. So you see, I have unlimited funds, but until political upheaval in my country settles, I must stay away. That is why I decided to explore as much of your great American West as I could."

"Huh?" Holten grunted in retrospect.

"What, Eli?"

"Just thinking. Our, ah, enjoyments together. I never made love to a member of the nobility before."

"And I have never made love with as beautiful and caring a man as Eli Holten. You have made it a rich, memorable experience. In so many ways, Eli."

"Huh," he grunted again.

"What, Eli?" she repeated.

" 'Many ways.' I'm remembering the afternoon on the trail, among the wildflowers and wild horses."

"Indeed memorable." More than wistful, an almost melancholy shade tinged her voice. "Mr. Sinclair has found me some fine men of Dimmick to escort me back to Dodge City and the train east."

Her mood was transmitted to Holten. "I guess that's the way it has to be."

"Before we say *adieu,* Eli, could we . . . ?"

Holten looked about him. "Here?"

"Here."

He moved to her for a pensive embrace. Their lips met and in the moist, velvet contact, gloom raced into the night to be filled by pent-up need and the overwhelming beauty of their closeness. Giselle broke from his arms to step back. He could feel her gaze fused on his as she plucked at the long row of tiny round buttons down the front of her dress.

"I'll put down my leather coat for us," he suggested.

Giselle stepped out of the dress, totally nude, and moved to recline on his spread jacket. She'd worn no undergarments in anticipation of just such a moment. It thrilled Holten and burnished his pride.

One side of his mouth lifted in a sardonic grin, suddenly remembering the night at Fort Rawlins and his romp with Doreen Thorne. Like Giselle, Doreen had come to his bed naked save for her dress. Women, he mused, were funny critters. Stepping out of his buckskin trousers, he moved to slide down beside Giselle to continue the precious preliminaries.

"Ummm, *très magnifique,*" Giselle murmured.

Eli sensed no sadness or finality in the surge of ecstasy that flooded over him. Something told him this would not be his last lovemaking with the beautiful and physically talented Countess Giselle de Triveaux.